I0552877

Net Switch

Denise Baer

Baer Books Press
Chicago   Hattingen

Baer Books Press

Published by Baer Books Press

Chicago | Hattingen
baerbookspress.com

Published in the United States of America
by Baer Books Press.

This edition published 2015.

Copyright @ 2011 by Denise Baer
www.authordenisebaer.com

First Publication, 2011

Library of Congress Control Number: 2014902415

Net Switch / Denise Baer.

ISBN-10: 0991326814
ISBN-13: 978-0-9913268-1-5

http://www.baerbookspress.com/

Designed by Denise Baer • Cover Art by Ana Cruz

In memory of my mother, Alma Baer,
for her sacrifices and influences.

*My dreams and successes are yours.
Even though I didn't get to sign a book
for you, I know you are with me in spirit,
and that I have made you proud.*

ACKNOWLEDGMENTS

It's a wonderful journey and blessing to have the opportunity to make up stories and share them with the world. I'd like to thank all the writers out there for their faith in themselves, and to the publishing world for its transformations. To all the readers out there, thank you for your love of words, other lives and worlds.

Thanks to Ana Cruz, http://www.anacruz-arts.com/, my book cover art designer. It was a joy to work with you, and I look forward to future collaborations.

Huge thanks to Kara McElhiny for her fantastic input. You dove into my story and gave valuable suggestions that moved it to another level. When I thought things were good, I invited my other beta readers, Nina Karlin and Steve Barber, and they undeniably supplied me with the positives and negatives to help pinch things together.

I want to thank my supporters, Barbara Riley and Joseph Sularz, for being my devoted blog readers and for their constant encouragement regarding my writing. When doubt crept up, it was you two who stifled my hesitations. I would also like to thank my friends at FINRA, Jacquee Broderick, Natalie Reed and Claudia Zavala, for your support and encouragement. It means so much that you are excited for my success. And a big thanks to June Kramin, my writer friend, who has been there for my IM's, rants and a great road trip. To Carol McKeone, who has always been there for me in all aspects of my life. Your support for my writing dates back years ago, and your enthusiasm still runs strong.

A special thanks to my mother, Alma Baer, who sacrificed much and allowed her children to blossom however they wanted to. You never stopped us from experiencing life. You will forever live in my heart and memories.

Finally, I want to thank Martin Haschka, for his love for me and belief in my abilities. This novel would have never come to fruition if it hadn't been for your encouragement and long hours.

You pushed me to pursue my dream and supported me beyond expectation. Du hast mein Herz.

ALSO BY DENISE BAER

Fogged Up Fairy Tale
Sipping a Mix of Verse (poetry)

"Mental institutions don't relieve the mind of misery, they only create more chaos where overcrowding exists. As the patient, I feel withdrawn from life because they, the doctors, are ignoring me and are not improving my situation so I can get back into society. This has been my home for over a year and it still troubles me to talk about what brought me here. My mind is my own prison and sharing it with anyone else won't change my predicament as long as the evil that put me here continues to enjoy freedom. Still, I know I must comply with their requests if I want a chance to be discharged from this miserable place."

I sense his discomfort as he shifts in his chair from time to time. I lean forward, placing my hand on his leg, and continue with my plan.

"I don't mean to start our visit by complaining. Every week I look forward to seeing you and you never fail me, so I apologize for my bitter mood. But have you ever felt as if the room's air is seeping out and your body starts itching from impatience? This place inflicts impatience; a cancerous growth caused by the restrictions. I can't even go outside without a shadow lurking over me. A mixture of antiseptics, urine and chlorine has seeped into my skin, making it my permanent fragrance.

"Please don't look at me that way. I can't bear it if you pity me. I need your strength and assistance to get me out of here. Take what I tell you about this place and use it in my defense."

He only shifts once.

"I was going to wait to tell you about my predicament, but I already started with a bad temperament so I might as well continue. As you know, I've kept a journal since I could remember. Well, the doctors have encouraged me to keep writing...they say it's therapeutic. I think they're just nosy and want to use my journal to their advantage to break my spirit. Anyway, at the end of this week I have a meeting with the doctors in which I'll give them my journal. If they feel my journal entries and attitude have improved, they'll decide whether or not to release me. Before I give them my journal, I need to share it with you. I want you to read it and understand what I've been through so you can help fight for my release. You are my last chance to get out of here. I need you more than ever."

A smile…he must be fine with it.

"Will you do this for me? I know it's presumptuous of me to ask, since you already make weekly visits, but I have no one else to turn to. Everyone abandoned me long ago. I promise to make it up to you if the doctors are convinced I'm rehabilitated and discharge me."

You're being pushy. Show him your gratitude.

"Where are my manners? Here I am asking for your help when I never thanked you for visiting me. You're the only one who takes the time out of your busy schedule. It's so good to see you again. You look as handsome as ever. Here. Here's my journal. I hope you won't think less of me after reading it."

SUNDAY, JANUARY 13, 2008: Good evening Friends,

A snowstorm hit the Chicago area this weekend making me a prisoner in my own home. I've sampled all the places in the area— Chinese food to pizza—that were willing to deliver IF I was willing to throw in a few extra dollars. Assholes. Even goodwill comes with a price. Anyway, I watched television for as long as possible until one program began resembling the next. I picked up the TV remote clicking the channel button up and down until I hit power to silence the room. It was then that I realized a chill had drifted into the living room. My feet hit the floor and I walked to the window, pressed my finger against the condensation, and started writing my initials. SH. (Look out world, Sydney Hayes is here!) I curled my hand into a fist, pressed the side of it against the window, and wiped it away.

I went back to the couch, threw the yellow chenille blanket over me, curled my toes into the fabric and pulled the blanket up to my chest before placing my laptop on my lap. I booted it up, read e-mails and joined a regional chat room through instant message. There was a list of names with emoticons and different colored conversations streaming across the screen, one after the other, moving faster than I could read them. (Great! At least I'm not the only loser doing nothing). I kept the default name 'Newbie' and tried to catch up on the conversation and join in when I felt confident enough. In the midst of the expressed boredom that bounced from one name to the other, I added my two cents about someone pissing off Mother Nature—maybe someone telling her she's fat. Nothing! My comment moved up the screen and disappeared in the frantic speed of the other typers.

While I was trying to keep up with the silent stream of conversations, a smaller window popped up from someone named Arcane texting LOL! and asking how I was doing. Mind you, this was my first time in chat (ever!), so I didn't know what to do other than close out of the window.

After a while, this unusual way of talking to people somewhat reassured me; I didn't feel alone anymore, like a loser, since reading that others were experiencing the same lethargy. A few minutes later, another window from Arcane popped up on top, again asking how I was doing. I thought, "This one is a persistent bugger" (Bugger. I love saying that with a British accent. You little buhg-er). *giggling buhger* The idea of someone entering my virtual space without an invitation bothered me. BUT…it was a chat room…where people come to talk to nameless, faceless others. It took a few seconds for me to find my place again—where to type and send a response. I said I was doing fine and he came back with "Good to hear. Hilarious what you said about Mother Nature" and so began our exchange.

Newbie: Thanks. I didn't think anyone noticed.

Arcane: Is this your first time here?

Newbie: Yeah, how did you know?

Arcane: Um…your username. I thought I would try to contact you again in case you accidentally closed the window.

My facial muscles clenched when I read his comment. I wasn't quite sure if he expected me to respond, but not much time passed before the conversation continued.

Arcane: How's the weather by you?

Newbie: Disastrous. I'm holed up in my condo waiting for the shovels and snowplows to dig me out.

Arcane: Tough winters in Chicago.

Newbie: That they are.

Arcane: Do you have another name besides Newbie?

I sat thinking about whether or not I should give my first name.

Arcane: No problem. Just asking. Would it be too rude if I ask if you're a woman? I like to know whether I should flirt or high-five you. That's an indication I'm a guy.

Again, I stared at my screen wondering how to respond to the question. I let his earlier intrusion pass, but now it felt like he was getting too personal. Asking how I'm doing is fine—but asking my name—too close for comfort.

Newbie: I gotta go. It was nice talking to you.

I closed out of the window, disconnected from chat, and sat staring straight ahead. My thoughts found the loneliness I've been trying to escape from, coaxing it back until my eyes squeezed together, expelling the tears. The bitterness of loneliness always comes unannounced…and uninvited.

Well, it's time for bed.

Good night, my friends, I'll see you tomorrow. Let's hope it stops snowing and I get out of this condo before I go mad. GGGAAAAHHH!

MONDAY, JANUARY 14, 2008: Hey Friends,

It's me again. The law firm I work for is closed for the day, so I started clearing out my overburdened closets (I've been ignoring them for so long!) to make room for future clutter. ☺ Grime and dust clung to my touch, eventually spreading over my body and into my mouth, coating my tongue. YUCK! My garbage is growing fat from being indoors, similar to how I am feeling.

Because you are fat.

You always say that when you get restless.

Stop! Massaging my temples, I walked to the living room window to smell the falling snow. Swollen flakes fell slowly and aimlessly like fire ash, accumulating on the ground and causing the snowplows to work overtime. Eventually the noise disappeared, and when I opened the window I could almost hear the snow effortlessly drop on top of the already accumulated snow. I hung my arm out the window and swooped down to get a handful of snow from the window sill. I stuck out my tongue and put it against the snow pile in my hand until water droplets fell onto my shirt. The rest was tossed out the window before I closed myself back inside, wiping my wet hand on my shirt where it was already wet.

I sat with the television off for some time. The ticking clock ricocheted off the walls. Internal whispers were getting louder to the point where television wouldn't drown them out. I needed to connect with others—even if it was an invisible world. I wanted to expel this creepy loneliness. It didn't take long to find the chat room from yesterday, so I entered again as Newbie. At first, I became transfixed on the colored dialogue screaming for attention. Each person threw out their feelings, assuming everyone sat licking their lips with anticipation about what they had to say. I started typing to snap out of my reverie, asking if someone would please have a talk with Mother Nature. A window popped up with Arcane's name and a "Hey!"(This guy again!) I strummed my fingers on my leg, debating whether or not I wanted to talk to him.

Of course you want to talk to him. Apparently, he's the only one willing to talk to you.

My shoulders lifted and fell with thoughts of knowing I had nothing else better to do.

Newbie: Hi. How was your day?

Arcane: Good. I didn't have work, so I caught up with things I've put off.

Newbie: Sounds like our days were the same.

Arcane: What do you have planned for tonight?

Newbie: Oh, I don't know. Maybe a glass of wine and some online conversation.

Arcane: I might join you, but I'll take a beer instead of wine.

We were keeping things simple—small talk about how much takeout food we could consume in a weekend. The lightness led to laughter. Arcane told me about a pizza he ordered the other day that had the makings of someone grooming themselves. He could have sworn he found a few fingernails underneath the gooey cheese (I think I threw up in my mouth) ☹. Then he proceeded to make me laugh with more stories, and when it was my turn to talk, his interest seemed genuine. Go Figure! I have to go into the virtual world to find someone I like.

We talked for several hours in our private chat about work and trying to see who could make the other laugh the most. The creepy loneliness that usually follows me from room to room during the day steps aside for Arcane. He is attentive to everything I say—a magnet drawing us together. Arcane wanted to know what I did for a living and what I did in my spare time. The information flowed as easily as the wine and I didn't realize how late it was or what I told him. I lifted the bottle to see how much I had drunk. EMPTY! Each glass of wine opened new discussions while stirring emotions. It was a combination of the stream of conversation, the wine, and the feeling I meant something to someone that made me like him more as we moved from one subject to the next. I mean…this happens all the time, right? People conversing in the virtual world? There is absolutely no reason for me to feel weird or worried…should I?

Arcane's strong whiskey personality tapered into a smooth finish. He never seems at a loss for words, yet still listening to me without drowning out my voice. He has a refreshing interest that appears to have been lost on my generation. Any subject, my work, social or family life—doesn't bore him. I told him I had a sister, and he confessed he had a brother. Our trade of information made things comfortable. I didn't feel like I was under a spotlight—giving of myself, yet unable to see who he was. He has definitely piqued my curiosity, which I plan to satisfy. The conversation ended with both of us saying we'd probably see each other here again sometime.

WEDNESDAY, JANUARY 16, 2008: Hey Friends,

I played catch-up the rest of the week at work, but my conversation with Arcane looped around in my head. It was difficult to focus at work. It has been years since I felt the flutter of butterflies in my stomach just thinking about someone, but Arcane causes this along with a stream of emotion. In such a short time, he has brought my senses to life. Arcane says the right things, makes me laugh and reaches out to me with unexpected surprise, like he has known me for years—my secret savant. I think I'm falling hard for this guy. It's crazy, I know, but he won't leave my thoughts.

Like today when I was at work in the copy room, making endless copies of a case, I found myself smiling at some of the things Arcane said—jokes and stories about his childhood. Then my smile wilted when I remembered how I suffered through his talks about old girlfriends. Bitches! No one else deserves a guy like Arcane more than me. Jealousy tugged at my soul. I tried laughing it off—telling myself it's ridiculous to think this way; however, infatuation has a tendency to bury common sense. I left the copy room, dropping off copies of the case with the attorneys' secretaries. My curt "Here" raised a few eyebrows even though I have an aloof attitude most of the time at work anyway. I have nothing in common with anyone at the firm. Most have families or a high maintenance night life—two things I don't care about.

I returned to my desk, still thinking about how Arcane and I connected. The different discussions feel like pieces of a puzzle that are starting to fit together—with the hope they form a complete picture. We mean nothing to each other—just two people passing the time on the internet—yet my head and heart want to paint another picture of us as a couple. His attention toward me tickles my heart, which seems to beat harder than Father Time. It doesn't matter that I haven't heard his voice or seen what he looks like. His company, his words and the fact we drank together is a big deal. It felt like a virtual date, but in my experience went a helluva lot better than many in my real life. This way allowed us to get to know one another—gather our words like threads and stitch them together to create a persona. Arcane makes me feel important, even if it was for only one night. Knowing I'll be going back to chat on Friday night—a night I normally reserve for relaxation—and seeing him there is helping me get through the week.

But the pessimistic me keeps whispering, '*You may never hear from him again*'.

To hell with pessimism! I'll make sure I'll see him again, even if it means I go into chat every night.

This has been my week so far. Talk to you later.

FRIDAY, JANUARY 18, 2008: Hey Friends!

It's Friday night and I crossed my fingers that Arcane would be online. After pouring a glass of wine, I sat at the computer wondering whether or not to log into chat.

Should I wait, so I don't seem desperate?

I tapped the desk with my pencil, looked at a blank screen with my mind rocking to the tune of "He's just not that into you." Years of being single has crushed my confidence when it comes to relationships.

Am I ready for disappointment? Will he be online, or worse yet, will I ever talk to him again?

Your life is full of fucking disappointment.

I rubbed my eyes and pressed my fingers hard into my eye sockets. The pressure became too much, so I removed my fingers and placed my hands on the laptop. I shook my head, sat up straight, rolled my shoulders back and typed out N-e-w-b-i-e on the keyboard and hit 'connect', letting my analytical self lose to my emotional self. What an exhilarating relief to act on a whim…or what others might consider acting irresponsibly. Impulsive is a better word. It makes my actions more fun and carefree. The endless wait for the system to detect my network seemed as long as waiting to text my vote for the next American Idol. Finally, all the conversations flashed up on the screen like a colorful rainbow as I searched for Arcane. My heart pumped up the corners of my mouth when I saw his name in dark blue.

Should I initiate conversation this time? Has he been on awhile and plans on logging off? Is he talking to someone?

I have mastered the art of confusion; often preventing myself from going forward with things. I ache from living a stale life, but it's security, my internal fortress. During my moment of hesitation he obliged me with a simple *hello*. This is how our conversation went:

Newbie: Happy Friday! How was your week?

Arcane: Hectic, but I made it through. How was yours?

Newbie: Good. I'm just glad the weekend is here.

Arcane: I hear ya. You drinking?

Newbie: Sure am. How about you?

Arcane: You know it.

Occasional pauses allowed me to sip my drink and move the conversation to more interesting, personal matters, such as plans for the weekend.

Arcane: So, did you miss me?

My eyes widened. It was as if he had read my thoughts throughout the week.

Newbie: Oh yeah. *smiles* You were always on my mind. *rolls eyes* Did you wait with anticipation to talk to me? *grins*

Arcane: Actually, yes.

No shit! In an instant, a cold breeze swept over me leaving me motionless. I let his words burn into my corneas. No way in a million years was I expecting this kind of response. Men don't react to me this way.

Arcane: I really enjoyed talking to you those few times and hoped you would be on tonight.

It's about time I found someone who is interested in me.

Ha! He's interested in getting in your pants.

I looked away from the screen, sighed, rolled my shoulders back and then turned my attention to his last statement.

Newbie: I did too.

I kept it short. I didn't want to ruin a simple enjoyment.

Arcane: *grins* I'm glad. I was afraid I was the only one who enjoyed the conversation.

Newbie: No! You weren't.

Arcane: I'd like to stop calling you Newbie, which is impersonal, so would you mind telling me your name…or make one up if that makes you feel better?

Should I give it to him or make one up? I could give him my first name. I mean, what's the big deal? I'm sure there are lots of Sydneys.

And Arcanes…and Caitlyns…and Ashleys

Newbie: Sydney.

Arcane: *smiles* Thanks. Now is that your real name?

I felt his ropes begin to loop around me. If he kept this up, I would become his captive in no time.

Why did you do that? You don't know him.

I blew out air to release the tension.

Newbie: It is. Is Arcane your real name?

Arcane: Yes. And yes, my parents were drunk when they named me. The name means 'requiring secret or mysterious knowledge'. I guess this means I must find out *your* secrets.

Newbie: LOL!

Arcane: Don't laugh, Sydney, it's imperative I learn everything about you, so there aren't any secrets left. That's the duty of my name. *smiles*

Newbie: What a duty. I can promise you my secrets are boring and insignificant.

Arcane: Tsk, tsk. Don't spoil the suspense for me. *winks*

He winked at me. Does that mean he's kidding or flirting?

Newbie: I'm more like a college thesis than suspense.

Arcane: That's good, Sydney. It means you're researchable. *winks* And at least in your early 20s.

Again he winked.

Am I reading too much into this?

He could be flirting and joking. I took a few more sips of wine to get a hold of myself.

Why would he think I'm in my early 20s? Do I sound immature?

Newbie: Ah, my 20s…such memories.

Arcane: Hmm…So you're older?

Newbie: I don't know, am I? It's your duty to find out all my secrets.

Arcane: Oh, I got a smart one here. A woman who can handle her own. Mmm…I love smart, older women.

Older? Wait! Does this mean he's in his 20s?

Newbie: LOL! Oh yeah, I'm so old. You're probably young enough to be my son.

Arcane: *smiles*

Newbie: Really?! Are you in your late teens, early 20s?

Arcane: Ah, Sydney. Age is but a number—

Newbie: Yeah, yeah, yada, yada. No, really, are you that young?

Arcane: I'm young enough to change careers, but old enough to know a good woman when I read one.

Newbie: Um… I'm not feeling comfortable now.

Arcane: Why? Because I might be young enough to be your son? We're talking about life in general. I'm not flirting with you Sydney…at least not yet.

Newbie: See. You're confusing me. People get arrested for things like this.

Arcane: Sydney, let me ease your mind. I'm not jail bait. We're just talking over a few drinks. Besides, you don't really want to stop talking to me.

At this moment, I realized how much I liked him. I drink his words like water, eager that it won't be long before I am drowning in them. Arcane knows what I'm thinking before I say it.

Newbie: *releases the breath she'd been holding* You're right.

Arcane: Thata girl.

Our conversation lightened between our third and fourth drinks, but then it took another turn.

Arcane: Tell me, Sydney, what's a beautiful woman like you doing home on a Friday night?

Newbie: How do you know I'm beautiful? That could be the

reason I'm home on a Friday night. And I wouldn't admit that to you.

Arcane: I know beauty and you're it. I can't believe your husband would leave you alone on this beautiful night.

Newbie: Huh.

Arcane: What?

Newbie: Nothing. I just realized how buzzed I am.

Arcane: Nice. I bet you look sexy as hell sitting on your couch with your laptop and glass of wine.

All of a sudden, it felt like an icicle was stabbing my skin.

How did he know that?

I put my glass on the floor, the laptop on the couch, and got up to look out the window.

Could he be across the courtyard from my condo?

I turned the light off and scanned the neighboring windows to look for signs of life. Too many of the windows were dark for me to know if someone was watching. I went to each window and pulled the shades down, taking a quick glance to make sure I didn't miss movement in one of the nearby homes. I moved back to the couch, sat down, put my laptop back on my lap and read his comments.

Arcane: Sydney? Are you there?

Arcane: Okay, I won't call you sexy.

Arcane: Come on, Sydney, talk to me.

Newbie: I'm here. Sorry, nature called.

Arcane: No problem. For a minute there, I thought the sexy comment had you fanning your face.

Newbie: Arcane?

Arcane: Yes?

Newbie: How did you know I was on my couch? Better yet, how do you know I have a laptop?

Arcane: Lucky guess, I suppose. Really. I had no idea.

He was so nonchalant about it I had to believe he was telling the truth.

Newbie: So…you're not going to call me sexy anymore?

Arcane: Er…it depends on if you want me to.

It was time I took control of the conversation. He seemed to know too much for my own good—perhaps I watered him with information like the wine watered my soul. The time had come to find out where Mr. Arcane was from and what made him tick.

Newbie: Where do you live?

Arcane: Why? Do you want to meet?

Newbie: Maybe.

Arcane: I live on the south side of Chicago. The Beverly area. Where are you?

The wine went down my throat like sandpaper.

He's right in my area. Am I glad or frightened?

Newbie: I'm sitting right next to you. *winks*

Arcane: I wish. Do you know what I'd do if you were sitting next to me?

My heart sped up. As much as he freaked me out by knowing too much, I wanted to know what he would do to me if I was there. Plenty of time has passed since my last relationship, leaving me with a vague recollection. With head and heart dried out, I am thirsty for a trickle of affection.

Newbie: No, what?

Arcane: I'd get you another glass of wine, put on some smooth music, and have you lie on the couch between my legs.

I closed my eyes and clenched my laptop. Even though I asked, his response was too intrusive for me. My body tensed as I repeated the words 'between my legs' out loud. But I lit the match—he just poured the gasoline. It was up to me to blow it out or cause an explosion. I knew the conversation would turn sexual, and even though he occupied my thoughts, I was hesitant about discussing sex with someone I barely knew.

Newbie: I think this playful discussion overstepped some boundaries. It was my fault. I started it and I'd like it to stop.

Arcane: Like you said, it's a playful discussion, but I disagree this overstepped any boundaries. We are the ones who set them, although I don't recall setting any. You're in the privacy of your own home. I'm not physically there to cross boundaries you may set, so where's the harm?

Newbie: The harm is we don't know each other and shouldn't be fantasizing about one another.

Arcane: Sydney. We've devoted more talking time than most married couples. I'd say we know each other enough to convey our desires. And I desire you.

Desire. A craving I've had for him since he threw me the first morsel. I want to know about his desires. I want to know what he'd do if he were here. Most of all, I want Arcane to let me forget about the years of lost love.

Newbie: You desire me? Why?

Arcane: Simple. You showed me that people can be 'real' online, and you seem like a photocopy of me...except you're a woman. What can I say, I love myself.

My laugh barked out into the room and before I knew it, I was asking him again what he'd do (to me) if he were here.

Arcane: Music...glass full...you lie between my legs. In other words, I'd hold you close until your body began to sleep and release the tension.

Newbie: Mmm...that sounds nice.

Arcane: My hands would occasionally touch a strand of your hair, rub your shoulders, and I'd kiss the top of your head.

I enjoyed his words and hearing how he'd take care of me. It felt as though I was experiencing it as he typed.

Arcane: Sydney?

Newbie: Yes?

Arcane: Do you have a mic on your computer?

Why? Did he want to actually talk? Did I want to talk?

A voice. This would change the playing field. I felt the two words "I do" ping-pong around my head until they found the hole and fell out.

Newbie: I do.

Arcane: Would you like to talk using voice instead of typing?

Newbie: Um…I don't know. We just met.

Arcane: I'm not asking to have a one night stand, just to talk instead of typing. That way our hands will be free to kick back and hold our drinks. *grins*

Newbie: Okay. Let me hook it up.

I pulled open the drawer where my external headphones and mic had been since the first day I bought them. The screen still held the last of our conversation. It seemed harmless enough. I plugged the mic in and straightened my posture. Taking a sip of courage, I cleared my throat and typed "ready".

I heard ringing.

Arcane said, "Hello? Sydney?"

My voice cracked as I replied, "Yes."

"Ah, there you are. You have a sexy voice."

I laughed and then said, "I bet you say that to all the women."

"And they believe me." There was a familiarity to his voice—an old song.

"Sydney, are you still there?"

"Yes. I'm sorry."

I could feel his smile when he said, "Don't be nervous. We're only talking. And you DO have a sexy voice."

I cleared my throat again and said, "Thank you. I like your voice, too."

"This old thang. Well, it has gotten me out of trouble a few times."

"I bet it got you into trouble, too."

"That it did."

Our breathing spoke when our words took a break. It wasn't as though we had nothing to say. It had more to do with what we shouldn't say.

Arcane took a gulp of his drink before saying, "As I was saying before, I'd make sure you were relaxed on the couch without a care in the world."

"You would, would you?"

"Yes. I can smell your hair from here—a hint of clean under a hard day's work."

I laughed. "Gee, thanks."

"My hands would massage your shoulders to loosen the work tension as my mouth trailed down your neck."

I couldn't help giggling. Talking and listening to him describe how he'd take care of me was awkward, yet he ignited something inside me. I felt myself getting wet thinking about his hands and mouth, so I closed my eyes to put his words into play.

"Would you like that, Sydney?"

I let out a long-awaited breath, and said, "I would."

"I'm glad because I know I would. I'd unbutton a few buttons on your shirt, and rest my hand on your breast as my lips lightly grazed your neck. My legs would open wider so your body would fit better in the contours of mine. I'd hear you moan, let out a sigh of need, and that would be my cue."

He stopped talking. I wasn't sure why, but I decided to say something.

"Cue for what?"

"Ah. I wanted to make sure you were experiencing this with me. You sometimes give me cues to proceed."

"I do? What kind of cue did I give you?"

"In response to lying back, your thighs would spread a few inches; you'd push down into the couch with your ass and slightly arch your back, allowing my hand to get a better grip on your breast."

"WOW! I had no idea I gave you this cue."

"It's subconscious. You've waited and wanted my hands and mouth on you. Now I plan to fulfill your fantasy."

I 'pfft' at his cockiness, and said, "I don't recall you in my fantasies."

"Yes you do. I'm the faceless guy who seduces you, violates you, and makes you submit to my needs."

I was replaying his words.

He even knows my fantasies. Or are these every woman's fantasies?

"I have to go, Arcane."

"Wait! Why? I'll stop with the fantasy."

"That isn't it. I have to—"

"No you don't. I freaked you out and now you're going to make up some lame excuse to get off voice."

What's wrong with hearing him describe your fantasy? You waited all week to hear from him, and now when he's talking sexual on voice you want to leave?

"I know you're still there, Sydney. Listen, if you don't want me to talk or ask about something then tell me. I won't if it isn't something you want to do."

The silence thickened. "Sydney? Please talk to me."

"I'm here."

Arcane let the silence gather my words.

"I like talking to you, but yeah, you did kind of freak me out."

"Let's change the subject. You can describe *my* fantasy."

We both laughed and continued talking into the early morning hours. Lighter subjects planted seeds in our relationship.

SATURDAY, JANUARY 19, 2008: What's up Friends?

What can I say? I dreamt and awoke thinking about Arcane—fantasies of getting to know him in the physical sense. Yesterday, we touched on so many subjects that I feel like I already know so much about him. But I don't. My hand began caressing my breast, moving down to where I pictured Arcane. It was a poor substitute for the man I desire, yet it was all I could count on now. I closed my eyes, dreaming about what he could possibly be like—an overall strength to submit to as dark, roasted eyes seared into my soul, stealing anything left of independence. His thick lips and tongue sliding along my inner and outer core until a wave of emotion rattled my bones and seeped between my legs.

I slammed my arms down on the bed and finally got up to a wintry day with a blinding sun reflecting off the snow (I so didn't want to get out of bed). Wrapping my robe tighter around me, I looked out the window, sipping coffee, squinting into the crystallized snow while thinking about Arcane and my early morning release. I turned to glance at the computer sitting on the cocktail table as if it whispered my name and then glanced back out the window. *Thank God I don't need to go anywhere.*

Is he still sleeping? Did he leave me a message?

After discussing so many things last night, and giving some information away, I had caved and given him my e-mail address. My curiosity and boredom got the best of me, so I woke up my laptop to check if he sent me anything—one new e-mail message from a Ramsey Cockinner. The name wasn't familiar, but I opened it anyway along with the attachment. My mouth dropped like a gallows trapdoor as my eyes locked on the picture of a guy lying on a bed, penis in hand with a message in the body of the e-mail, "For you, dear Sydney. Think of me during your alone time. Heart, Arcane".

My face caught fire and I closed the attachment (and slammed the lid of my computer). Unbelievable! The gall he had to send me such a picture. During our talks, inhibitions flying away, I didn't recall inviting such a bold move.

Does he think this is cute?

DAMN HIM! Up to this point I thought he was perfect. Did he send that as if I'm some whore who gets off on picking up strangers on the internet? I closed my eyes, took in deep breaths, formed a circle with my lips and released the air. This slow motion continued several times before I opened my eyes again.

When my anger—mixed with embarrassment—subsided, I reopened the attachment to inspect it more closely. Messy, dark hair hung in chunks around his face with dark, perfect, symmetrical eyes looking directly at me with want and a wily grin. Arcane's skin, the top coating of Crème Brulee—shiny and sweet—his muscular curves smooth and inviting. The picture is impressive—mocking and challenging—worst of all he has the personality to enhance his strong beauty.

I don't recall how long I sat staring at a part of him I wished was inside of me, but an instant message popped up and brought me back to reality. My eyes drifted over to Arcane's IM, "Mornin', Beautiful."

I had mixed feelings about the picture he sent so I wasn't quite sure how to respond. On the one hand, I was insulted that he thought so low of me—like a perverse loner—but on the other, he trusted me enough to send it. With the picture still opened, staring at his pose and handsome features, my insides melted and leaked out. I typed a simple "Good morning".

Arcane: Did you just wake up?

Sydney: No. I've been up for a few hours. What are your plans today?

Arcane: to

Arcane: see

Arcane: you

My fingers stopped mid-air, reading each word as it appeared. I wasn't sure if he was waiting for a response or goofing around. Even after a few in-depth conversations, I still find it difficult to decipher whether or not he is joking.

Arcane: Are you busy? We live close by, so why not hook up?

Close by? I never told him where I lived.

Are you sure you didn't? You popped off the cork and poured out your life to him last night. An inner warning went off when you gave him your first name. You shouldn't have started this with someone you don't know.

But we do know each other. I'm not some loner looking to divulge my secrets like a 900 number call.

I dropped my head, covered my face with my hands and rubbed my forehead. The permeating sun through the window summoned me to get up and glance around the courtyard. All seemed deserted.

But somehow he knows.

I thought back to last night's conversation—picking it apart like a turkey carcass. There were moments of light banter, sexual seasoning and his hunger to know things about me. When it came to specifics, I always made sure I kept it general without giving too much information. He asked what I did for a living, and I told him I was a secretary.

Arcane: Sydney. Take a shower, eat something and think about it. I'm heading into the shower to put my guy at ease by thinking of you. *winks* I'll check back later.

Things are moving too fast. He knows things he shouldn't, says things he shouldn't, yet it is easy to talk to him. I closed the living room blinds, moved to the couch and threw a blanket over me.

This is my fault. I let my loneliness make me vulnerable and now he is feeding off it. It's one thing to get to know him with wireless streams between us, but the idea of a full, in-person meeting so soon is unnerving. I rested my head against the arm of the couch, facing his picture and message.

Arcane doesn't have a mark on him, other than a tattoo on his right hip of a naked woman straddling an anchor with three hairy 6's protruding out of her.

Did he get the tattoo on a dare, to be funny, or does he think low of women?

His arched eyebrows frame his dark eyes, partially covered by restless strands. His nose shoots straight down with enough width to balance his meaty lips. He is hypnotizing, erotic and disturbing. I feel as if he is playing my heart like a guitar, plucking the strings with his looks using words to poison my cautiousness.

Some time passed while I was gazing at his picture. I left the instant messaging window up with his last comment while I showered and thought about how to answer him.

We need and want each other, but he looks about twenty years younger than me.

It wouldn't be right of me to get involved with someone so young.

Could my heart even handle an emotional attachment to a possible fling?

He looks good enough to eat and dangerous enough to stay clear of. My body grows hungry from the thought of him—personality and appearance—I finally have to admit that he tapped into my soul last Monday.

I walked back to the computer and typed, "What do you have in mind?"

I had no idea what would happen next, but this simple question offered up so many wonderful possibilities…or maybe not. Still, I told him where I lived.

The internet offers the opportunity of charades, except now I had unlocked the door to truth. No more confidence behind a screen name or beauty behind the mystery—my manners and flaws would be exposed for ridicule and heartbreak. Even though these consequences entered my mind, I was only focused on being a part of Arcane's life and filling my lonely days and nights.

Enthusiasm stifles inhibitions. It took me several hours to get ready. After putting my makeup on with precision, I pulled my hair back, turned to the right, left, and then front to see if my hair looked better up. Taking the hair away from my face showed too much of me, so I let it fall and stuck my tongue out at myself in the mirror.

By the living room windows, I looked down on the walkway that circled around, veering off into each entryway. My insides were like popping popcorn. To stop the heat from melting my skin, I pressed my forehead against the cold window and closed my eyes.

Is this really what you want? If not, you still have time to cancel.

I want this. I'm tired of being lonely. I want someone to love me.

The gate buzzer rang and my eyes flipped open. I hesitated for a few buzzes before letting him in the gate. I ran back to the window to watch him walk toward the entry. Instead of going straight to my door, he turned left and walked to the opposite side, looking at the address above him.

He was showcasing his goods and I bought into it, watching every step he took. I watched his thigh muscles clench then release the fabric of his jeans. His hair resembled the picture—dark with chunks outlining his face. The leather jacket and scarf garnished his confidence as I felt mine evaporate. He made his way all the way around the walkway until once again the buzzer called me.

My heart was about to pop out of my chest. With my back against the hallway door, I pressed my hand against my heart, trying to calm its excitement. I smiled and let my head rest against the door and then a laugh escaped. Still smiling and laughing, I wrapped my hand around my mouth to stifle the noise. I was giddy!

Arcane is a luxury. I can't settle down.

I looked out the peephole and listened to the echo of his breathing. Arcane took his time, and before making the last flight up, he paused on the landing and looked out onto the courtyard. He approached the door and I opened it before he could knock. We looked at each other, but now it was his turn to scope out the goods. His eyes fell to my black shoes, slowly rising up over my hips, pausing at my stomach before proceeding. He smiled when he got to my breasts—bulging a bit from the blouse—and then his eyes rested on my face.

Arcane tilted his head, bit his lower lip, and said, "Hello, Sydney."

His mixture of boyish charm and sensuality claimed me. I couldn't fight it, nor did I want to. Arcane is every woman's fantasy, and he plays the fantasy to his advantage.

In what felt like slow motion, Arcane rested his right forearm against the door jamb, leaned in and brushed his lips against my cheek, lifting my hair with his fingers and whispering, "Like I asked, what's a beautiful woman like you doing home on a Friday night?"

I tilted my head, bit my lower lip and with my eyes swaying his way, responded, "It's Saturday."

I followed up with a smile.

I opened the door wider and backed into it. Arcane prowled my condo, lapping up as much information about me as possible. I took cover in the kitchen and was fighting with the wine opener when he approached, bringing his arms around me, pressing up against my back and pulling the cork out with ease. (OMG!) His lips swooped in on the back of my neck, hovering, restless until he turned me around and surrounded my lips with his. His seductive moves hypnotized me, and it wasn't long before we engaged touch and taste over every inch of our bodies.

Arcane is young—he doesn't rush matters; appreciative and cognizant of my tenderness and surprise. He understands how to fulfill a woman's desires at the same time making me want to please him even more. He doesn't care about or mention age and treats me as if I have the taut body of a twenty-year-old.

I didn't have a problem lying next to him, but my adrenalin kept me awake. I snuck out of bed to tell you about my day. Magical, wouldn't you agree? I can't believe he's still interested after seeing me.

Oops…I hear someone *nudge* moving around. Talk to you later.

WEDNESDAY, JANUARY 23, 2008: Friends,

I thought I'd stop by and share my crazy thoughts.

I've seen Arcane every day since we first met. I have never had a lover put so much time into pleasing and being pleased and (now) I find myself—my body—crying for him daily. It hurts to leave for work, knowing I'll be without him and this obsession is growing each day. Arcane seems unaffected by our time together. He enjoys the experience and continues to make everything close to perfect, but his disconnect is evident. I try, even beg at times, to find out what I need to do to make him lose sleep over me.

Usually with a laugh, he responds by saying something like, "I adore you, Sydney, isn't that enough? Must I want to kill myself for you?"

Yes! I do! I want him to lose sleep over me…suffer from constant dreams of me.

My internal pain and need will not allow his words to shake me awake enough to step back and accept how things really are…that I love a man who merely enjoys my company. My work is beginning to suffer, along with things in the condo. When I'm not with him, I'm thinking about him—and when that isn't enough, I pleasure myself thinking about him fulfilling one of my many desires. Sometimes I have to stop and catch my breath because my feelings for him are so strong they knock the wind out of me when I think of his abandonment.

How did I allow my feelings to run wild? I have to stop making him my life. Give me strength, my friends. Good night.

FRIDAY, FEBRUARY 22, 2008: Hello Friends,

I'm sorry it's been a while since I've written. In the five weeks I have known Arcane, my contact with family and friends has been limited, too. My sister, Carolyn, called to tell me she broke her wrist tripping over a basket of clothes. I told her I was sorry to hear about it, and would stop on by sometime during the week to see her. The week went by without me popping over. A friend called crying that she miscarried. I lowered my voice, gave her my condolences, and lied that I had the stomach flu. I focus on Arcane and his needs leaving little time for others. After all, I sat many times on the sidelines waiting for friends' calendars to free up from their boyfriends/spouses. This is my time.

Arcane never calls, so I never know when he'll show up. To keep him happy, I make sure I have the things he likes in my refrigerator and cabinets. He keeps me charged in his presence, but I'm starting to feel drained in his absence.

My relaxing Friday nights of solitude and drinks have turned into sessions of pleasing Arcane. As busy as I am with work, it never occurs to me to ask him to pick something up; nor does he ever bother. Weakened from his hours of silence, moments when I sit waiting for the phone to ring, leave me giving him more. What little scraps of compliments he tosses my way, I gather for the times I hunger during his punishing silence. His careless whispers deafen me from my own. Our relationship has already fallen into a cadence of silently assigned duties. His cortisone-injected personality creates anxiety (I find I exhibit when in his presence). When Arcane shows up, I feel a burden to please.

sighs Gotta go.

SATURDAY, FEBRUARY 23, 2008: Friends,

Life has changed forever. Arcane and I planned to go out to dinner last night. When I opened the door, I couldn't hide my disappointment in the way he was dressed. He showed up in flip flops, ripped jeans and a t-shirt. During our times in the chat room, I mentioned my dislike of flip flops and the overall messy appearance men think women find attractive. It was one thing for him to dress this way if he was sick or we were lying around the condo, but it upset me after I put in the time to look nice for him— the curves of my freshly cleansed body in an inviting soft, purple angora sweater, long jean skirt and black knee-high boots.

"What's wrong, Sydney? You don't care for the way I look?"

"Well, you could have dressed a little nicer."

"I'm sure there are plenty of women out there who wouldn't be disappointed in the way I look, and would probably even be pleased about it."

I turned and walked into the living room. Before I reached the couch, he grabbed my arm and jerked me around to face him.

He punctuated the move by applying pressure to my arms, saying, "If you want, I'll leave and find someone else who wants to be with me; someone who doesn't want to change who I am."

Arcane squeezed my arms harder as he spoke. It hurt…it really hurt. My eyes stretched open in disbelief.

"Ow! You're hurting me, Arcane. Let me go."

He released my arms immediately and I rubbed them to ease the pain. Tears of confusion and embarrassment pooled in my eyes (I couldn't believe this sudden change). I looked away, but I felt his stare so I bowed my head and went into the washroom. When I came out, Arcane wasn't in the living room or kitchen, so I eased toward the bedroom where I found him lying on his back on the bed looking up at the ceiling. He turned to me and held out his arms. I went to him, allowing his arms to wrap around and hold me close. Nothing needed to be said, but he spoke anyway.

"I'm sorry you expected something nicer. I didn't think it—"

"It's fine. I guess I'm just tired."

We laid there for some time before he took my hand and pushed it into his pants. The negative mood appeared to have aroused him, but my efforts to follow through fell short. As much as I wanted to please him, I didn't have the energy.

My less than enthusiastic actions ignited something inside him. He grabbed my hand and hair, pulling me up.

I grabbed at his hand (the one that pulled at my hair)—trying to get him to release it, wincing. I didn't understand...

"Let go! What did I do? Let go of me, Arcane."

He rolled on top of me and pinned my arms down.

"Shut up! First you make me feel like I'm not good enough for you, and now you're trying to humor me."

"What? I'm not trying to humor—"

He spit out, "I don't want to hear it. You will please me the way I want it."

He used my body like a wooden board. When he tired of my protests, he hit me (hard!).

I woke to the sound of his breathing.

Arcane had raped and sodomized me.

He slept, fulfilled as I limped to the washroom. I had played

Russian Roulette in that chat room and lost. I turned on the shower and scrubbed the semen and blood that leaked out from both ends, lightly touching the scratches and bite marks decorating my inner thighs, stomach and arms. In the dim lighting of the nightlight, I sat in the shower; head resting on my bent knees, hoping the sound of the water would drown out my cries. I watched, dazed, as a part of me swirled around and down the drain with the blood and semen. When my body showed signs of shriveling, I turned off the shower, grabbed a towel, and rested my head on it until the darkness of my dreams saved me for the time being.

I HATE ARCANE!!

TUESDAY, JUNE 4, 1985: Dear Friend,

(sighs) It's Caitlyn.

My mom is gone, locked up in jail for things she did to me. I should have been a better kid...maybe things would have been different between us. Since she's not around, I don't have anywhere else to go. The only person I thought was eager and willing to help me is Cal Birch, but when I arrived at Cal's house hungry, tired, and full of hope, all he greeted me with was angry lust and heated demands.

He grabbed my backpack, tossed it on the floor of the living room, grabbed my upper arms, pulled me within inches of his face and said, "Well, Caitlyn, you ready to be mine?"

"Yours? I thought you were going to help me."

Cal's nicotine breath made me want to throw up when he said, "Sure I'll help you. I'll help you onto my cock. I'll give you a place to stay, food to eat, but you do as you're told. You understand me, bitch?"

"But Cal—"

He took a step back, released my arm and brought his hand down hard across the left side of my face. My cheek felt like it ballooned—the stinging heat watering my eyes. I fell a few steps back, brought my hand to my face, and slid my tongue along my lower lip. Blood. My tears didn't sway Cal from his mean state. He grabbed my hair and dragged me to a back room where he threw me on a bed and began to tie my wrists and ankles to the bedposts. Shock and fright made me obey. Besides, I have no other choice. Cal has always said he wanted to take care of me, 'cept he never told me what he considered 'care'. His easy going way and understanding when I used to complain about my mom and other men, is gone. Cal needs something or someone to take his anger out on...someone he can blame because of his problems...and that someone is me NOW!

Once secured, Cal cut off all my clothes. I closed my eyes to block out the humiliation. I should be used to this by now. This isn't the first time I've been in this position (literally) before and (apparently) not the last. But how? How is anyone supposed to get use to this treatment?

I felt the bed dip between my legs, and then Cal said, "Open your eyes."

I opened my eyes. Cal was leering down at me with a wooden spoon in his hand.

He licked his lips and said, "We're gonna have fun together."

Why did you let him tie you up? You should have fought back.

For what?! Where am I going to go?

I'm sorry I'm a disappointment, friend. You're the only one I trust. The only one I can tell about my daily sadness. Please forgive me. I'll be back soon…I hope.

SATURDAY (night), FEBRUARY 23, 2008: Dear Friends,

I return to you humiliated and in pain. Friday night turned out horribly wrong. I don't know what I'm going to do…how I'll get over Arcane's deception. As I write this I still can't stop crying…but I have no one else to blame but me.

When I woke yesterday morning still lying in the tub, I knew Arcane had left because the air felt lighter. Balancing my arms on the sides of the tub to lift my assaulted body out, I took a deep breath and looked in the mirror. A stranger stared back at me; an aged woman with red, swollen eyes and Arcane's unfinished artwork of black and blue with small purple lines. I invited the tears, as I do now, opened the washroom door, looked around and waited for sound before exiting. The bed sheets were on the floor and I could see last night's damage on the bed. As if I was in a trance, I moved to the front door to lock and bolt lock it. I returned to the bedroom, pulled the sheets off the bed and threw them in the garbage. I closed all the blinds and curled up in the middle of my bed, hugging two pillows and wondering what I had done to deserve last night's rage. My family's calls went unanswered, and it wasn't until the sun began nodding off when Arcane decided to call. His name flashed on my phone display, bringing back the pain. I knew I hated him, but wasn't sure how I was going to get rid of him without provoking this monster.

I hATE ARCANE!!

How does a funny, great-looking guy turn into an animal? Better yet, how did I miss the signs?

You didn't. You knew he was trouble from the beginning, but you didn't care.

I did care. He was nice. He made me laugh and I felt comfortable being with him.

How so? He sucked the energy from you. You were pathetically needy.

I pressed the fatty part of my palms against my ears—I needed to block out the blame.

It isn't my fault.

His control had seeped into our relationship, filling the cracks with demands.

It only took a few ignored phone calls before I heard him ringing the bell. I thanked God for not getting around to having a key made for him. For once, procrastination was my saving grace. The buzzing echoed throughout the courtyard every time Arcane pressed it. I pulled the pillow over my head to stop the ringing in my ears...to hide the tears...to hide from shame. When his anger got the best of him, he held the buzzer in. The neighbors were yelling out of their windows for him to knock it off, but that only made him do it more. Under the pillow, I buried my face into the bed, begging for him to quit it.

Soon after, the buzzer stopped so I removed the pillow. I heard arguing and then shouts as the police tried to reason with him. The courtyard acoustics pulled the scuffle toward me, magnifying Arcane's unruly restrain. His shouts, "You bitch. You whore," blasted through the courtyard.

I'm not. I'm not a whore. I loved him. Can't you see that? Can't he see that?

The police calmed Arcane down before they rang my buzzer. I'm guessing they wanted to find out what was going on, but it was much easier to ignore the situation than face my tormenter. From my opened window, I could hear the police giving Arcane an ultimatum; leave or go to jail. I heard him shout, "Fine!" Then I heard a car door open, start and screech out of its space down the street. I put my hands together in a prayer pose and pressed them against my forehead. (Thank you!) The cops' walkie talkies went off indicating they had another issue to deal with. In my bedroom, I clenched the pillow as my body shivered involuntarily just thinking about the coming days.

I told you you're worthless.

Please, friends, don't…don't point your fingers and say you told me so. I can't bear it if all of you blame me for it. It's bad enough knowing I was careless.

I need sleep. Let's hope he's gone forever.

SUNDAY, FEBRUARY 24, 2008: Dear Friends,

I thought I slept off the fear and sadness, but a new day brings more. When I looked at my phone, it showed fifty missed calls and ten messages from Arcane. The first several messages filled my ears with words of hatred and then the messages altered into sobs of apology. SERIOUSLY?! An apology for what he did? I'LL NEVER FORGIVE HIM!! I went through each message deleting his poisonous words. He even threatened me that if I didn't pick up the phone he'd make my life miserable. I thought to myself, 'Hasn't he already done so?' His name-calling bit and dug deeper into my already battered spirit. I needed another shower to scrub away the grime I felt after listening to him. Under the showerhead, the water pounded my skin the way Arcane had pounded my dignity and emotions—his presence continues to seep into daily routines. It doesn't matter how often I go over and over Friday night in my head, nothing I had done excuses what he did to me. I let the water massage my scalp as I dropped my head, pressing my hands against the tiles in front of me to brace for the noises I pulled from my gut. The water streamed into my mouth as I spit it out with my cries. I let anger and self-pity battle it out.

When I was spent, I shut the shower off so my skin could iron out the wrinkles. The water didn't cleanse me from anxiety, and the cancerous emptiness kept spreading within. I still feel dirty. In my cold kitchen, I paced its length, chewing on my hair as I waited for the coffee to brew. Staring straight ahead at nothing in particular, I gnawed on my hair transfixed on thoughts of the past few months. Back and forth, chewing and mesmerized—a collision of emotion slowly hardening from recent events. When I got to the back door of the kitchen, I stopped, slipped my finger under a kitchen blind slat and lifted it to check the weather. Shit! Arcane! He was sleeping on my porch.

I HATE ARCANE!!

You get what you deserve.

I've been good. Why do I deserve this?

Because you're irresponsible.

But I wished on a falling star—not a fallen angel.

A quick release of the slat caused the kitchen blinds to move and make noise, so I put my hand against them to control the movement, squeezing my eyes in prayer that he didn't wake up.

Being on the third floor has its advantages and disadvantages. I am high enough where no one could see him laying there in wait. I moved into the living room so he couldn't hear me pace as I chewed my fingernails.

If I ignore him and stay in all day, will he eventually leave?

My heart pounded louder and my hands shook when I reached for my cell phone.

I noticed a little post-it on my display, which indicates a text message. I flipped the phone open, went to my message and started reading it as I eased down onto the couch.

Arcane: i gave u love, a social life and great sex, so u can see why im confused. 1 minute were fine & the next u don't want me. what the hell, syd. i luv u.

I HATE ARCANE!!

He loves me? HE LOVES ME?! HE NEVER LOVED ME!! I snapped the phone shut, shocked by his bullshit words. My vision blurred and I was feeling puzzled and scared by his reckless views and actions. I flipped my phone back open.

His calm won't last.

I dialed 9-1-1.

I had to call the police. Who knew what he'd do next? Within minutes the police rang my bell. Oh...it gets worse. The officers— one male, one female—stood in my living room arguing that there was nothing they could do.

The male officer, Mike O'Connor, said, "Miss, he's not back there. We can't press charges against someone for trespassing when they're not even here."

I pressed my fist against my mouth as I looked out the window then back at the officers. Officer O'Connor's eyes narrowed and zoomed in on me when he spoke. I think he was trying to intimidate me. He folded his arms over his wide chest, spread his legs shoulder-width apart, and extinguished his breath like a fire-eating dragon. His hostility pulled the nerves right out of my skin.

Why is he acting this way? I didn't do anything.

Probably because you pulled this fat cop away from his donuts.

He's scaring me.

He's pissed. Your stalker is long gone and you're wasting his time.

I pulled at my hair to stop the anxiousness and then hugged my arms when I said, "I understand that officer, but what am I supposed to do? He could come back and kill me. Is that what needs to happen for something to be done?"

The female officer, Katie Flannigan, stepped forward sensing my terror.

"Miss, by law we can't press charges, but we can go and talk to him if you'd like."

O'Connor dropped his arms and shook his head walking away from me. (What an asshole!) Officer Flannigan clicked her tongue at him and then looked at me.

"If you give us his address, we'll go over there and have a talk with him."

I felt my face change colors.

Damn it! This totally makes me look so stupid.

I bit my lip and whispered, "I don't know where he lives…"

Flannigan and O'Connor turned to me—skepticism swept across their faces.

"What do you mean you don't know where he lives? I thought he was your boyfriend?" O'Connor demanded.

I cleared my throat and said, "He is, but I've never been to his place. We met last month in an online chat room. Every time we were together it was either here or we went out."

Flannigan let air escape loudly from her mouth and looked out the window.

"Well, miss—"

"Sydney. Sydney Hayes"

"Well, Sydney, there's nothing we can do then. I'd like to help you, really, but I can't without an address," Flannigan said.

As you can imagine, I was desperate for them to catch him. I walked over to my laptop, picked it up and said, "Could you get it from my computer? You know…check the IP address."

"Miss, we're not a forensics team," O'Connor blurted. "If something more concrete were to happen, the police and higher-ups would get involved, but a simple squabble between two people who apparently barely know each other isn't really grounds for forensics testing." His sarcasm dripped like a leaky faucet. He was such a jerk! The way he treated me only added to my fear. My face crumpled, tears sinking into creases. My hands gripped the laptop tight. I put it down and remained where I was standing…to hell with walking them to the door.

I don't need to be treated like this by them.

O'Connor put his hat on with his bloated fingers and he turned toward the door. Flannigan followed, but turned back to me before leaving.

"Here's my card. Call me if something else happens or if he comes back, okay?"

No it's not okay.

You're on your own.

He'll slip up.

I'm hoping it's not when he kills me.

I HATE ARCANE!!

FRIDAY, FEBRUARY 29, 2008: Hi Friends,

I thought I got rid of Arcane because the week went by without any sign of him. Since my walk to the train station is a few blocks away, I was relieved when I didn't find him lurking in the bushes or behind a tree. I mean, he IS a psycho, so of course it's only normal I looked out my window—moving my head to the sway of the pendulum for signs of Arcane. But today...after work...my luck ran out. My guard must have taken a nap. When I opened my condo's security gate, Arcane grabbed the gate and slipped in behind me before I could close it. My feet scrambled for ground, but he seemed to glide effortlessly, securing my arm. I jerked it back. He hadn't made an appearance all week! Why now? I wanted to SCREAM! In the cool early evening air, I could feel my face darkening...my hands balled into fists. But I didn't scream or lose my cool in any way.

"What are you doing here?"

"I need to talk to you. Please talk to me."

"There's nothing to talk about. You got what you wanted, so leave me alone."

I was moving toward my door when he caught my arm again. I snatched it back, shouting, "Just leave me alone!"

Parentheses of confusion cupped his eyes and mouth.

"Where's all this coming from, Syd? Please? Let's go up to your condo and talk."

"Arcane, we are not going upstairs, and there isn't anything to talk about." I folded my arms to show I wouldn't budge (tough gal) as I tried to still my trembling legs. They were as loose and wobbly as noodles.

He folded his arms, saying, "What's going on, Sydney? One minute we're making love and the next you're calling the cops on me. What happened?"

The shock began to curdle and my entire body straightened in defense. I thought, 'This is a joke, right? He couldn't honestly believe he didn't do anything wrong?' No. This was a ploy to play me again…to earn my trust and then shatter it. I kept my voice even—unwavering to show I was not playing his game.

"Arcane, if you don't know what you did to me then you need help."

"Tell me what I did to get this treatment from you."

SHIT! He was making me relive it. My eyes watered and narrowed. Staring right at him, stressing each word, I said, "You. Raped. And. Sodomized. Me."

His mouth dropped open, playing innocent. He put his hand on his chest as if appalled by my accusation. "I what? You. Wanted. It."

I HATE ARCANE!!

I felt my shouts rumble around me. "Wanted it?! I said 'no', which means stop! I cried. You told me I was to please you, so how is that wanting it?!"

He scanned the courtyard, turned toward me, lowered his voice and responded, "You said it was a fantasy of yours. To be taken against your will."

I looked down, too repulsed to look at him. "You didn't do it for me. You did it for your own pleasure. When we had our fantasy discussion, I even admitted I wouldn't want to act out all my fantasies in real life—that's why they're called *fantasies*!"

I turned toward my outer door and then decided against opening it. Only turning my head to look over my right shoulder, eyebrows crinkled, I said, "Please leave."

Arcane turned to go. With one last look, he turned his head to look over his shoulder, eyebrows crumpled over his brooding eyes then left, slamming the gate behind him.

SUNDAY, MARCH 11, 1990: Dear Friend,

It's me, Caitlyn.

I finally got up the strength to leave. When Cal stumbled into the bedroom and fell on the bed, I looked down at him, kicked his leg out of the way and walked out of the house. He didn't realize what was happening until I was halfway down the block. I pictured the ripped screen door creaking open as it balanced on its rusty hinges.

I smiled to myself when Cal Birch yelled, "If you take one more fucking step, your ass better not come back here again. You hear me, bitch?!"

I hATE CAL !!

So I kept walking down the street without looking back. I knew he was too drunk to follow me...too drunk to bother chasing something he got tired of. In the distance I heard the screen door slam shut and then silence—closing on the last five years. Thank God! To be honest, I never thought this day would ever come.

I have counted the days until now. Five years of abuse at the hands of the only person I could call family. Every day I prayed for either my day of freedom or for a painful, unfortunate death for Cal. God must have some pity for me.

Little by little, I had stolen money from Cal until I had enough to last a month on the road. This morning I showered, dressed and stuffed the things that I needed into a dusty backpack—the same one I had when I first showed up on Cal's doorstep.

Now I am waiting in the train station (to get out of the suburbs and go back to the inner city of Chicago) to search for what I lost...and find myself again—Caitlyn Hayes. She's been dormant for so long.

Until we meet again...

SUNDAY, MARCH 2, 2008: Hi Friends,

It took half of the weekend to recuperate from our altercation. I didn't bother going on my computer, keeping its lid closed to keep all intrusions away, and I have avoided leaving my condo. The calmness I previously complained about has returned and I feel like I am becoming my old self again (the self before Arcane). I have been sleeping in and when I woke, I kept busy cleaning the condo, changing things to distance me from *him*. There was enough on television this weekend to keep me occupied—my favorite marathon shows and plenty of movies. Even though I know Arcane is unstable, a part of me still wishes things had worked out because I had grown to love him, and his absence reminds me of what I had always wanted—a relationship (I know I sound pathetically needy).

I have decided not to tell anyone, except you, about what he did to me. Since that night, my memory has begun to betray me—the details sometimes separate from the events. Other times I vividly remember the physical and emotional pain; curled up under the covers or on the bathroom floor, crying, I give self-pity its parade of much needed attention. I have that right for what he did to me. I praise myself and swear at him in my bouts of anger. BUT pity abandons me—leaving me groveling for loss of memory. Even though the physical pain has dissolved, it's the visuals of his empty eyes and mechanical, forceful actions of humiliation that continue to slap my brain.

It's hard to explain how I feel to someone who hasn't experienced it. NOT that I would want anyone to, God no!

Tomorrow is a work day so it's time I get some sleep. Good night.

MONDAY, MARCH 10, 2008: Dear Friends,

What's happening to me?

This morning, my alarm clock decided to sleep in, so I had little time to get ready for work. I wasn't late but whenever I wake up late the rest of the day falls apart. As I was getting ready, I started a list of things I need to do for the upcoming week, scribbling some grocery items and tasks on a piece of paper. Lists and notes have become my memory…even post-it notes on doors to remind me of something. Before I left for work, I walked through the condo one more time to make sure I unplugged everything and the windows and doors were locked.

A big case is going to trial next week and the attorneys I work for had me making copies and phone calls all day, which was good because I didn't think about Arcane. My neck and feet hurt from standing at the copier for hours and I got dizzy a few times from the monotony of turning from table to copier. Instead of setting aside time for lunch, I inhaled it, which left the feeling of a lump in my throat. The phone calls poured in from the State's Attorney's secretary requesting faxed documents; witnesses complained about their required day to appear in court and my attorneys shoveled out demands. Busy was best, even if I struggled to keep current on their requests, let alone accomplish them by the end of the day.

Before I knew it—it was 6:00 p.m. I let out a loud sigh and sat back in my seat, exhausted from everything I have done and overwhelmed by what still needed completing.

One of the attorneys, Richard Bradshaw, came out of his office, asking, "Can you fax this right away to the prosecutor's office? They'll need to review it tomorrow."

"Okay, but afterwards can I go home? I'm tired and would like to get rested for another big day."

"Fine. Fine. Please be here early tomorrow. I need a few things done before John arrives," he impatiently replied.

I couldn't wait to get home to trade in my work clothes for sweats and snuggle up in front of the television with a cup of tea. When I got home, my bag hit the floor as always. I moaned as I glanced at the list sitting on my counter and turned my back on it, deciding to put off my responsibilities for another day.

It's Monday, a day of getting back into the swing of work—my way of convincing myself it's all right to procrastinate.

I filled the carafe with water and programmed the microwave for four minutes. I picked the list up to look over it.

I stopped breathing when I saw the words CHANGE LOCKS.

Those two words vacuumed the air out of the condo. I let the list float back onto the counter, backing up to the door. My hand wrapped around the kitchen doorknob, turning it to test the lock.

Locked.

I opened it to check the screen door.

Locked.

THEY'RE LOCKED! HOW?!

My arm trembled as I closed the door, walking on jelly legs to get the phone. I crossed the length of my kitchen to get the phone. The words collected in my throat like dried toast.

I waited for the police by the kitchen door, my eyes floating around looking for something out of place—any sign that Arcane was here. Damn him! My eyes were the only things willing to move for the sake of sanity, as the rest of my body suction-cupped to the door for safety. The buzzer unstuck me as I ran to it, buzzing them up. I pressed my eye against the peephole, willing them to move faster. Two male cops came up the stairs. I didn't care that they were different cops, I just wanted someone with me to search my small confines, to find proof Arcane was here.

I flung the door open, startling the cops enough to draw their guns. In my already fragile state this made me scream. My hands rose in surrender as I fell back into the door. They apologetically put their guns back in the holsters.

"Miss, everything's going to be fine."

Fine? I wanted to laugh…a wild laugh to emphasize how wrong they are.

My tears dripped as I responded, "No it won't. He was here…in my condo." I sucked in a mouthful of air.

Officer Kennedy, the name on his tag, raised his hands in surrender and said, "Okay. Okay, Miss. We'll take a look. Can we come in?"

My head shook so hard it felt as though it might crack off my neck. I moved against the door to give them room to enter. They stepped into the kitchen and Officer Kennedy took out a pad of paper.

The other officer, Jackson, said, "Do you have any reason to believe someone is still in your condo?"

I couldn't control my body's convulsions. The harder I tried, the more my body shook. The panic of knowing he was here, let alone the possibility of him still being around, deprived me of the simplest of functions.

Officer Jackson placed his hand on my arm and said, "It's all right. We're here. I think it's best you step outside the door while we search the area, okay?"

He helped me to the door, closing it with an inch to spare. Officer Jackson at least acted concerned. I heard them opening up the closets and moving the shower curtain. Not much to the place, so not much of a search. The door opened, inviting me back inside.

Officer Kennedy said, "We checked and no one is here. I know you're upset, but we need to ask you a few questions, okay?"

They were kind enough to wait until my vibrating body returned somewhat to normal. I saw them through tears and listened to their muffled words over my heavy breathing.

Officer Kennedy asked, "What makes you think someone was in your condo? According to dispatch, you said something was written on a piece of paper. Can we see that piece of paper?"

I pointed toward the list and said, "There. He wrote 'change locks.'"

The officers exchanged looks that indicated they were beginning to suspect I was losing my mind.

"Check your records," I pleaded. "I called last weekend stating my boyfriend—at the time—was on my back porch. He's stalking me."

Officer Kennedy said, "Do you have a copy of the police report? If not, I can call the station for the information."

My hands couldn't open the drawer fast enough, scattering papers everywhere in a frantic search to find it. When I did, I practically hit the officer when handing it to him.

"Calm down and let me look it over," Officer Kennedy said.

Again, they looked at each other before he started reading it.

Why does everyone think I'm making this up?

He's gotcha.

You never even bothered to find out Arcane's last name.

I chewed on the inside of my right cheek, twirling a piece of hair around my finger and pulling on it. Their eyes wandered from the police report to me and back to the report. I let go of my hair and stood up straight, hoping this would show them I was serious.

You don't have to stick out your tits.

Officer Kennedy looked up with disapproval and asked, "It says here you met this boyfriend in a chat room. Is that right?"

"Yes. It was during the snowstorm and I was stranded inside. We got to know each other."

"But it says here you don't know where he lives. Is that correct?"

Arcane got me. He really knew what he was doing by keeping himself invisible to me. Now I'm the one being dismembered. I rolled my hands into balls, fighting the urge to scream.

I looked down, knowing exactly what they were thinking: 'This bimbo meets some guy off the internet, invites him over, never gets his address and now wants us to do something about it'.

They're not far off.

My voice cracked as I responded with a simple, "Yes."

"It also states you don't know his last name." Officer Kennedy felt the need to make me feel like shit.

I looked directly at him and said, "I know it sounds bad. I know how stupid I was to invite someone over I didn't know, so I don't need you to rub it in my face."

Officer Kennedy let out a breath, rubbed his eyes and continued looking over the report. Maybe because he's older, he doesn't allow for such carelessness.

Officer Jackson seemed more understanding and decided to step in.

"Miss—"

"Sydney."

"Sydney. Are you positive you didn't write that on the list? Maybe you wanted to change the locks because you gave this boyfriend of yours a key?"

"No. I never gave him a key. I'm thankful for that."

He walked to the door, opened it and looked at the frame.

"It doesn't look like a break-in. Let me check the other door and windows."

While Officer Jackson inspected my bedroom windows, Officer Kennedy glanced my way with a troubled look. I wanted to smack him and shout in his face that I made a mistake; that it didn't mean I should be crucified for it. I folded my arms and glared back.

Do it! Who the hell is he to judge you?

Officer Jackson came back into the kitchen and said. "I can't find any evidence of forced entry. Are you sure you didn't give him a key?"

I shook my head vehemently 'no' before he even finished the sentence.

"Maybe he got a hold of your key and made a copy?"

"I guess that's a possibility."

Officer Kennedy said, "Then I'd advise you to change the locks—as he *apparently* stated."

"What? You advise? Aren't you going to dust the place for fingerprints? Do you want my e-mails from him?"

Officer Jackson spoke. "Sydney, nothing's been uprooted or harmed here. There's no reason for us to take fingerprints. You already admitted he's been here, so his fingerprints will be all over the doorknob anyway. Unless there's been an actual crime—"

I yelled, "What?! I have to get hurt—again—before something is done?"

Officer Jackson asked, "Again? Did he hurt you?"

I shook my head when I said, "Forget it" and walked to the living room to hide my disbelief. Both officers followed me, but it was Officer Jackson who spoke.

"That's pretty much it. It can be argued you wrote that on the list. The writing doesn't really look that much different and your credibility is questionable. You don't know where he lives. You don't even know his last name."

My words dangled on my tongue like an autumn leaf, cracked from the strain of the moment. I let the words fall to the floor—dead.

I turned my head to the hand on my shoulder.

Officer Jackson looked down at me with sympathetic eyes, "I know this is hard for you. I wish we had more to follow up on. Is there somewhere you can stay until the locks are changed?"

A barely audible "yes" came out, so I nodded my head to assist.

Officer Kennedy handed me a copy of the police report as Officer Jackson handed me one of his cards.

"Call me if you need to."

Famous last words.

I followed them to the door, shut and locked it and put his card next to Officer Flannigan's.

I can't let Arcane run me out of my place...so stupid of me not to even ask for his full name. And I slept with him! It never even occurred to me that I didn't know his name or where he lived. I'll find him though. I'm not going to let him take me down.

"Let him try to kill me," I said out loud to myself.

Before I go to bed, I'll be putting a knife under my pillow.

I hATE ArCANE!!

Will you guys stick by me? I'm going to need your strength. Tomorrow's another day, right?

MONDAY, MARCH 22, 1993: Dear Friend,

It's Caitlyn. I know…it's been a while.

What can I say? I had lots to do after leaving Cal's. I found a cheap apartment in a scary part of town. I had to go with cheap instead of real nice. Hell, I lived with Cal for all those years…being able to pee when I want to is a treat. The wallpaper is peeling off in areas, the toilet lid is broken in half and the bathroom mirror has chunks missing from it. If I stand a little to the right of the mirror, I can see half of my face. Good enough.

Not long after finding a place to live, I got a waitressing job…a few blow jobs in the back room and I was hired on the spot. LOL! Oh well, I guess a girl's gotta do what a girl's gotta do. I take the bus south to the diner, and on my way home, I sometimes stop and walk over to this classic condo complex. The building has a different design with castle-like features—something I've read about in fairytales.

The reason I go there is because this is where Carolyn Baker lives. I found out she has something of mine, and as soon as I can afford it, I'll get it back from her. In the meantime, I just want to check up on her…make sure she doesn't move. Carolyn is thin, dresses boring and has a weakness about her (funny, I actually like her). I've heard her talk a few times and she talks softly. People enjoy talking to her. Maybe someday we'll become good friends.

When I go there, I walk around the place, reading the names on the gate buzzers and sometimes sneaking in to sit in the courtyard. It's calming, and for the time being, I can pretend I live there. One day when I stopped by, Carolyn was walking home from the train and someone called her name—that's how I knew it. To avoid her seeing me, I crossed the street and pretended to look at a car as Carolyn waited for the other person to catch up.

This is the only exciting news I can share with you at the moment. It's been lonely without you, so I'll try to write more.

SUNDAY, MARCH 23, 2008: Hello Friends,

Happy Easter! I celebrated the day with my mother and sister with a smile and an 'everything's fine' attitude. There is no reason to involve them with my Arcane troubles. We stood in the kitchen preparing the appetizers while eating them at the same time. This is what I love the most about getting together with my mother and sister—impromptu moments—the relaxed closeness of us picking at food that hasn't been formally served. I uncorked the dry red wine, poured us all a glass and made a toast.

"To us." I held up my glass. "May we have many, many more holidays together."

We all clinked glasses and took a sip. My mother wrapped an arm around mine and Carolyn's waists and spoke, saying, "It's so wonderful to have my girls with me. It's too bad your father couldn't be here, but I know he's looking down upon us smiling."

I kissed my mom on the forehead and moved to the other side of the counter. Discussing my father always makes me sad. I was a daddy's girl and my mom and Carolyn did the mother/daughter things, like shopping while I hung out with my dad.

My favorite moments with my father were when he would bring me to his work. One of the top architects at the firm, my dad would set up a makeshift table next to his desk so I could draw all kinds of pictures. Out of the pictures I made, my dad hung up a picture I made of all of us.

Why did he go?

He didn't want the responsibility anymore.

I wish he stuck around. Things would be different.

I pressed the glass against my forehead then put the rim to my lips, hesitating before guzzling the rest of my wine.

After my father's heart gave out, ten years ago, the gap between my mother and I grew steadily. It wasn't that we didn't care about each other or love each other; it was my way of hiding from pain. Carolyn and my mom rely more on each other; however, when I come around I know that they miss me—try to bring me closer.

We sat down for dinner, dishing out the foods. The silence of the room was magnified by the clinking of silverware and glasses. Normal felt so comforting, mixing in light conversation between bites.

And now I'm exhausted from keeping up a happy façade while constantly worrying about when Arcane will make another appearance. It was nice to pretend he didn't exist—even if it was just for the day. I wish you all a good night (and a Happy Easter!). Sweet dreams.

SUNDAY, APRIL 3, 1988: Dear Friend,

It's Caitlyn again. (sighs)

No matter what I do, Cal is never pleased. Today is Easter Sunday, so I thought a nice dinner would be nice…well, as nice as I could make it with whatever foods I could find in the refrigerator and kitchen cabinets. I mixed peas with mayonnaise, cut off the mold from the edges of the lunchmeat and covered it with barbeque sauce. The only thing I could find for dessert was vanilla pudding. It wasn't the best, but I smiled to myself that I attempted to make it a special day—the resurrection of our Lord. Unfortunately, Cal came home in a nasty mood and didn't care about Easter Sunday. Now that I think of it, Cal's atheist, which makes sense as to why he reacted the way he did.

Cal walked into the house, slammed the screen door and cursed as he made his way to the kitchen. I was standing by the sink when he entered, stopped and looked at the table of food.

"What the hell is this shit?"

I turned and said, "It's Easter so I thought I'd make us dinner."

Cal's laughter gripped and shook me until I stood completely still with my head bowed—shoulders scrunched up tight. He walked up to the table and brushed his arm across pushing everything on the floor.

"You think I fucking care about what day it is or that I'd even eat this shit?"

"I'm sorry. It was all that was in—"

He came around the table, grabbed my arm and dragged me to the back bedroom. Cal tied me up, ripped off my clothes and said, "Yeah, let's celebrate."

Why haven't I learned by now? Cal is soulless.

What I have learned is not to cry or plead; it only makes him more sadistic. I closed my eyes and pictured celebrating Easter with a mother and sister.

You should have never moved in with him.

I was lost. I needed somewhere to go. Where was I to go?

Not here. He will continue to destroy you.

I'm already destroyed.

After Cal was spent, I laid there staring at the ceiling until he woke, untied me and pushed me off the bed. I got up and moved into the living room where I finally found solace talking to you. My friend, you have no idea how much you mean to me. I've lost everyone else…please don't ever leave me.

I hear him moving around in bed. I better hurry up and say good-bye for now.

WEDNESDAY, MARCH 26, 2008: Friends,

It was a horrible day. I don't even know where to begin…life is so unfair.

When I first woke, I thought the abnormalities of my life where Arcane is concerned had disappeared. I hadn't heard or felt his invisible stalking since the last incident. Work keeps me busy with the trial underway and my weekends once again echo loneliness; except now I embrace it. It has given me a chance to settle into life and lasso my sanity long enough to tame it.

I've already told you about the big case my firm is working on. The trial is bringing in plenty of money for the firm, requiring overtime to make sure every day of trial has the paperwork and exhibits ready. I either sit at my desk typing away or in the copy room photocopying piles of documents, but majority of the time I've been spending in the conference room with Richard going over a checklist of 'completed' and 'need to do items'. I can honestly say, after working closely with him on this case, that he isn't a bad boss. We've ordered lunches and dinners that Richard paid for out of his pocket. A few times we even went out for drinks to unwind and try to get the trial off our minds. It's an innocent way of getting to know one another, expectations for work, and for two single people to enjoy a drink as friends.

Only once has our work life rolled over into our personal lives. Vodka tends to invite and console what might otherwise not need consoling. Richard and I were sitting at a bar pouring our hearts out over a few drinks. My fingers became numb and when I stared into his eyes, feeling the depth of emptiness that waited for me at home, it encouraged me to extend a hand—lightly brushing away the hair from his face. With mixed emotions and driven by loneliness, lips anchored to lips, life vests for the time being, we could feel desirable again. Or in my case…just feel. I woke up at Richard's place drenched in sweat, but shivering from the cold mistake of the evening. I dressed and slinked away like a prowler in the night. I wanted to die when I got home…worried about having to face him at work. But we both dismissed the incident by pretending the evening never existed, and over the weeks since it happened, we fell back into work mode. Richard and I can even joke from time to time.

Everything was fine today on my way to work, but when I walked into the office I hit a brick wall. I was expecting to see Richard waiting for me at the reception desk, ready with demands and a handful of papers to copy. I even picked up coffees for us since he has spent his own money on lunches and dinners. As I walked down the hallway, I saw heads shaking and secretaries crying. My face contorted with confusion, looking at each person as they quickly averted their eyes. John Miller was sitting at my desk on the phone. He held a finger up indicating 'one minute' and turned away from me. I heard him say, "I'll be there" and "He'll be fine" before hanging up the phone.

John turned back to me and said, "Can I talk to you in my office?"

He got up and walked to his office without waiting for a response. I didn't understand his abruptness and was worried I was losing my job. Rewinding through yesterday, I searched for a clue or slip-up that might give me some inkling of what was going on.

Would people really be that upset and/or crying if I was being fired? No. No they wouldn't. This has to do with something else.

John closed the door of his office behind us.

"Have a seat, Sydney."

"What's wrong? Why is everyone crying?"

"I don't know how else to say this, so I'm just going to come out and say it. Richard had an accident last night."

"An accident? What kind—"

"Well, it wasn't exactly an accident. When Richard left the office last night and headed to his car, someone approached him in the parking lot. From what we know there was an argument and then this person threw acid in Richard's face. He's at General Memorial in critical condition."

I couldn't believe it. My mouth went slack as I fell back into the chair, staring as if John had just slapped me.

"I'm going to the hospital after we're done. Sydney, are you all right?"

I felt my eyes water as I thought about our working relationship. Richard turned out to be funny. As much as I thought he was an asshole in the beginning, he turned out to be a good guy. He knew how to separate work from personal relationships. It wasn't until I was sitting there thinking about him, our one-time sexual escapade, when I realized how much I admired him. Richard had worked hard to get where he is and he wasn't going to jeopardize that for anything. Most people disliked Richard's serious nature, yet they still admired his work ethics.

How could anyone be all right after hearing this kind of news?

I wiped my eyes and shook my head in disbelief.

"I know this is a shock for you. You've been working close—"

"No. No. Who did this to him?"

"They're not sure. Richard was only able to give a few details before slipping into unconsciousness."

My hands gripped the armrests. "This can't be! We were just working here yesterday on the final exhibits. He let me go home earlier than normal because of all the work I put in."

"I know, Sydney, I know. I wish I could give you good news, but I can't. This was a big blow to all of us. The police are looking into any recent cases Richard tried or threats he might have received. I realize this is tough, but I'll need you to cooperate with the police in collecting data and information from his computer and office. Can you do that?"

I took deep breaths, trying to stop crying. I shook my head, closing my eyes to squeeze the rest of the tears out.

"Yes. Yes, anything…"

"Thanks, Sydney. I knew I could count on you. The crime lab is here, so I'll let them in once you've collected yourself."

"I'm fine, John," I reassured him. "Shocked, but fine. They should start the investigation as soon as possible. Please call me from the hospital with a status."

"I'll call Barbara, who will keep you all updated on his progress," he said.

I nodded numbly and went toward the door. Before leaving, I turned and asked, "Was Richard able to give a description?"

"No. All he was able to say was 'Newbies lie about what they want.' It doesn't mean anything to… Sydney, what's…"

I ran out of his office and into the washroom.

Newbie? Oh my God. Please God, tell me it wasn't him.

I HATE ARCANE!!

My eyes shut tight as I purged anything still existing in my stomach. The cold, hard bathroom floor resonated of Arcane's actions. I placed my hand against the stall wall, attempting to get up. My weak legs made it difficult to stand, let alone move, so I slouched, staring down. A tear dropped into the toilet sending ripples out to the rim. That's how all of this can be summed up. A ripple effect, except the ripples are starting to become large waves. I pressed my hands against the opposite walls to push away the guilt that started pressing against me.

My cries and struggle to breathe drowned out the knock on the bathroom stall door. With every release of tears came a full body seizure, weakening every muscle in my body.

As I sucked in a large amount of air I heard, "Sydney? Are you all right? John said you ran in here."

Am I all right? Why does everyone keep asking me that? One of my bosses was assaulted and will be permanently damaged by some monster I met online a few months ago.

"Sydney?"

"What?"

"It's Barbara. Can I get you something, honey?"

"No thanks."

"Why don't you go home? I can help the police with whatever they need."

I opened the stall door, looking away to avoid a pity look and moved to the sink. Barbara rubbed my arm as I splashed water on my face. When I looked in the mirror, I saw myself decaying. My face grew older before my eyes and my body slumped forward from defeat.

"It's okay, sweetie. I can take care of it," Barbara offered.

Looking at Barbara through the mirror, I said, "I think I better go home. I'm not feeling well."

Before she responded, I stumbled out the door and headed for my desk to collect my belongings.

My hazy commute home was forgettable. I fell on my bed and released all my fear and sadness into my sheets.

Richard is innocent. How could Arcane hurt someone he doesn't even know?

Don't blame anyone else but yourself. Did you think he'd really be interested in you?

I pushed my fingers into my ears scratching to erase these thoughts. When I pulled them out, there were traces of blood on the tips. I washed my hands, grabbed my journal and decided to tell you about what happened. Isn't it terrible? I don't know how I'm going to live with this guilt. I'm going to be leaning on you for a bit. Well…thanks for listening.

WEDNESDAY, MARCH 29, 1995: Dear Friend,

Caitlyn is back!

I have been following Carolyn Baker for about two years now. Recently, I've noticed a man walking with Carolyn from the train to her condo. He exudes confidence, and his appearance is sinfully delicious. I have never been intimate with a man of such class—always in a suit and tie. Hot damn! (I can think of a million things I would do to this man and holding hands isn't one of them…unless he's on top). LOL!

I followed him by tracing his steps, and found out who he was. For hours I sat at the Harold Washington Library, looking for information on Richard Bradshaw. He is an associate at a law firm in downtown Chicago. I started following him. The more I followed and researched him, the more I wanted to be with Richard—a treasure of traits I can only dream about.

This obsession had to become reality. One evening, I followed him into the parking garage of his job. It was late, and no one was around. His car was parked near the staircase entrance where there were paint buckets and others filled with a pungent smell. A ladder and carpenter's tools were nearby, too.

I approached him with my sexiest swagger and stopped a few feet away from him. All the while staring at him, I pulled my skirt up just enough to show my thong.

His eyes narrowed when he said, "Are you kidding me? I don't pay for sex."

I didn't like the way he was looking at me, so I figured I needed to spice things up. Another step bridged the gap between us and I raised my fitted skirt higher. My tongue drifted along my lips as my hands slid my skirt up just above my pelvic bone. I moved my legs shoulder width apart, brought my right hand to my mouth and began sucking on my fingers, moving them in and out.

His face contorted.

I said, "Come on. I can fulfill anything you want."

I gave a sly smile and attempted to adjust his tie.

He slapped my hands out of the way, and said, "Get the hell out of here before I call the cops. Do you honestly think I'd waste my time with someone like you?"

I fell back a bit, surprised by his words. I looked away for moment to breathe.

I turned back to him, locked eyes and said through clenched teeth, "You bastard. Who do you think you are talking to me like that? Do you think you're better than me?"

He laughed. Laughed! Well, I was going to show him who is better than who. No one laughs at me.

I walked over to the buckets and picked up the one that smelled the worst. Richard went to open his car door and I threw the contents of the bucket at him. He screamed in agony as he frantically tried to wipe off his face. I was shocked when I saw the skin on his face turn red and starting to bubble. I ran to my car and left.

Why did you do that?

He laughed. Cal used to laugh at me. My mother used to laugh at me. I won't let anyone laugh at me again!

Now you've done it. You have to leave. They'll be looking for you.

All I wanted was for someone to care about me. Why did he have to laugh?

TUESDAY, APRIL 1, 2008: Dear Friends,

It's April Fool's day, but I've been a fool this entire year. I am still having a hard time dealing with Richard's situation. Today I returned to work. Even though I was bailing on John, I took the rest of last week off to console my own guilt and avoid the possibility of people seeing right through me.

Could they perhaps smell the greenery of the guilty—the poison ivy I touched and spread to others?

I didn't want them to figure out that one night I invited danger over and he greedily accepted.

So, last Saturday morning, the sun shone through the cracks of the blinds, but I dismissed it by pulling the covers over my head as I had done the two days prior. My sister and mother called a few times to check up on me after they heard what had happened to Richard. They didn't know him, but they knew I worked for him for a while and was taking this hard.

Over the past few months, I have pushed my mother and sister away. I ignored their kindness for Arcane, who never did care about me. I felt guilty (as I laid in bed) when they offered to go grocery shopping for me, so I declined, telling them it would be good for me to get out. Time passed and I found reasons why I didn't need the food or fresh air.

The red letters of the alarm clock showed 10:00 a.m. I knew my condo couldn't protect me forever. After Arcane's mysterious visit, I had the locks and bolts changed, yet I still feel vulnerable. I cry for being stupid. I cry for Arcane's actions. I cry for Richard. But most of all I cry at the thought of someone being so cruel, and that I fell in love with such cruelty. To be wrong about something so obvious leaves me uncertain about any future decisions.

Finally, I threw the covers off and headed to the washroom to look fear in the eye and give it a pep talk. The mirror had become a stranger to me over the past few weeks, (GAH! I understand why) so I took some time to reintroduce myself. Creases stretched around my eyes and mouth—arms hung lifelessly. I tilted my head, watching my neck strain, and leaned into the mirror. My fingertips pulled down on my lower lids then I let the flesh fall back into place. I scrunched my face, stuck my tongue out and laughed. I slipped into clean, warm clothes and put the kettle on. I had stayed away from my laptop, but figured by now it might be safe to check my e-mails and browse the internet.

I had thirty new e-mail messages.

The first one had the subject line, "Oh Sydney? Look what I have for you." The second said, "Sydney, are you ignoring me?" And the third said, "This is for Sydney and everyone else's viewing pleasure." I clicked on the first one and then on a link in the body of the e-mail to a YouTube video. The video popped up, loaded for a minute and then I saw myself naked on the bed with Arcane's face buried between my legs. I can't even describe what this did to me. Somehow the air in my lungs refused to move. My body began to shake as I watched him violate me without his face ever being seen. He had videotaped me without my knowledge, turned it into porn…I had the lead role. The screen blurred from tears and I wiped them away as fast as they accumulated. The video showed my face and then him straddling it. It showed every part of me.

My body set like cement—mouth clenched to suppress an animalistic cry.

At first only my eyes rolled down the screen, resting upon poisonous words written by viewers—daggers—anything capable of damage. My fingers trembled as I fumbled for enough composure to hold the mouse and scroll down through the comments.

Bastid: How can he fuck that fat bitch?

InnocentTilGuilty: Dude, she's got holes so who cares.

In their comments, the men cheered and stated what to do to me next. Those comments were easier to take than the comments from women about spitting on my face, blood leaking from my lip and that Arcane should tie me up and give me what I really deserve. I wasn't sure what they meant by deserve. The women were merciless, painting me as a whore. The cruelty pounded in with every letter.

How could they say that without knowing me?

You are a whore. Look what you did to Richard.

I lost control of my senses, of who I was, where I was, as I began throwing things around, screaming, "No!" I spun through the condo destroying things in my path until my left hand went through a window and I collapsed, staring at the ceiling and praying the distorted whiteness was heaven.

I woke to the sound of a monitor and a throbbing hand. When I tried to wipe my face, I couldn't move either of my arms. I screamed and a nurse came running in.

"It's okay, honey," someone said to me.

"No, it's not! Get these off!"

"It's okay, calm down. You're in the hospital—"

I lifted my upper body and yelled, "Take these off!"

"We put them on for your own protection."

"I don't need this kind of protection. Take them off now, bitch!"

"Now, let's watch our mouth. I can't take them off you. Please lie down and relax until I get the doctor."

I glared at her, but I knew she wasn't going to release the restraints. I lowered myself back onto the bed and shifted my sights to yet another white ceiling—this one with dots for me to count or go mad trying.

"I'll let the doctor know you are awake."

You were hesitant on giving him your first name. You should have gone with your gut feeling from the beginning.

I didn't think being on a first name basis on a computer would create such hellish events.

You can't trust anyone. Sooner or later, they'll all let you down.

The fury and pain rolled down my cheeks, dampening the pillow. I drew in a deep breath and let it linger before it drifted out of my mouth. My eyes became fixed on the ceiling, even as I was aware that someone had entered the room.

My sister, Carolyn, hurried to my bedside. She put her hand on my cheek and turned my face toward her.

"Sydney, what happened? After mom and I couldn't get a hold of you, I went to your condo but couldn't get in. My key wouldn't work. That's when I called the police and we found you on the living room floor."

I moved my head back to the specks on the ceiling that had begun to look like vast stars set in the clouds. The locks. I guess changing them didn't matter.

"Just get me out of here," I responded in monotone.

"Sydney—"

Without moving my head, I rolled my eyes toward her. Through clenched teeth I said, "Get. Me. Out. Carolyn."

I heard someone else come into the room and Carolyn moved to the only visitor chair to make room for my mom.

"Sydney—"

In a whispered, menacing voice I heard myself say, "Get me out of here." I balled up my hands into fists.

My mom brushed the hair away from my forehead, leaned down and kissed me.

She moved away slightly and said, "I'm trying, baby. They want to run a few tests on you."

"For what? I had a breakdown. People *have* breakdowns."

"I know sweetie, but in order for them to release you they need to make sure you're all right."

Narrowing my eyes, I said more calmly, "I rarely ask for anything from you, but I'm asking now. If you love me, you will get them to release me. I'm fine…really."

She just nodded to avoid upsetting me and joined my sister.

The doctor came in with a smile, asking, "How is the patient doing this morning?"

"My name is Sydney and I'm doing fine."

He let out a little laugh and said, "Good."

My eyes followed him as he looked me over and tried to gage my emotional condition.

"Sydney, I'm going to take off the restraints, okay?"

Sarcasm. "Oh, no, I love them on."

He ignored my comment and took them off. I rubbed my wrists to get the circulation back in them, all the while the doctor watched me.

"When can I get out of here?"

"Do you feel you're all right to go home?"

"Yes."

"You came here in a fragile state. I'd like you to talk to someone."

"What do you think we're doing?" I snipped.

My mom stood and said, "Sydney, don't be rude."

I sighed and looked away.

"I'm going to have someone come talk to you for a little bit. If they feel you're fine to leave, then you can see the psychologist on an outpatient basis, ok?"

He gave my mother a not–so-subtle look and left without waiting for a response from me.

Now I'm home in my unsecure condo, feeling insecure and waiting for the next move. Arcane continues to terrorize me…I don't know how much more I can take. Keep me strong, friends.

MONDAY, AUGUST 6, 1985: Dear Friend,

They say children fear losing their parents. Not me. Not Caitlyn.

My father is nowhere to be found and my mom is locked away for a long time. In my case, I would probably say my biggest fear is being alone.

What am I going to do now? I wandered the streets after my mother was convicted of a list of crimes, some I can't even pronounce. It was dark before I made my way back to my mom's house. Inside, I locked the doors and windows letting the sweltering heat intensify sweat. I need to sweat out all my anger. I looked around my mother's room and found a box of pictures on the floor by the bed. The bed creaked when I sat down to shuffle through the pictures. "Just one", I said to myself as I placed the top picture at the bottom of the pile and then took the next top picture placing it on the bottom and picking up speed until I was back to the first picture. NOTHING! I looked down at the pile in my hand, tears falling on the top one then I lifted my arm and threw the pile against the wall. Impact. My intense sadness made me laugh as I watched the pictures hit the wall and spread around the chair and floor.

Spread. Something my mom was good at. All the pictures were of my mother in sexual positions with her lovers. Not one of me. NOT ONE! I hoped for at least one picture of me, but I guess I was expecting too much. It was proof that I meant nothing to my mom…to no one. Men. Sex. Two important things she needed in life.

My laughter subsided. Suddenly, even the sadness stopped hurting. I dropped my head in defeat and headed to the kitchen, my tangled hair falling around my face.

(Loser. Loser Abuser). Yeah, that's what I am…a loser abuser.

I took out each item from the silverware drawer, inspected it and placed it back. On the right side of the drawer was a thick carving knife, so I took it out of the drawer and held it in my left hand. I chewed on the side of my cheek and tucked my straggly hair behind my ear with my right hand. Pushing my back against the kitchen counter, I moved my feet out, lowering myself to the floor. Light shot off the knife at each angle I turned it to as I focused on the blade and what it could do. I opened my right hand, placed the tip in the middle and pushed down until a trickle of blood rolled into one of the cracks in my hand. When the blood started to dry, I took the blade and began tracing all the lines in my palm.

Doesn't it hurt?

Hurt? Ah, nothing like I've already been…

Blood dripped on my shirt as I unbuttoned my blouse.

I didn't know what I'd do next, but at that moment, I turned my emotional pain into physical pain.

I'm so alone. No…I know you're here…but it's different. Help me figure out what to do next. Where and what am I going to do?

WEDNESDAY, APRIL 8, 2008: Hello Friends,

I didn't tell anyone at work about my hospitalization. OMG! Could you imagine how fast the gossip would travel? I'm glad the doctor released me over the weekend, albeit with a drug prescription and written instructions to follow up with a psychologist. The images of that video repeatedly play in my head like a scratched record and the humiliation is preventing me from sharing my disgrace with colleagues, family and friends.

Finally you keep your mouth shut about everything—everyone.

Not only do I avoid sharing, but I cling to the notion that no one saw the torrential rain of humiliation; angles and areas of me presented to the world in a defiled fashion. I question why he sought mental and physical abuse on me; why he chose me as prey instead of someone more deserving of punishment. Outside of living in Chicago, there isn't a link between us. I wasn't the only lonely person around, nor was vulnerability the only thing I was capable of committing to.

That's it. I need to change the playing field of Arcane's cat and mouse chase; one he has controlled for too long. It's time I make a move he can't control. Each disturbing incident involving Arcane is cutting off veins and arteries, hardening me and causing me to disregard other people's feelings. Where once thriving highways of life ran through me, now endless dead ends take their place. Along with relying on you, I've relied on self-absorption, coddling woes like a childless woman, and thinking about how I could release myself from Arcane's steely grip.

Every time I step outside my condo I'm on the defense, as if everyone looking in my direction has seen the video. In my head, they are all judging my appearance or what I have done. When I catch them staring I yell, "What the hell are you looking at?!" The fear of someone I know getting a hold of the video, along with the world seeing it, is making my anxiety worse.

I feel like I'm breaking apart.

A lot has happened. Give yourself a break.

I have been to the psychologist a few times, but her idea of treatment entails me talking the entire session (without her input) then referring me to a psychiatrist to prescribe something else. Can you believe that? I am perfectly capable of talking to myself and popping pills. I don't need prompting or approval from anyone, let alone someone costing $150.00 a visit.

My frailty causes me to tremble at the slightest touch. I'm losing weight; though not intentionally. (Huh, I shouldn't really complain about that. I've wanted to lose weight for...forever!) I went to the hair salon for a change—to start cutting Arcane out of my life. Did you notice the change?

THURSDAY, APRIL 24, 2008: Friends,

It was time for me to visit Richard. If I want to get control of my life then I need to face my mistakes. The hospital released him a week ago, but he was still facing years of plastic surgeries from the acid burns. The weight of guilt for indirectly causing Richard's injuries is like someone constantly pushing down on my shoulders while I struggle to stand. I'm counting on some of my guilt slipping away after meeting with Richard, but I'm scared of what Arcane did to him. Before I left, I called his sister to see if it was all right for me to stop by. She was happy to hear from me and said Richard would like a visitor. The Phantom of the Opera. Michael Myers. Jason. In my mind, I pictured all of these masked roles. Driving to his house felt like a trip to the cemetery of a newly deceased family member. Church music played in my head as tears found their escape. I pulled over a few blocks away to compose myself.

The images I conjured up in my head to prepare for the sight of Richard didn't compare to the face-to-face. It took my breath away. I didn't want to react the way I did, but a quick intake of air followed with an "Oh" said it all. AWFUL! And I'm talking about his looks and my response (So much for guilt dissipating). Richard's face wasn't bandaged as I had secretly hoped. When Arcane threw the acid, Richard turned and was only hit on the right side of his face from the cheek to his chin to the back of his ear; the red, puckered flesh swollen to abnormal proportions. Large sections of tough, crimson skin gathered, creating the look of a red elephant. In some areas it bubbled and his ear no longer resembled an ear.

"I apologize for the way I look, Sydney. I'm supposed to let the flesh breathe sometimes, and I didn't calculate the time right." Richard turned his head to conceal his Mr. Hyde side.

"My God, Richard, there's no need for you to apologize. No, I should apologize for reacting the way I did," I said.

I bent my head to hide my embarrassment.

You did this to him. Don't ever forget it. Fucking look at him, he at least deserves that much.

Richard reached over, put his hand on mine and said, "Sydney, it will be all right. I have several surgeries set up and—"

I can't. I didn't mean...

I couldn't look at him. Seeing him pushed me closer to a confession. *They're my sins!* Didn't God care about Richard…or me? Richard will need surgeries for his disfiguration. It was me who brought this upon him. I lost sight of who I was for the beauty of a man I knew nothing about it. I gambled an entire hand on Arcane and lost the pot—along with who I truly was.

I cradled my face in my hands as I shook my head back and forth, saying, "I'm sorry. I'm so sorry."

Silence followed as my words disintegrated into the room.

"Thank you for visiting," he finally said.

"It was my pleasure and nice to see you," I managed.

These words have been said a million times, yet the wrong ones to say at the moment—a natural response to an unnatural situation. He smiled at me and I managed to find a small one for him and then I left with the knowledge that I had inadvertently changed his life, too.

I'm drained from shame. It's amazing how one poor choice we make in life can alter the lives of others. I wish I never met him…I wish he was never born.

I HATE ARCANE!!

FRIDAY, JUNE 13, 2008: Dear Friends,

The unbelievable happened to me three weeks ago. I know I'll lose it every so often as I tell you about it, so please be patient. After I saw Richard, days passed without hearing from Arcane. I grew weary of constantly looking over my shoulder and hoped he had lost interest in terrorizing me. The next thing I knew it was Memorial weekend. I took that day off to head out of town to clear my conscience and rebuild my independence. By six that morning, miles separated me from home, the wind playing with the blaring radio. My arms flailed around the car as I screamed along to the song "Crazy" by Gnarls Barkley. It was an hour into the drive when all of a sudden my tire blew, (I couldn't believe my bad luck) forcing me to pull over and call for road service. They told me it would take at least an hour before someone could make it out.

It wasn't fair. All I wanted was one weekend to get away from the past months. I slammed my hands on the steering wheel and then rested my head on the tops of them. It was the last thing I deserved after all I have been through. A special weekend filled with new ways to relax awaited me at the end of this worn road. My head gradually rose, my eyes scanning the never ending highway. It made me think of the unknowns that lay ahead. Fear. Anger. I missed the monotony of life before Arcane, when nothing was a surprise. When the only fear I clung to was the thought of another lonely weekend. Now, I always feel angry and my anger flies out and grabs at the easiest victim it can find—a Tasmanian Devil in disguise.

I'm unsure if I am describing myself or Arcane.

Weather reports had predicted a bright day for my travels, but it turned out the sun took the day off, leaving a congested sky of clouds. Out in the distance I could hear an animal wailing as though the air curled around the sound and flipped it around. An uncontrollable shiver came over me even though I had the windows closed. I leaned down to the floor on the passenger's side to get a water bottle. When I sat back up, I saw a car in the rearview mirror sitting behind me, the dark windows prevented me from seeing inside. Everything around me got darker...I can't be sure if it was my imagination or not. It didn't matter though. I knew it was him—I could feel it.

My eyes shot to the door locks, but before I could lock them, the passenger side opened. Instinctively, my body shoved against the door, still frantically clicking the door lock. *Click. Click.* My worst fear slid into the passenger seat, closed the door and looked straight ahead without saying a word. I pressed my back harder against the door without taking my eyes off him.

"Tsk, tsk. Going somewhere, Sydney? I don't remember getting an invite," he said in a low, even tone.

Similar to my hand still grasping the door handle, my eyes refused to veer away from him. The rest of him remained still as he turned his head toward me and smiled.

"I've missed you, Sydney."

My tears blinded me. I felt the bile slosh around in my throat, so I swallowed fast. Arcane enjoys this and I give him the power to continue on. He makes me fear him, and this fear is what stopped me from striking back.

Punch the shit out of him.

"Are you mad at me?" he asked.

Every nerve in my body swelled and increased my internal heat. Images of what he did to Richard—to ME—flashed in my head and before I could stop myself I started hitting him. I slapped his face and arms, pulled his hair and screamed that I hated him. I jabbed my nails into his skin, like stabbing an ice pick into ice until I felt his skin accumulate under my nails. Strands of his hair tangled between my fingers. Good! I was inflicting some pain on him. But he laughed...and that laugh triggered a fury inside me, so I put more power behind my punches. My body lashed out at him until Arcane got tired of me and grabbed my wrists, holding them out between us.

"Let go, you asshole!"

I pulled my arms toward me, but I couldn't shake his hold. My hands opened and I looked at the strands of his hair stuck between my fingers…streaks of blood on them and his face. With a twisted smile, I shifted my amusement from my hands to his face. I smiled. It felt so good to smile. For that split second, I didn't think about the consequences of my satisfaction.

Anger shifted from me to Arcane when my smile zapped him. Clamping both my wrists in one hand, he grabbed my neck with his other and threw me up against the window, applying pressure to my windpipe. My eyes widened when he cut off my airflow. I was able to free one of my hands to grab at his wrist, but this only made him apply more pressure. My hand hit his arm and then everything went black.

***

Darkness was better than what I woke up to. I felt someone moving my shoulder and a sharp pain shot up my legs when I moved my head.

"Stay still, miss. My name is Pete. I came to change your tire and found you like this."

Like what?

When I tried to move my legs, I screamed as excruciating pain came from between my legs. I felt something inside me and started to cry.

Between my screams, I asked, "What's wrong? Why can't I move?"

Pete brushed away the hair on my forehead. "You'll be all right. I called an ambulance."

I forced a whisper and asked, "Why? What did he do to me?"

"Who? Do you know who did this to you?"

I was able to get a 'yes' out before passing out.

Don't blame anyone but yourself. You are so obsessed with attention.

I'm not blaming anyone. It's my fault I'm in this mess.

***

After being unconscious for a few days, I woke to find my legs full of welts and a blood-soaked pad under me. That BASTARD had used the lug wrench on my vagina and rectum, tearing them both. Because of internal damage, they had to do a hysterectomy and a sphincter repair. The pain didn't compare to the lifelong scar he left. He tore any possible dreams of children from thought and discarded them like the removal of my uterus.

I HATE ARCANE!!

I stared at yet another ceiling as the doctor described the injuries and what they had needed to do to stop the bleeding in order to save my life. The doctor's voice sounded like he was begging for understanding. I squeezed my eyes as tight as possible to shift focus from his words. The words "we had to" and "we had no other choice" were deafening.

I'll have no other choice but to leave town, I thought.

No other choice but to get rid of material things and start fresh somewhere else. No other choice but to become someone else, leave behind the things I have grown to love, the look I have become satisfied with and the person I have become. The things I have achieved up until this point, all my dreams of a healthy relationship, ripped from the present and buried in the past.

"The bleeding wouldn't stop…" the doctor's words kept interrupting my thoughts.

No other choice but to move.

"We had to…"

I have to leave before he finds me again.

"You had internal damage…"

A new life.

I was told the recovery time would be around three months, but the doctor was talking physical time. Emotionally, Arcane damaged me the first time he popped up on my computer screen asking how I was doing—a veiled attempt at being human.

It's been three weeks and I still can't believe all that's happened to me. If I can't believe it, I sure as hell won't try to explain it to anyone else. My mother and sister tried to find out how this could happen by sliding questions like an under the table deal, yet the words wouldn't form. I hugged silence until the questions vanished.

So it's now onto a new life, my friends.

FRIDAY, JULY 20, 1984: Dear Friend,

It's me, Caitlyn.

I can't stop crying. I've lost so much over the past few weeks...blood...body parts...nothing was by choice. My mother hasn't paid much attention to my needs, which put me in the hospital with an infection. The infection spread to my ovaries and bleeding persisted. In order for the doctors to stop the infection from spreading further, they needed to do a hysterectomy. The doctors consulted with my mother, and without talking to me about it, she responded with a hasty "yes".

Aside from my birth, (although who knows if that's where I was born) I have never needed treatment in a hospital. It smelled so bad and it made me feel vulnerable. I laid on the cold, metal bed, arms straight against my sides, staring at the buzzing ceiling lights while I waited in the pre-op room. Chemicals drifted around and I shivered from loneliness...the unknown...the unfairness of life. Metal froze my body—a thin blanket outlined my form. Tears rolled down the sides of my face, dampening the pillow. I didn't bother to wipe them away.

A nurse came in to insert the needle for the IV and prep me for surgery. She gathered my hair, twisted it and put it in a mesh hat that fit around my head. Neither one of us spoke. It was much easier for me to lose myself in the freckled white ceiling.

Then my number came up. I gripped the sheet as the bed swiveled down the hall to the operating room. I tried to focus on the lights, but they rolled past, one after the other.

Inside the operating room, everyone took their places, and the anesthesiologist put a mask over my face and said, "Now count backwards from 100."

"100..."

I'll never be able to have children.

The anesthesiologist said, "I can't hear you, Caitlyn."

"99"

You have to go to the police and tell them.

"Keep going, you're doing great."

"98"

But I'll have nowhere to live.

Do you really want to stay with her after all she has done to you?

MONDAY, AUGUST 18, 2008: Hello Friends,

I finally got out of the hospital after months of painful physical recovery. The time has come for me to focus on my emotional healing. My chat room encounter had shattered my life—my confidence is melting like a snowman in the summer sun. In order to break away from my clutter, I need to change the scenery and work on restoring order in my life…and in my heart.

During my recovery, I looked into places to live. Carolyn gave me brochures for Seattle and the surrounding areas. The west coast landscape is more appealing than the stifling east coast, so I found a real estate agent online to look for places in and around Seattle. There is a nice apartment for rent on Puget Sound, ready for me to move into, which has set everything in motion. Even the name 'Puget Sound' sounds so exotic. An escape. Sounds of the ocean becoming my wakeup call. I let John know of my plans and he understood. He even put me in contact with a friend of his in the Seattle area, except I decided not to contact his friend, to minimize the number of people who know my whereabouts.

The time came for me to say good-bye to my place, my sister and mother. They had a hard time seeing me move so far away, yet didn't push it because of all I had been through (they'll have a cheap vacation spot). We hugged, cried and I got in my car, set up the GPS and headed for a new life—new rhythm. At the beginning of the trip, I couldn't help looking back through the rearview mirror to check if anyone was following. It wasn't until Wyoming that I began to relax after convincing myself I was alone on the road. BUT, and that's a big but, I took precautions before my road trip. I kept my phone in my lap the entire time, and put a baseball bat underneath my seat.

The drive took longer than it should have because I took my time. Even though my physical injuries have healed, my mental anguish pulled deep from within. I constantly reenacted everything, from when I met Arcane to my last hospitalization, grinding my teeth to the point of pain when anger at him—or myself—was high. Sometimes I got so mad at myself for my stupidity…the caution I took in the beginning was a silent warning. I had allowed him to possess me mentally and physically and his hold still hasn't let up. During the drive, when self-torture lay dormant, I'd grab my camera from the passenger seat to take pictures when this country's beauty marks came into view; or when I encountered the birth of a sunrise, or the fall of a sunset.

It helped me pretend this was a road trip, instead of the beginning of a new identity—a new name.

If I want this to work, I have to change it all. Sydney lives in the past disappearing with my injuries. It's now up to 'Ashley' to set things straight, and of course, I still always have you.

THURSDAY, MARCH 30, 1995: Friend,

It's Caitlyn.

What have I done? I ruined everything! EVERYTHING! I tried to be nice…offered all I have to him, but he laughed. The laughter bounced around in my ears, like banging drums, irritating till the point I couldn't take it anymore. He didn't even care about my feelings. Oh why? Why did I think he'd be any different?

It didn't dawn on me until I woke up this morning, what I had done. I needed to get out of there, so I stuffed anything that would fit into my backpack and headed for the train station. I never covered my face. Richard can identify me…describe me to police…then they'll put out flyers and an APB (whatever that is—I always hear it on television). A disappearing act should be easy for me. I don't have much of an identity in society, and since I didn't give my real name to the owners of the apartment complex, no one will be following me.

I'm heading for Seattle, Washington. After I left Cal, I found out that the west coast is where I'll find one of the things I've been looking for. It's been so long, and I want to be loved. Damn it! I deserve it.

I bought a one-way Amtrak ticket, found a quiet compartment, threw my bag above the seat, and watched the train smoke gather around the station before pulling out. The country is whipping by as I look out the window, erasing my mind of what I have done and who I am leaving behind.

This journey will give me more options. I can't sit and think about what I did to Richard. It's done and over with. I need to concentrate on the future…a future you'll always be a part of.

FRIDAY, AUGUST 29, 2008: Dear Friends,

What a trip?! It was scary and exhilarating—the beauty of the land and new experiences ahead…and I like my apartment. When I was closing in on Seattle, I contacted the manager of the building to set up a time for us to meet. Timing was perfect. The smell of fresh paint scented the bare apartment. When I walked through it with the manager, the wood floorboards creaked in some areas and there were nicks, which simply enhanced the charm of the place. The creaks will offer security in letting me know if someone is in the apartment. My hand wandered over the wooden windowsills that balanced the wall lined windows in the living room area. The windows cast a large amount of light into the room and adjacent kitchen, and from here I could see a four way street—the hustle and bustle of people coming and going. From the front door, we walked down the hallway to find a bathroom to the right—the bedroom to the left. I wanted enough room to move around, but not enough for anyone else to.

This is perfect! The compact feel and second floor location provides an added feeling of safety (No porch for Arcane to sleep on).

Don't even mention him.

I have no expectations of Seattle, only the hope of healing and moving on with my new alias. It cries a lot in Seattle, something I do inside and out, so its temperament coincides with my own. I funnel my pain through a glass of wine each night, feeling it seep into my blood and flow throughout my body as it massages it to sleep. We all need something to keep us company—my company just happens to come in a glass.

My new apartment is my escape and therapy, and I'm still taking the time to enjoy my new home. The kitchen is completely different from my old one—cabinets forming a U-shape above the countertops and appliances. I sometimes stand in the middle while the water for my tea heats up and I smile—even if only for a moment—at the thought of a quiet life. Then I sit down at the table, cupping my mug and thinking about the stages of my life. I can't believe how much has changed in seven months and my own carelessness is to blame. I keep to myself, appearing standoffish— a defense mechanism. I only use my computer to keep in touch with my sister and mother, browse online sales and read celebrity gossip. My old e-mail accounts have been wiped out and replaced.

I don't have it in me anymore to work at a fast-paced job, so I traded that stressful way of life for an artsy, laid-back lifestyle. What better place to blend into an artsy life than in Seattle? Unfortunately, this type of job forces me to interact with people, but I am able to balance a customer service attitude and privacy. Out of the multiple Peace, Love & Latte locations, I landed a job at one of the many in a five-mile radius. It just so happened that they lost one of their employees (the beauty of timing). It is within walking distance to my apartment, and it is appealing to the owners to have someone close who can keep an eye on things and even lock up if they aren't around. The owners are a hippie '60s couple who like the employees to be creative with their attire, and have few demands other than to keep the freebies to a minimum.

Stop fucking jumping at the sound of the bell—they're going to fire your ass.

When the bell jingles, I can't help thinking that it might be him. It takes time to adjust to new things and try to forget about the old.

You better adjust quickly before they find out about everything.

After a few weeks of getting accustomed to making coffee, lattes, cappuccinos and frappuccinos, I will learn the cash register. Right now, I just listen to the different dialect and try to copy it when I'm at home. It won't hurt to blend in. I'm hoping over time the owners will soon trust me enough to make me a manager with more hours.

Solitude no longer bothers me. When I feel the need to reach out to someone I contact my mother or sister. They know not to say where I live or give out other important information to anyone. I didn't tell them I changed my name because I didn't want to hurt my mother's feelings.

I'm beat. This moving thing has wiped me out. See ya soon.

TUESDAY, SEPTEMBER 23, 2008: Hello Friends,

Things are looking up in my life. As I wished, I was made manager and got more hours than most…and I don't take days off, as the rest of the crew does. Everyone's nice for the most part, although I can't help laughing at the '60s couple. They are a strange pair; always walking around humming old tunes or dancing around the room—their own world of coffee, drugs and rock and roll (I can't say for sure whether or not they get high, but sometimes I wonder by the way they act).

When I arrived at work today, the sun was still sleeping and the cool night air still hung around. I arrived to find the owners there with most of the work started. I closed the door behind me and joined in. The quietness while we worked let my mind drift off and at times even go into sleep mode—as if I was sleep walking. Still in this semi-unconscious state of mind, someone knocked on the window. I was oblivious and didn't hear, continuing to place napkins and flyers on the tables. The '60s woman walked over to the door, shot me an annoyed look, and unlocked the door. It took a few moments before I realized how my thoughts had consumed me and just how that must have come across. I apologized to her and the male patron.

The wife smiled and went back behind the counter as the patron stepped up to order. The '60s couple always work the register when they are there. I finished setting the tables and then went to the coffee machines to fix his order. He tried to start a conversation while I made his cappuccino. Due to my lack of participation, his voice simmered and the splash of the cappuccino machine took over. I kept my head down, added the foam, capped his drink and looked up when I handed it to him with a soft "Enjoy."

He took a sip, held it up toward me and said, "Best cappuccino ever made."

I looked up from cleaning the counter. He smiled and winked at me.

"She's a keeper," he said to the owners.

We all looked at each other. I was surprised by his comment as he casually left the store. It is rare for anyone to speak to me because I mainly keep to myself, hidden behind the coffee machines.

It is the only 'out of the ordinary' thing that has happened since I've been here. Oh well, maybe I'll see him again…maybe I won't.

WEDNESDAY, OCTOBER 8, 2008: Dear Friends,

It's a steady life. Nothing eventful happening…days flow one into the next without notice. I avoid friendships, but I must admit it can get lonely at times. Not that I don't appreciate you, because I do. Work is going well—it's a break from the quietness that lives within me. I enjoy making the different drinks, hot and cold, and sometimes even wander out of the store during my breaks with a Chai Tea in hand to people watch. Life in Seattle differs so much from Chicago. It's a laid-back lifestyle, which is strange considering the coffee consumption is twice as much. The people are polite, but distant. Their greetings and courteous manners of opening doors for you and letting you cross the street are genuinely nice. It is a camouflage for the lack of invites or general acceptance into a group. Not that I am looking for such invites— just an observation of being seen—not attached. Seattleites will stop to let you pass, wave, smile and then move on forgetting they ever encountered you. One might say there is a loss of intimacy in Seattle—a perfect place for me to call home.

I am beginning to fit into Seattle's mold. My physical wounds have left some scars—Arcane's tattoos—a reminder for the rest of my life. The emotional wounds seem to float around like ghosts…moving about…swooping down during my daily tasks. Once in a while I'll stop to investigate my surroundings, listening for the unexpected and even looking over my shoulder to catch the ghost. So far, it hasn't surfaced.

The '60s couple decided to sleep in with the rest of the world today, so I got there early to get everything set up. I turned the machines on before setting the tables. It worried me to be alone at the store that early in the morning, but once I got things going for the morning rush, my body's rigidity began to soften. Nobody ever comes in before business hours. It's like they all are waiting for the machines to come to life and for the aroma to pull them out of bed. I stuffed the napkin holders until they expanded on the sides, a few flopping over the canister. I went to the table by the large front window, took a chair off the table and flipped it over to place it on the floor. While flipping the second chair I heard a knock on the window. Shit! (Someone had to come this early). I dropped the chair to the floor and gripped the top of it. My head turned toward the second knock and I found the same gentleman, who had stopped by a couple of weeks ago and complimented me on the cappuccino, waving to get my attention. Through the window he asked if I could let him in so he could get a coffee.

I said, "No. We're not open yet," shaking my head to enforce my words.

I was freaking out. I moved to the door to make sure I had relocked it after I came in and he shadowed my movement to the door. OMG! (It was locked. Locked. I didn't have to worry about changing the locks). I shook my head, looked down, mouthing to myself, "It's not him." I backed away from the door, twirling my hair between my fingers with my right hand, and then putting it in my mouth. I looked outside to see if anyone else was around—the quiet street sent a chill through me. I wrapped my arms around the front of me, gripping my elbows. I let the words, "It's not him" scroll around my head.

"Please? I start work in a half hour and need my coffee fix," he pleaded.

I took another step back to add more distance between us.

"I'm sorry. We don't open for another half hour and the machines aren't ready."

He frowned, slumped forward and said, "Well…thanks anyway."

Once he was out of sight, I dropped my arms and shoulders and hurried behind the counter. It was a much safer distance. For a second I felt bad lying to the guy. He seemed nice enough. Arcane had 'seemed' nice, too.

Nice is overrated.

I worked until 5:00 p.m. and then decided to eat out somewhere since I had my journal with me. Usually I eat at home, rarely making public appearances other than at work or taking an occasional shopping trip. Today I decided to get some fresh air—I wasn't ready to face the stillness of my apartment. I headed to a deli not far from the shop. In a corner booth, I sat with my turkey and swiss sandwich and my book of writings (poetry and stories). Words poured onto the pages with no rhyme or reason, so I stopped for a moment to look out the window, to slow them down and put the words into a more cohesive language.

Release your fears. Release your sadness. Release your anger.

As I opened my voice to the pages, a shadow crept over my words.

Was this the ghost I'd kept a watch out for?

I closed my eyes to focus and reduce the winds that started to swirl inside.

Please tell me Arcane didn't find me already? I've worked so hard to change my location and identity. If it's this easy for him to find me, it will be easy for him to start torturing me again.

My eyes opened and I looked up, expecting to see Arcane smiling down. Instead, I saw the man from this morning. Silently releasing the breath I held, I clenched my jaw to stifle the anger that was rising inside.

Who invited him over? What happened to the Seattle attitude of smile and move along?

"Sorry about scaring you this morning. I figured that's probably why you didn't open the door. I understand," he offered.

Who cares if he understands?

My thoughts remained in my head as I responded with a short, "Thanks." I saw him eyeing my book, so I slid my hand over what I had written.

"I see you're busy. Didn't mean to bother you, but I wanted to let you know 'I get it'. Next time I'll make sure someone is there with you, or come around when you're actually open."

I nodded and thought, *why is he going out of his way to tell me this?*

He winked at me and finally left. I watched him walk out of the deli and down the street, craning my neck as he disappeared. His substantial height must have fought with many a doorway, although his slouched saunter suggests he has grown tired of bending down. His hair falls in different directions as if on command and his cocoa eyes are hypnotizing. A trickle of feelings I boxed up when I came here has now escaped.

Don't even think about it.

I know...I shouldn't even be going down that road.

Damn right. Remember why you're here.

I shook my head and returned to my book.

I don't need distractions. There is no room for relationships—the focus is purely on surviving, right? I don't hear you...you're not convincing me.

SUNDAY, OCTOBER, 12, 2008: Hey Friends,

You'll never believe what happened today. A plus is that I had the day off work. The rain lashed out and the cold autumn wind enticed me to stay cuddled up on the couch. It has been a while since I had a Sunday off (being alone and an outsider, I tend to work the days most employees want off, which is fine with me). My butt had been lounging since the morning, so I walked around to get the blood flowing again and headed into the kitchen to get a plate, fork and spoons for my Chinese food delivery.

I went to the living room windows, put my feet close to the radiator and looked out onto the dreary day. The few people who had the courage to venture out were beaten and chased into the nearest shelter. For the first time since I had arrived in Seattle I felt lonely…a feeling of déjà vu. Bad weather. Loneliness. I glanced at the computer and whispered to the room, "no way".

The doorbell rang so I headed for the door, scooping up the money as I went by the table.

I looked through the peephole and asked, "Who is it?"

"Here for Miss Ashley. Chinese."

Ashley. I'm still not used to the sound of my name.

I opened the door, exchanging food for money. He bowed his head slightly and said, "Thank you". Just as I turned my glance from him, I caught a glimpse of another man coming to a stop at an apartment door adjacent to mine. You'll never believe who it was because I didn't at first. As he began unlocking his door, he looked up to extend a polite nod and we locked eyes.

It was "Cocoa Eyes" from the coffee shop! He took a step forward suggesting he wanted to talk to me.

Waving his finger toward me he said, "Hey, I know where you're from."

I backed up into my doorway a little and said, "Hi."

"I didn't know you lived here. How long have you been here?"

"About three months now."

"Nice. I've been here a few years and I like it. Lease it from a friend who moved to Canada. How do you like it here?"

"It's nice. I like that it isn't far from work."

"Yeah, you got it made." He looked down at the menu stapled to the Chinese food bag and said, "Good choice. That's probably the best Chinese food around here. I don't care *what* their kitchen looks like."

He saw my face drop and said, "I'm kidding. I've never been in their kitchen."

I laughed and looked down at my feet.

Finally, I found the guts and said, "I want to thank you for what you said at the deli the other day. You caught me off guard, so I didn't respond the way I wanted to. Thanks for understanding."

Why are you talking to him? Whatever happened to no relationships?

But this isn't a relationship. I'm just talking.

That's what you did with the other guy—talked until he stalked.

I tilted my head to the right, lifted my right shoulder and rubbed my ear against it.

He cocked his head, leaned forward with his right hand out and said, "No problem. By the way, my name is Garrett. Garrett Hart."

I looked at his hand and gradually my right hand came forward until ours connected and I said, "Nice to meet you."

Garrett let out a laugh and said, "Do you mind sharing your name, or shall I refer to you as 'Peace, Love & Latte Gal'?"

My face warmed up and I said, "Ashley. Ashley Powell."

"Pleased to meet you, Ashley."

"Likewise."

"If you need anything…something fixed…want to know where something is…to hang out…just knock on my door. The pleasure would be all mine."

I had been averting his eyes, but then looked into them, saying, "Thanks for the offers. I appreciate it."

"I know some cool places to go to, so the offer is always open."

This time I just nodded, the words "the pleasure would be all mine" reverberated in my head. My threat alert went from green (low) to blue (guarded).

Mr. Friendly wants to fix things or hang out. I recall another guy with a great personality inching his way into my life in much the same way.

I moved my leg inside the doorway and leaned backward to position my body inside the safety of my apartment.

Yep, he noticed my movement because he ended the conversation by saying, "Well, you take care and I'm sure I'll see you soon."

"You, too," I said, trying not to sound shaken.

As I was closing my door a twinge of guilt hit me and I popped my head back out into the hallway and said, "It was nice meeting you, Garrett."

"Likewise."

I know what you're thinking, but you're wrong. I have no intention of getting involved. It's…well, it's nice to know someone close by that's all.

Time for bed. I'm still stuffed from the Chinese food.

WEDNESDAY, OCTOBER 15, 2008: Friends,

I don't know what's happening to me. The cycle is beginning again and it's scaring the hell out of me. I've let fantasy rule over common sense. The more I fight any possibility of a relationship the more I want it. At one time I befriended solitude and now I want it to go away. Like the illusions I created of Arcane, I'm starting to compile and do the same with Garrett. I have only seen him a few times, yet my memory keeps outlining his build, tracing his average-width nose to his thin lips and drowning in the warmth of his eyes. When he approached me at the deli I noticed a scar on his right temple, resembling a crescent moon. In comparison to my past loves he doesn't quite fit the 'interesting' mold, but apparently the interesting mold doesn't enhance the quality of my life. The laid-back grunge appearance always came off to me as lazy. Garrett wears it in a trendy way. The few times I've seen him his clothes look more like they fit his body than struggling to stay on—wrinkles formed from wear, not from residing on the bedroom floor.

This morning as I was making a latte and thinking of Garrett, I heard a familiar voice say, "Hello neighbor."

I looked up, surprised and embarrassed by my thoughts (he had read my mind) LOL! then I smiled and said, "Hi. How have you been?"

"Good. It's amazing; we live right across the hall and mostly see each other outside of our apartments. How are you doing?"

"Fine. Keeping busy with work and such."

"And such. Hmm…I never quite knew what 'and such' was."

I laughed, but I didn't remark.

"I was wondering if you were busy this Friday?"

"I'm working."

"Yeah, I figured that, but what about afterwards?"

Was he asking me out on a date…and did I want to go?

I do think about him, but loneliness makes you do things you wouldn't ordinarily do.

Or would you?

Looking back on my life, I realize that I tend to lean toward companionship. I've always needed someone to feel complete…to have security…to make me happy.

Was I ever happy with who I am? Better yet…WILL I ever be happy with who I am?

For a while, after Arcane, I grew secure with being alone. It is safe and uncomplicated. I've thought of Garrett often, and whether it has to do with being lonely or interested, I started to think that maybe it wouldn't hurt to have a friend. At least it's the excuse I feed myself in order to reach out and push loneliness to the curb.

"Hellooo? Ashley? Did you forget we were talking?"

I blushed and said, "No, of course not. I'm not doing anything after work."

"Then would you like to join me at the Autumn Festival?"

"There's an Autumn Festival?"

Garrett turned to the patrons in the coffee shop, saying, "Okay, who was responsible for filling Ashley in on our festivities?"

People glanced around at one another, clueless.

I felt my face simmer with an all too familiar feeling of awkwardness.

"Ashley, our Autumn Festival is known throughout the nation. We have fresh apple cider, pumpkin-carving contests, games, a King and Queen Inauguration, and—most importantly—a community effort in making this the most joyous occasion throughout the year."

My eyebrows rose as I said, "Really? It's that popular? Are you the festival's promoter? "

"Well… no and no, but I wanted to get your attention and see if I could coax a little excitement."

I shook my head and said, "You are something else."

"Why thank you, Ms. Ashley. So, will you do me the honors of escorting me to the Autumn Festival?"

I looked him over and then made eye contact.

The whole town will be there, so he can't hurt you. Besides, he lives across the hall from you and nothing has happened. He hasn't tried to break in or jump you in the hallway.

"I'd like that," I said.

What?! What happened to NO RELATIONSHIPS?! You screwed up your life doing the same thing—taking danger over loneliness. Why?

"Then I'll pick you up across the hall…let's say around three?"

"I work until five."

"Then six it is."

I handed him his latte and thanked him for the invite.

"My pleasure, Ashley. Have a good rest of the week."

"Likewise."

What am I supposed to do? Be rude? Be alone for the rest of my life? It's not a date. He invited me to a festival...as friends. Please don't make me feel guilty for not wanting to be alone. I hate being alone and you know that. I gotta go.

FRIDAY, OCTOBER 17, 2008: Dear Friends,

I'm sorry for my abruptness. You know your opinions mean a lot to me, but you have to listen and understand where I'm coming from. Nothing's happened with Garrett and me…we're becoming friends. I need a friend. What if Arcane shows up? Who will help me out? I'm getting to know him so I'll have some protection. So I accepted to go with Garrett to the Autumn Festival. It's done and over with and now I want to tell you how it went.

No lies. I was nervous…so nervous. My hands shook with a caffeine-like high waiting for Garrett to pick me up. I kept my attire simple and warm. Not having much of a wardrobe made the decision that much easier. My thick, black sweater hung straight down, covering the top of my faded, loose jeans. I chose black, water-resistant shoes for comfort and to protect me from the unpredictable rain. Not worrying about what to wear made me think of it as more of a hanging out thing rather than a date, which I figured might be how he was viewing it, too. As the minutes clicked closer to six I started second-guessing my choice of clothing.

Even though it wasn't a date I could still look nice. I don't have many clothes that fit in the 'nice' category though. What would he think?

Who cares what he thinks?

I don't want him to think I'm a slob.

I pulled on my sleeves, bit my lip in frustration and then I started down the hallway to look in the mirror again.

Too late—the doorbell rang. I turned back and rubbed my hands together, hoping to calm the shakes.

I pulled on my long coat, but it was too constraining. The doorbell rang again, so I threw the coat on the couch and slid into my Pea Coat and answered the door. Before I could catch it, my jaw fell at the way Garrett looked. He had a thick leather jacket on over a brown sweater; dark, worn jeans and black Jackhammer boots. It looked like he had put some thought into his attire and he wore everything well. The brown enhanced his cocoa eyes. His cologne drifted into my apartment and I found myself stepping out into the hallway, pulling the door closed behind me.

He laughed, saying, "You're in a hurry."

I moved to the side.

Garrett's smile was infectious...like he was so comfortable wearing it. It spread far, revealing white, straight teeth with a few slightly angled.

"You look pretty."

I looked down at my appearance then back to him and said, "Thanks. You look...handsome."

"WOW! And here I was aiming for 'not bad'."

The last time I have seen him I thought his humor was to make fun of me, but it seems he uses it to soften moments of awkwardness or lighten the mood.

"Come on, beautiful, let's show these Seattleites how to have fun."

He bent his arm in my direction and I put mine through. I couldn't help tensing when I replayed "Come on, beautiful..." in my head. Arcane was the first guy to ever call me beautiful...somehow I gave him ownership of the words.

As we walked to the Autumn Festival, I asked, "So where is the festival? I never even asked where we were heading."

"Have you been to the famous Pike Place Market?"

"No."

"Miss Ashley, you need to get out more. We're about five blocks away from it and you haven't heard of it?"

I just shook my head and smiled.

"Well let me tell ya about it. Pike Place Market is a farmer's and fishmonger market. It's open every day of the week, all year round, and you can buy everything from fruits and vegetables and fish to crafts and clothing."

"Sounds like a shopper's paradise."

"Oh it is…that it is. And for the Autumn Festival, they change for the theme and add booths that are specific to the season. There are booths and booths of things to eat and buy, so are you ready to eat hearty and shop 'til you drop?"

I marveled at his enthusiasm and responded, "I'm always up for eating, but not so much into shopping."

"A woman after my own heart."

We continued to walk with my arm through his to the Autumn Festival. Just as Garrett described, the booths were filled with food, drinks and crafts throughout the building. Outside the market area, tents were set up for contests; pumpkin-carving, apple-bobbing and Pin the Tail on the Donkey, to name a few. Garrett took my hand and led me to an outside tent where people were dancing to a live band. Smoke from grills and smells of food filled the air as bodies moved in close to keep warm.

No one looked familiar—it made me feel alive. This was a new start on life. I didn't have Arcane following me…or the humiliating videotape. I found myself taking it all in—the people dancing, children running around, witnessing the overall enjoyment of the city. Out of the corner of my eye I saw Garrett looking at me, so I turned my head in his direction. He handed me a beer and grinned as though he knew what I was thinking. We stood for a while, not talking, just watching the people having fun.

As the night progressed, I blew on my hands to warm them from the dropping temperatures. Garrett took my hand and led me to a booth that sold leather goods.

"Hey Michelle, what do you have for us this year?"

"Garrett!" The woman hugged him and shook my hand.

To me she said, "Ah-h, I know what you need."

Michelle guided us to a rack of gloves and went to help some other people who were interested in the leather coats.

"Try them on," Garrett said.

I looked at the price tag, a habit I got into after my yearly salary was more than cut in half, and said, "It's nice of you to think of me, but I'll be fine. I have gloves at home. I just didn't think I would need them."

"Just try one on. You'll love them."

"Garrett, I'm sure I will, but I have gloves at home." I found myself taking offense—like he was pressuring me into doing something I didn't want to do. I jammed my hands into my pockets and took a few steps back.

He sensed it, put his hands in his pockets, moved closer, and said, "She's a friend and will give a good discount."

I looked up at him, reached for the black gloves with fur inside and reluctantly tried them on. In an instant, they warmed my hands and the soft leather made it easy to bend and flex my fingers. My eyes widened with my mouth.

"You like them, don't you?"

"Yes. They're beautiful and warm. Unfortunately, I …"

He took them from me and paid Michelle without a word.

I followed him out of the booth and said, "Garrett, I can't accept those. You shouldn't have done that. Maybe she'll take them back."

He stopped, turned toward me and put his forefinger to his lips to indicate he wanted me to be quiet. "Ashley, I bought you these. Be polite and accept them graciously."

"You don't understand, Garrett—"

"Yeah, I do. Believe it or not, I do. You left your home to escape demons, but they seem to have followed you here. I want to be friends—maybe even more than that—but I'm not pushing anything. After tonight we might even realize we don't have much in common. We can see where this takes us, though you'll have to be open to whatever. Now take these gloves, thank me, and let's not make a big production out of it."

Shame over my behavior made it impossible to be mad.

Am I that transparent? How does he know I'm trying to escape demons?

I took the gloves from him and whispered, "Thank you."

We went back to the band area and had a few more beers. Garrett doesn't frighten me. Actually, he does the opposite—he makes me feel at ease. Maybe it has to do with being straightforward and calling me out on my feelings. CD tracks played during the band's breaks and one of my favorite Van Morrison songs came on—*Into the Mystic*. I found myself swaying to the music and hugging my arms. Garrett slid behind me, put his arms around me and swayed along. At first my body went rigid, but it wasn't long before I softened and leaned into him.

Later, we decided on a warm meal of chili in bread bowls—perfect autumn food—and found a bench to sit on. We ate and people-watched, enjoying each other's company in silence.

Garrett spoke first. "We lucked out with the weather. They're not even forecasting any rain this weekend."

"When does the festival end?"

"Sunday at 6:00 p.m. An hour after crowning a new King and Queen."

"What do the King and Queen do?"

"The King and Queen are high school kids who will continue to do what they are being recognized for, except now they will have an article about their high grades, community service and popularity. It's more recognition of their good deeds than an expectation."

"That's nice."

He looked right at me and said, "Yeah, it is." We locked eyes. This time he looked away first.

The festival ended at 11:00 and we were one of the last to leave. We wandered the streets looking at the booths, stopping to talk to someone Garrett knew and just naturally finding relief with silence when words weren't needed. I believe he didn't want to pry too much into my life, maybe time would answer his questions, and I didn't ask much to avoid suggesting questions were all right. So, we started our relationship by keeping our secrets in a jar. If we want to share them, each of us will have to take the lid off when and if we're ready.

We arrived back at our apartments and he took my shoulders, leaned in, gave my forehead a friendly kiss and said, "Thanks for a great evening, Ashley. I hope you had fun."

I was surprised, but I also knew he wasn't expecting anything. Still, I felt a wave of disappointment that he didn't kiss me on the lips.

My feelings were undeniable when I grinned and said, "I had a great time. Thanks for asking me to go. I appreciate it, Garrett."

As he started down the hallway, he turned back and said, "Well, you better get inside, young lady."

I was still looking his way as he said it and I smiled as I unlocked my door, quickly waving and closing the door behind me. Once inside, I made sure I put the chain on and double-checked the locks before pressing my back against it. The evening made me feel alive, and for the first time since January, my life felt ordinary again.

I was deep in thought about our evening as I opened the closet to hang up my coat. With my hand still on the doorknob, it hit me.

Didn't I throw my long coat on the couch? Or DID I hang it up?

Do you remember?

I stood staring into the closet, my heart rate picking up speed, looking at my coat.

My reflexes kicked in and I released the handle as though it was on fire, backed into the door and moved over to see as much of the apartment as possible. My heart was beating wildly in my ears as fear paralyzed my body.

Scanning the room, I saw that the couch and pillows were untouched and the drapes opened, as I had left them. My muscles softened and I began to move around the rooms.

I closed the drapes and crept down the hallway, stopping halfway and moving back to the kitchen. Grabbing a knife, I headed to my bedroom, opening doors and looking around. There were no signs that anyone had been in my apartment.

No message from Arcane.

I put the knife under one of my pillows and changed for bed.

It was a long day, but wonderful. I'm not going to let thoughts of *him* ruin it. Good night.

FRIDAY, OCTOBER 31, 2008: Hey Friends,

I had an embarrassing day and that's putting it mildly. It's the day of ghosts and goblins and I had the pleasure of closing because the '60s couple wanted to be home dressed as Frankenstein and the Bride of Frankenstein to hand out candy. If you ever saw them, you'd think to yourself, 'They don't really have to dress up to scare the hell out of anyone.' I'm so mean. But they went all out with decorations. A spider web covered half the ceiling with a big, fuzzy spider hanging from it. Each table had plastic skulls filled with candy. Black and orange lights lit up the windows and a ghost—basically a sheet—flew back and forth through the room on a string while eerie music played in the background.

We had a packed house most of the afternoon and into the evening. Children gathered their candy while parents warmed their hands and insides with coffee or tea. Some of the kids shrieked at the sight of the spider and ghost, but would soon recover when they'd see candy waiting for them. My eardrums felt like they were swelling from the screeching children. The coffee machines held up to the challenge, unlike my feet, which ached from standing and turning in the same area for hours.

Later in the evening, a man came in dressed from head to toe as a vampire. He had long nails and fangs, a whiteout face with blood droplets coming from his mouth and a long, black cape that covered most of his body. When he walked in the kids ran, screaming for their parents to look at the vampire. He lunged at a few of the kids, making their screams earth-shattering and then came up to order.

"I'll take a large cappuccino with a shot of blood," he droned, remaining in character with a full-on Transylvanian accent.

The cashier, Cathy, responded, "I'm sorry, we're all out of blood. How about whole milk?"

He laughed and said, "Great substitution, but let's go with fat-free."

The children screamed and scattered as he walked over by me to supervise the making of his cappuccino.

"Hello, Dahling."

Without looking up, I said, "Hello, Count Dracula."

"You look tired, my dear. Would you like me to bite your neck so you can come alive?"

"Ooo…very tempting—yet I'll have to take a pass."

"That's too bad; I'd love to control you."

My arms stopped in mid-air as memories of Arcane smacked me in the face. The room felt like it was caving in and I was having trouble breathing. I backed away from the coffee machines and grabbed at my shirt to get more air. Panic shook my body.

He's here! Oh God…how?

What are they looking at? Stop staring!

The counter stopped me from backing up further and before I knew it, the vampire came behind, pressed his hand on my lower back and lowered me toward the floor.

He whispered, "That's right, breathe Ashley. Everything's fine—concentrate on breathing. I didn't mean to scare you. It's Garrett."

He spoke with a steady tone—calming—and I felt my lungs opening up. I hugged his arm and made a conscious effort to regulate my breathing. I was embarrassed by my panic attack and began to cry. Garrett rubbed my back, continuing to talk to me in his soothing voice. I don't know how long I was hunched over, crying and trying to control my attack.

When I finally brought my breathing to a regular pace, I lifted my head to find a crowd around us.

Garrett helped me into a standing position and said, "She's fine everyone. You can go back to your candy and coffee. No harm done—I didn't bite her!"

People smiled, took one last look, seeming to accept his reassurance, and returned to what they were doing.

He stepped in front of me to block everyone's stares. I found myself leaning against his chest, my face wet. A line had formed during my episode and I let out a moan. Garrett wiped my tears away.

"It's okay, Ashley. Take your time—no one's rushing you. Why don't you head to the washroom to chill for a minute?"

In the washroom, I threw some water on my face and dabbed it dry before blowing my nose. I looked in the mirror replaying what had just happened.

Is this how I'm always going to feel?

Stop acting like a scared cat. He's not here.

Words…actions…they all seem to thread through Arcane's needle. If I keep this up, I'll lose my job and my apartment.

Snap out of it! Nothing's happened to prove he's here. You're letting your mind play games.

I patted my hair down and returned to the coffee machines. Cathy asked, "Are you okay, Ashley? I can make the coffee if you want."

"No, No. I appreciate it. I'll be all right. What do we have?"

Garrett took his coffee and sat at a nearby table, keeping an eye on me. Every now and then I looked up to see him watching me or reading and gratitude replaced shame. He stayed until closing and walked me home.

I appreciate his assistance and can't even begin to describe how thankful I am that he didn't ask questions—he let the incident blow away in the wind. I guess he has his own secrets he wants to keep in a vault. I know that opening my Pandora's Box would eventually force his open...

Better to keep the box locked as long as possible.

Yes, and I told you it was a good idea for me to become friends with him. He's protecting me. I hope you're starting to accept Garrett for what he is and isn't—Arcane.

It's time for this ghoul to get to bed. I have another full day ahead of me.

SATURDAY, NOVEMBER 8, 2008: Friends!

This time I did good. I'm going to tell you how wonderful Garrett was to me yesterday and you, by the end, will like him as much as I do…well, maybe not as much, but close. Because I worked on Halloween, the '60s couple let me have the day off, which is a rare occurrence. In the late afternoon, I stood in my living room wondering what to do, not use to having so much time on my hands. No sooner did I think about calling Garrett when there was a knock on the door.

With a bouquet of flowers in one hand, a bottle of wine in the other and Chinese takeout under his arm, Garrett greeted me, saying, "I hope you don't have plans tonight."

My heart began to sweat.

This man…this man who doesn't know anything about me—hasn't asked any questions—comes around with his arms full of wonderful things to make it a special night.

Without thinking, I took his face in my hands and kissed him on the lips. LOL! I know, I was so shocked that I did that.

Taken aback by my boldness, my right hand touched my lips and my left hand flew up in a halting motion as I stepped back, saying, "I don't know what came over me. I'm sorry. I didn't mean to do that." How embarrassing.

After striking a devious grin, he said, "Too bad. I was hoping there was more of that to come. Since there won't be, can you take some of these things from me?"

I looked at his full arms and quickly grabbed the takeout and flowers.

"These are beautiful. Thank you, Garrett."

I brought the bag and flowers into the kitchen, and he put the wine on the table before looking around. Every once in a while I looked up to see what he was doing.

Arcane had also walked around, soaking up as much information he could find.

Garrett is different. He's only wandering, not prowling.

You keep thinking that.

I shook my head to silence my fears.

Garrett has shown nothing but kindness and friendship. Arcane took possession right away.

I trimmed the flower stems—consisting of Geraniums and Marigolds—splitting them between a couple of glasses. Since I never expected to get flowers, my place is devoid of vases. After I set the table, I watched Garrett as he browsed my apartment with the interest and curiosity of an art historian trying to find a clue or understanding of who I am or where I came from. He looked at things, smiled and then replaced them.

He stopped at the one and only picture I have in the apartment of my mother, sister and me, taken a year ago at my sister's house. Garrett picked it up, studying our faces. My hair was long and blonde and I was heavier—a huge contrast to the short, dark brown hair I wear now—atop a size four.

Garrett realized I was watching him, so he replaced the picture, clapped his hands together and said, "Let's eat."

Stuffed, we sat next to each other on the couch, sipping wine and watching the movies he had since retrieved from his apartment— *The Fugitive* and *Underworld*.

"I brought *Underworld* so you could see where we vampires come from," he teased.

I fell asleep during *The Fugitive*. When I woke, I found myself sleeping between Garrett's legs on his chest as he slept, too. I hated to wake him to ask him to leave. I pulled the blanket from the back of the couch and was about to get up, but his eyes opened with a whispered 'no' as he pulled me back to him, wrapping his arms around me. Smiling to myself, I covered us both with the blanket. He kissed my hair and we fell back to sleep.

I don't think I've slept that good since last year.

Do you agree that he's a good guy? Gotta get to work. Talk to you later.

WEDNESDAY, DECEMBER 2, 1998: Dear Friend,

YAY! It's Caitlyn.

I think I encountered a miracle. Today, I went into the Seattle Art Museum to pass the time before going to work. It was cold and rainy out (shocker, right?), so I walked around admiring the beautiful artwork. In one of the rooms, I saw a teenager with a frail, older woman. The woman was pointing at a painting, describing what it represented and explaining the brush strokes. The teenager's mouth was slightly opened as he moved his attention from the painting to the woman. There was something about his face that seemed familiar.

For the rest of the time, I watched them interact, and at a comfortable distance, followed them through the rooms. I heard the woman call his name, and he referred to her as his mother. I inched my way closer. When the woman wandered off to the next room, leaving the teenager admiring a painting, I stood right next to him and stared at his face. It took him a minute or so to realize I was next to him.

The teenager took a step back and his eyebrows scrunched up.

I said, "I'm sorry, I don't mean to stare. My name is Caitlyn and you happen to look like someone I used to know."

He responded, "Well, I don't know you."

"I apologize. I must be mistaken," and I walked away.

A miracle. I followed them home and decided to keep track of him.

Leave him alone. You're only going to make things worse.

I'm not bothering him.

No, but you're following him.

There's no law against it.

He's a good-looking boy. I only pray his life turns out to be wonderful.

I'm cold and tired. I'll talk to you soon.

SUNDAY, NOVEMBER 9, 2008: Hey Friends,

I learned a valuable lesson: I shouldn't risk losing the only friend I have in Seattle. I'm not going to lie that my feelings for Garrett are past the friendship stage, but that's not why I could have lost him today. I've put a wedge of secrets between us, and that wedge happened to cut us today. Let me explain.

The weather was out of character—warm and sunny. I only had to work until 2:00 p.m. and then the rest of the day was mine. Over the weekend, Garrett and I didn't see much of each other so I was surprised to find him sitting in a car in front of the coffee shop when I got out of work. It occurred to me that I didn't even know he owned a car. I'd only seen him walking. Then again, being in our area, I don't drive my car much either because everything is within reach.

Garrett lifted his sunglasses and asked, "Would you like to join me for a country ride?"

A break from the usual landscape on such a warm day sounded like what I really needed.

"I'd love to."

We drove down roads I didn't know existed in this part of the country, eventually coming upon forestland. He got out, grabbing a large duffle bag. I hesitated for a moment before joining him.

Alone in the forest…no one knows where I'm at…Garrett carrying a duffel bag.

He's not Arcane.

But I didn't think Arcane was Arcane either.

You're being distrustful when there's no reason for it.

We walked down a crunchy, leafed path as the sun shot through the tall, semi-bare trees. Yellows, browns, oranges and reds still clung to life and those that had lost the battle decorated the foliage and grounds. Garrett moved like a man on a mission, turning a few times to make sure I was still following. The smell of the woods and witnessing its sleep preparation for winter made me hug my arms and smile. The forest felt like a place for thoughts and an opportunity to connect with nature. Being a city girl, I've never really had many opportunities to venture over to this part of Mother Nature's home. The stillness of the forest, birds flying overhead, calmed my prior apprehension.

We climbed over large overgrown roots and then I heard water. It took a few more minutes before Garrett stopped and pointed. A small waterfall poured into a pond surrounded by tree stumps and dirt mounds. I got out my cell phone and took a picture of Garrett in front of the waterfall that was sprinkled with dark green moss at its base. I watched as he dropped the duffel bag, unzipped it and began to remove the contents. He took two corners of a red plaid blanket, tossed it up and let it float in the air until falling lightly to the ground. His hand kept digging inside for foods and drinks, such as cheese, sausage and beer, and another blanket. Garrett's thoughtfulness and spontaneity lightens my heart.

He planted himself on the blanket, saying, "Come join me, beautiful."

I dislike the word, or what I think of as 'Arcane's web', but Garrett's kindness didn't deserve a rebuttal. Sitting across from him, I looked at the food and my stomach rumbled.

Garrett laughed. "Someone's hungry."

He reached into his duffel bag and pulled out small paper plates, handing me one.

"Sorry, the china was in the dishwasher," he said, winking.

"This is wonderful. I can't believe you thought of doing all this. I...I..."

"I know." And he does. He knows how grateful I am for his kindness.

We filled our plates, opened our beers and sat listening to the forest chatter at us.

"Good day?"

I looked at him and said, "It is now."

"Then I can pat myself on the back for being a Good Samaritan?"

"I guess that would depend on if you think I'm in trouble and need saving."

"I didn't mean that. I—"

I looked away, whispering, "I know."

"Since you brought it up...am I someone you would want saving you?"

The food stuck to my throat and I swallowed hard before I could answer 'yes'. Garrett took my plate and put it aside, taking my hands and pulling me toward him. He covered us with the blanket. His touches, kisses and words gently charmed me into opening up and letting him feel me—inside and out.

Our eyes searched to memorize each other's faces, our mouths gradually exploring until their hunger matched our prior stomachs. Garrett slid his hands up and down my body, feeling its contours and I shadowed his actions. His hand slid under my shirt, fingertips barely touching my skin, and his hand cupped my breast. He gently caressed along the cup of my bra with his thumb, pushing his fingers underneath to rub my nipple. I took a quick breath, sucking in some of his, indicating my surprise—mixed with desire—as we continued to search one another.

His hands drifted to my belly where he circled my belly button then gently put his finger in, wiggling it inside. The pleasant vibration migrated between my legs and my underwear began soaking up the moisture his touch created.

It ended as fast as it began. I turned away and pushed up into a sitting position, trying to return my breathing to a normal speed, and said, "No. No, I can't."

I pulled my shirt and coat down, folding my arms in front and rocking backward and forward, looking toward the waterfall. I battled with wanting Garrett, remembering what happened with Arcane and listening to your rhetoric in my head.

Garrett sat up and bent his knees in front of him, resting his arms on top. He also looked straight ahead without a word.

I let him down. I ruined a good thing. Why do I keep comparing him to Arcane? He's not a game! He's the real thing!

I started to cry. "I'm sorry. I shouldn't have let it get this far. I'm really sorry, Garrett."

He sat for a second, letting out a sigh, and then responded, "It's fine, Ashley."

I continued to feel sorry for myself, but he didn't move to console me. The forest stopped talking, as if listening to our missing conversation, making the silence unbearable.

Garrett continued gazing at the waterfall, saying, "You know, Ashley, I know you're running from something. I know you're scared and don't trust anyone. I get that. We haven't known each other that long, but I'm going to ask one thing from you."

Between gasps, I responded, "What?"

"Talk to me."

"I do talk to you—"

"Answering my questions or throwing small compliments out isn't talking. Don't get me wrong, I like compliments except when I'm with friends and want my conversations to have depth."

I took a napkin and used it to wipe my nose. It took everything I had to look at him.

"I'll try."

"I guess that's all I can ask."

The sun was setting, so we packed everything up and headed to the car. On the drive back I rested my head against the headrest. Embarrassment caused me to turn away from Garrett; especially in light of all the nice things he's done for me.

He isn't Arcane. Arcane never extended himself outside of compliments. If I learned anything, I learned selfishness from him.

I thought about what Garrett said and I knew I could lose the only friend I have in Seattle. Garrett placed his hand over mine, our fingers entwined and rested on my left thigh.

I won't lose him. He's my friend…I feel safe with him. Doesn't that mean anything?

There's no reason for me to go on. The day is done and Garrett and I are all right.

MONDAY, NOVEMBER 17, 2008: Friends,

You won't believe what happened to Garrett and me today.

We had planned to see the midnight movie, *The Illusionist.* so he stopped by the coffee shop to help me clean up to get out of there faster.

"Did the '60s couple make it in today?" he asked.

It's a running joke between us that the '60s couple has a tendency to party hard and get up slow after the weekends.

"The wife called me to say she ate something bad last night."

"Yeah, her husband."

OMG! I couldn't stop laughing. I don't know anyone else in my life who has ever made me laugh like he does.

"I can't believe you said that. You're bad."

"And you love it."

"You're right."

"Come on, we have half an hour to get there, get our popcorn and get the best seats in the house."

"Oh. Which are those?"

"Dead center, baby."

We got to the theater just as the previews were playing. Garrett requested extra butter on the popcorn, loaded it with salt and handed me a large Coke. My heart sped up just watching his seasoning fetish.

Once inside the lightly populated theater, Garrett raced to the middle and ran down the aisle for center seats.

He dove into the popcorn with verve—afraid I might eat it all, I guess. I had a hard time getting any popcorn with his hand scooping and shoving it into his mouth. Hilarious! How could someone so mature and considerate still be such a child? As I continued to try to score some popcorn, a custodian came down the aisle, flashed his flashlight at us and asked for our tickets.

Garrett looked at him like he was kidding, but when the custodian didn't leave, Garrett sighed and asked me if I had my ticket. I patted myself down and looked around on the floor (crap!).

"I think I tossed mine on the ground somewhere."

The custodian said, "Then I'm going to have to ask you to leave."

Garrett spoke up and said, "What? Are you kidding? No one holds onto their ticket stubs."

"Sir, if you don't have a ticket, you can't stay."

"Why are you only asking us? We bought tickets."

"Someone saw the both of you sneak in, so I'm asking you to show me your tickets."

Even in the dimly lit theater, I could see Garrett's scowl redden. His body stiffened, eyes set on the custodian like a fire torch to wood. It was the first time I have seen him really upset about something. But I didn't blame him…I was pretty pissed too.

Can you believe someone making up such a lie?

Maybe the custodian wanted to feel like a big shot, randomly picked us and blamed it on someone else. He was creating such a scene…or maybe we were because we tossed our tickets.

"Dude, you're taking your job way too seriously. People don't hold onto their ticket stubs," Garrett said. He turned around and asked the people behind us if they had their tickets. They took their stubs out of their coat pockets and showed them to the custodian.

The custodian gave Garrett a snide look and said, "Ticket stubs or get out."

Then I started getting embarrassed. I got up and said, "Garrett, forget it. Let's just go."

"No! We're being accused of sneaking in here because some asshole said we did."

People around us started telling us to get the hell out—that we were ruining the movie for them. I wanted to put a hood over my head to avoid anyone actually recognizing me.

The custodian said, "Sir, I don't want to have to call the police. Please just go."

I took Garrett's hand, pulling him in the opposite direction of the custodian.

"Come on, Garrett, we can see it another time."

He hesitated then let me lead us out.

When we got outside, he threw the popcorn and said, "What the fuck? Are they kidding? Who the hell would accuse us of not paying? I'd like to find that asshole and punch the shit out of them."

I put my hands in my pockets as we walked to the car. Garrett was infuriated by the accusation. He buried his hands in his pockets and walked next to me back to his car.

"I don't know," I said, trying to dismiss the whole incident and calm Garrett. "It's no big deal. We can come another time or rent it."

We drove in silence as we both tried to calm our nerves. I kissed him on the cheek and thanked him for a nice night.

He scoffed and said, "At least you can tell your kids you were kicked out of a theater for not paying."

I cringed at the "kids" comment.

Un-fucking-believable, huh? I'm not mad for being kicked out as much as I am for Garrett being upset. He was looking forward to seeing the movie…I was too. Oh well, we can rent it and eat all the popcorn we want…if he's willing to share it. LOL!

TUESDAY, NOVEMBER 18, 2008: Dear Friends,

If I thought yesterday was bad, then today was a nightmare. It started in the morning and snowballed from there.

As soon as I woke up I got in the shower to rub away yesterday's blues and then I made my way into the kitchen. While the coffee brewed, I went to the window to peek out of the blinds—another day of a weeping Mother Nature. When I went back to the kitchen, something on the table caught my eye. I stopped to see what it was.

"No. It can't be," I whispered.

My knees buckled and my arm hit the table when I collapsed to the floor, sending a movie ticket stub floating through the air—as if in slow motion.

So he was the 'someone' who said we snuck into the movie? Is this my ticket?

I used the wall to get up. My feet slipped a few times as I pushed against the wall for security, and then I moved to the door in a trance. I was about to unlock it but leaned against it instead. My head felt heavy and my limbs hung like wet blankets. The room began shrinking and I could hear someone say, "He's here", realizing it was my own strained voice that uttered the words. I slid to the floor, my lips kissing my knees. I stared blankly down the stretched hallway.

I did everything to protect my identity. Moved, changed my looks and pretty much kept to myself. My mother and sister are the only ones who know where I live.

Why does Arcane want to ruin my life?

How did he find me?

But you didn't keep to yourself. You hooked up with some guy, AGAIN, you hardly know because of your insecurity of being alone.

I was released from self-torture for the time being when there was a knock on the door.

"Ashley, are you in there?"

Garrett.

I closed my eyes to block out the noise.

"Ashley?"

Don't be an idiot and let him in.

The knocking persisted.

Go away, go away.

"Hey, I passed the coffee shop and saw you weren't there. Did you oversleep? Ash?"

Don't say anything. He'll leave when he gets tired. It's best to keep this to yourself.

I lifted my head and tried to hold it steady to focus on his words.

"Ash! Come on, open the door."

You'll ruin everything if you open that fucking door—you and you alone!

But I need him.

Bullshit—

If you do need him, then open the door...but be careful about what you say.

The phone rang. My head whipped toward it and I gasped, but I didn't move, just gazed in its direction.

"Ash? I'm worried. If you're in there, open the door!"

I ran my fingers through my hair and rubbed my scalp.

I need time...give me time.

Garrett banged on the door again after he heard the phone ring. The pounding returned my attention to him. I grabbed the doorknob to lift myself up, slid the chain over and opened the door. He stepped forward and I fell into his arms, hugging him tight to help with the weight of fear.

Garrett held me close against him, swaying and rubbing my back, asking what was wrong. He finally shut the door.

The swaying started to still me and he kept repeating, "It's going to be okay, Ash. I'm here now."

Garrett guided us to the couch and sat down, pulling me onto his lap. I rested my head on his shoulder and locked my arms around his neck.

"Ash, let me call the Wilsons. I'll tell them you're sick. Someone will need to get down there to open up."

Still in somewhat of a trance, I pointed to my cell phone. Garrett shuffled through the contact list and called the Wilsons, saying that I was vomiting and wouldn't be in.

"Everything's fine. They got it under control," he said.

He stretched my legs out and hugged me close. I knew he was trying to figure out how to help me, but all he could do was console me...pretty much what I wanted.

Garrett kissed my cheek and said, "Ashley, you gotta tell me what happened. I can't help you unless you tell me."

I had to tell him.

There was no way I could fight Arcane alone, and there was no way I was going to lose Garrett over this asshole. It was time.

"He was here, Garrett. The monster I thought I escaped from is here—in Seattle."

Instead of bombarding me with questions, he waited until I explained who *he* was. I started from the beginning, leaving nothing out and ending with the good-bye to my mother and sister.

"I'm the one on the right," I said, pointing to the picture Garrett had been looking at the first night he was in my apartment. "I thought moving and changing my appearance would lose him. And…"

I paused. Garrett's only known me as Ashley. Could this admission be a deal breaker?

"…and my name is Sydney, not Ashley. I thought I could lose him by creating an alias, but he's back. I apologize for lying to you, Garrett. I couldn't let anyone know my real name. It would be—"

"A risk. I understand Ashley. Or Sydney."

"Ashley. I need to remain Ashley because of my job and lease…security."

Revealing the truth felt like a massage—pain for a moment and then all the tension went away. I simultaneously felt alive and tired. The secret—a leech—sucked on my energy all this time.

"I'm speechless. Now I understand why you cringed yesterday when I made the 'kids' comment. To be honest, many things are now making sense—your apprehension and mistrust to start with. Shit, if someone did that to me, I don't know if I could ever recover. I don't know how you managed to go on."

"You just go on. It's that or die. I guess I wasn't ready to meet death."

I sat up, moved over to the space next to him and said, "Garrett, you've been nothing but kind to me. Your thoughtfulness threw me off after dealing with Arcane and I didn't know how to react. I owe you—"

"Ash. No. Let's not start throwing out apologies. You did what you did to survive."

We sat looking at each other. I let his words soak in as he continued to examine my face like it was his first time seeing it; a new revelation—a new look. His finger moved the strands of hair from my face, his thumb traced my eyebrow and then his hand slid to the back of my neck, carefully closing the gap until our lips stopped a breath away. I looked down at his lips and then back up to his eyes, letting him know it was all right. Our lips pressed together and held, feeling the warmth before moving in sync. Our eyes closed and opened in harmony as feelings began to rise to the next level. When we moved a few inches apart, I bashfully smiled at the tingling of my lips and his puppy dog eyes.

Kissing him was an incredible feeling. Not that we hadn't kissed before, but it was different this time. This time truth lay in our laps, validating genuine feelings.

Garrett asked, "Are you all right?"

Am I all right? Right at that moment, I wanted our feelings to keep going, yet they were too sensitive to rush.

"I'm fine. I'm more than fine. Telling you everything was like a weight lifted off me. I've felt so tensed having to cover up my identity and what happened with Arcane." And I was—fine, I mean.

You're really not. But don't even think about confessing everything!

Why do you do that? Why do you argue about how you feel?

Because revealing everything to Garrett isn't going to get rid of all the tension. You'll still continue to think about Arcane.

He looked away and then asked, "Not to change the subject, but why do you think he was here?"

I took a deep breath and dove in, saying, "This morning I found a movie ticket stub on my kitchen table. Remember, I threw mine on the movie theater floor? When I noticed it, I lost it because I knew it was him. This is his game. He does little things to let me know he's around. Plays with my mind to the point where I begin second-guessing myself. He won't stop until he's ready to stop, and I have no idea when that will be."

"What are you saying? That's his ticket?"

I nodded 'yes' and I could tell things were starting to make sense to him.

"Do you think he is the one that said we snuck into the movie?"

I nodded again.

Garrett swallowed hard. I knew he was thinking about Arcane and churning the idea of him being so close to us. He got up from the couch and began to pace.

"If he left that ticket then that means he was in the apartment."

I looked up at him in agreement. He started turning on lights, opening doors, closets and checking under the bed. I followed behind, looking to see if anything was missing. Arcane left no signs of intrusion—other than his ticket—which didn't prove anything.

"We need to call the police."

"For what, Garrett? For them to tell me there's nothing they can do?"

"They need to know there's a psycho in town."

I looked down, shaking my head and said, "What am I going to say? 'A psycho is here and he left a movie ticket in my apartment?' The police can't do anything until there's proof or Arcane actually does something—to me I guess. Trust me, I've already been through this a couple of times with the police."

"For Christ's sake, Syd, I mean Ash. Didn't he do enough to you?"

He slid his hand through his hair, crinkling his eyebrows in disgust.

"Garrett, I know you want to help, and I thank you for it. I know how the police work and I tried to have him arrested in Chicago, but they couldn't without sufficient evidence."

"I don't care. You need to at least go down to the police station, explain what's happened and file a report—that way, if something happens it's on record."

"Gee thanks, now I have something to look forward to."

I scrunched my eyebrows, sighed and ran my fingers through my hair.

"I'm not kidding and you know what I mean. If anything happens, meaning he'll slip up, they always do. Why don't you get dressed and then we'll go to the station together?"

This was unexpected. Feelings or not, I didn't expect him to invest this kind of time. I got off the couch, my hand gently squeezed his as I kissed his shoulder, whispering, "Thank you."

He went into the kitchen to get some coffee and called in to work to let them know he wouldn't be in.

***

When we arrived at the station a few cops sat at their desks on phones, so we walked to the front desk and asked to speak to an officer. Officer Miller told us to take a seat then left the desk and went to one of the officers on the phone. The one on the phone looked over his shoulder at us, wrapped up his conversation and waved us back.

He stood an inch taller than Garrett and his hand swallowed mine when we shook.

"I'm Officer Callahan. Have a seat." Gesturing to chairs across from his desk, he continued, saying, "Officer Miller said you wanted to talk to an officer. What can I do for you?"

Garrett took control of the situation.

"Yes. My name is Garrett, a neighbor of Ashley's. We have reason to believe someone is stalking her."

Callahan's expression changed and he cleared his throat before proceeding. "That's a serious charge. What makes you think she's being stalked?"

"How much time do you have?"

Callahan brought us into a conference room and gave us something to drink. In the privacy of the large room, I related the same story I told Garrett, in addition to my real name and the incident with the movie ticket stub.

When I finished, Callahan leaned back and said, "I'll have to verify the police reports."

"I understand, but at the time there wasn't much information for them to go on. Like I said, I met Arcane on the internet, never got his last name or went to his house. The police said that without evidence of wrongdoing they wouldn't even bother checking my computer to try and trace him."

"Stalking can be a hard thing to prove, and the Chicago police are right. Unless they catch him in the act, their hands are tied."

Garrett sat back hard, letting out a heavy sigh and said, "That's crap. So what? You can't do anything unless he kills her?"

Callahan gave him a disapproving stare and I placed my hand on his to calm him. Garrett was taking this hard, which made me want him more.

Callahan said, "I realize this is frustrating. Our laws need updating and improvement. The laws leave the person stalked vulnerable due to the need for concrete evidence. That's why so many stalkers accomplish what they set out to do—hurt, and in some cases, murder."

"Oh, I'm sure she feels much better now," Garrett retorted.

"You better watch your tone, boy. I understand it's frustrating, but you don't need to talk—"

"I'm sorry, Officer Callahan. Garrett's just concerned about my safety. He recently found out about all of this, so it's fairly new to him."

Callahan sat back, thinking, as Garrett looked around the room. I stroked Garrett's arm and then took his hand in mine. As much as Garrett frustrated Callahan, he made me feel safe—my knight in shining armor. I had never had someone look out for me like this— someone fighting in my corner. It felt incredible.

Callahan looked at me and said, "Here's what I'm going to do. I'll contact the Chicago Police Department and ask them to fax me the police reports. After I review them, I'll contact you and ask you to reiterate everything, but I'll record it this time."

Garrett got up, pushed his chair and said, "Are you kidding me? That's what you're going to do?"

Callahan got up, towering over the table and pointed at Garrett as his voice rose.

"Sit down. I don't want to hear another word out of your mouth, do you hear me?"

I tugged on Garrett's arm, pulling him back to his chair.

"It's fine," I said, "I'll tell it again."

Callahan sat back down and asked me, "Is there somewhere you can stay while I verify your story?"

"With me. She's staying with me."

Callahan shot back, "What did I say? I don't want to hear another word from you."

"He's right. I'll stay with him."

Callahan eased off. "I'm sorry I can't do more for you right now, but once I get the reports I'll see what I can do."

"I appreciate your time, Officer Callahan."

Garrett and Callahan nodded at each other and we left the station.

***

Back at my apartment I put a few things in a duffle bag. Garrett thinks it's better if I don't go back to my place at all for a few days.

I dropped my stuff off at his apartment and we went to rent videos, stopping at a deli on the way back. We chose a table in the corner by the window. I couldn't keep myself from staring outside, searching faces.

He's out there somewhere. After all I did for protection, he's found me.

Garrett reached across the table, put his hand on top of mine and said, "Don't do this. You'll drive yourself nuts looking for him."

We returned to his apartment, exhausted. Our earlier thought of watching videos went out the window. He took my hand and we went into the bedroom. Fully clothed, we slipped under the covers and slept until the evening hours.

I woke before Garrett and watched his chest rise and fall, his quiet face wiped of concern. Telling him was the best thing. I'm scared as hell about what Arcane has in store for me, but at least I'm not alone.

I'm lucky, friends.

THURSDAY, NOVEMBER 20, 2008: OMG! Friends,

Last night was one of the best days of my life…a magical release. It started out with Garrett insisting I take the pepper spray he had in his kitchen drawer. His mother gave it to him years ago, and he never bothered to throw it away. It was so sweet that he wanted to keep me safe. I told him it wasn't necessary, but he argued until I gave in. I feel silly carrying it because I only work across the street. Besides, it wouldn't help anyway—Arcane works in the shadows. I'll see him when the game is about to end. I'm sure he didn't come this far to end it so soon.

The middle of the week is always slower at the store, so I filled the time cleaning the coffee machines and thinking about the ghost from the past.

He'll always be in my life.

He will as long as you let him.

When Garrett finished work he came by and watched over me; which meant drinking several cups of coffee. By the time I was done with work he was bouncing off the walls. We left the coffee shop walking hand-in-hand swinging our arms, acting as if everything was all right. With us—things are. Our relationship has gone from friends to romance.

I took a bath before getting into my pajamas. When I came back into the living room Garrett was in the kitchen making us something to eat, so I grabbed a movie to put it on. The movie dropped to the floor when I screamed and Garrett ran in asking what was wrong.

I pointed, and said. "Did you rent that movie?"

The movie *Identity* stared back at us.

"No, I got three comedies."

He put the movie aside and said he'd ask for his money back when we returned the others. Garrett didn't find it strange, but I know Arcane did it. I have a feeling things are going to start occurring more often than not until we catch him.

"Ashley, it was a coincidence…that's all it was."

We put on *When Harry Met Sally*, but I couldn't quit looking at the movie *Identity*. I didn't argue with him, but Garrett was the only one laughing during the movie. Seeing my heart wasn't into it, he put his arm around me and pulled me closer. His heartbeat, the warmth of his arms, helped alleviate thoughts of Arcane. I curled my legs underneath me, put my head against his arm and my hand on his thigh.

I looked at his legs and for the first time noticed the muscles buckling out of his calves and thighs. Garrett let out a sigh then casually moved my hand away when I unconsciously began caressing his leg. I wasn't trying to play games, but doing this made his body react, so I placed my hands in my lap. His chest rose and fell in an even rhythm except during the occasional wave of laughter. The warmth of his arms and the normalcy of the moment were sedating and the weight of my eyelids soon won out.

The clock ticked—1:00 a.m. I turned away from it to face Garrett. I watched him sleep, the gentleness of his breathing, his content face…handsome as ever. I moved closer and pressed my lips against his. Startled, his eyes opened then he put his arms around me, pulling me close. His kisses moved from soft and slow, to asking for permission, to gently demanding—a wanting to explore. My body responded. This is when the magic began.

For the first time since I met Arcane, maybe in my life, I didn't fear anything. Garrett had awakened my emotions and I gave my all to our lovemaking. The caresses, desires and release—nothing escaped my want to please and give him what he deserved. I hung up my inhibitions for the night and continued to express to Garrett what his protection meant to me.

The time was perfect. I'm staying with him, holding onto his protection. I have waited for this moment. The perfect fit. I can't wait for it to happen again. LOL! Later...

THURSDAY, NOVEMBER 27, 2008: Friends,

Happy Thanksgiving! Unfortunately, the holiday didn't close the coffee shop…well, not for the entire day. People need their fix while doing last minute shopping. Since I was the only one at work without family and friends, I was the winner—scheduled to work until 3:00 p.m. at time and a half. I really didn't want to go. I wanted to stay at the apartment with Garrett. Since I couldn't be there, I thought about the night before and early this morning. I could feel Garrett's touch on my skin and I still wore his scent.

I haven't told him…I'm not sure if I will, but I. LOVE. HIM.

I LOVE GARRETH

There was a steady flow of people all morning, except Garrett wasn't one of them. I thought he might surprise me. He called a few times to see how I was holding up and to thank me for a wonderful night…I mean it was sweet…but no visit. Did I sexually fulfill him or is he disappointed? When he called he complimented me, showed concern, but I still found myself heading down a line of self-questioning. By the end of the work day, I convinced myself that he was going to tell me he wanted to just be friends.

Don't you know how to take things slow? You take things to a higher level than the person you're with.

I never told him I loved him. THAT would be taking things to a higher level.

The smell of turkey dinners drifted throughout the hallway as I made my way to Garrett's apartment. I knocked a few times and when he opened the door, a seasoned breeze met me as Garrett put his arm around my waist, pulled me toward him and kissed me.

"I missed you," he whispered.

He said he missed me. I'm so stupid. He missed me.

I hugged him back, saying, "You have no idea how much I missed you."

Garrett hung up my coat while I went into the kitchen and looked around.

"Geez, someone's been busy. I'll go get changed and help you out."

When I came back into the kitchen, wearing less constricting clothes, he held his hand up indicating 'stop' and shook his head 'no'.

"No worries. I. Am. The. Man. I timed this perfectly. If you want, you can pour us a glass of wine, which you'll find in the refrigerator."

Did I finally find him because of all my prior suffering? Is he too good to be true? No!

As I poured the wine, I looked at all the food he made and then back at him, asking, "Are we expecting anyone else?"

"Not that I'm aware of."

"Okay…I'm hungry."

"We don't have to eat it all today."

He dipped his finger in the mashed potatoes, scooped some up and put it by my mouth.

"We're both off tomorrow and there's nothing like leftover turkey after hours of sex."

I opened my mouth and took the potatoes off his finger, seducing him with my tongue. My hips pressed against him, my right knee moving up his leg and applying gentle pressure to his groin. After thinking he was going to dump me, and then seeing the dinner he cooked, I couldn't help it...I was horny as hell. I wanted the rawness of it, like a vampire's reaction to the scent of blood.

Looking into his eyes, I said, "We can start things off with an appetizer if you'd like."

I took his lower lip between my lips and drew it into my mouth, sucking until it began to swell. Garrett's breathing increased a bit, then he put his hands on my hips and kissed me with an intense want. We moved away from the stove to the wall as his hands glided everywhere—groping and fondling—inhaling large gasps of air to last until the next breath. It didn't take long before my pants were off and Garrett's pants down to his ankles. His fingers plunged inside me, prepping me to take him, his tongue darting in and out of my mouth, kissing down my neck to my breasts. I pressed my head against the wall, pushing my breasts out to the rise and fall of his touch. He lifted my right leg and penetrated me, moving fast like time was running out. I was ready to take him in deep. His hands gripped under my ass and lifted me up, pressing me against the wall. I wrapped my legs around his waist for leverage as I bounced up and down to the rhythm of his thrusts. We sighed and moaned in pleasure. Somewhere in the backdrop the oven timer went off, but we ignored it as he pushed hard and deep into me until our bodies started to spasm. I wrapped my arms around him as his body tensed and he released inside me. It was several minutes before we regained control of our breathing. I let my legs slide down his, causing him to slip out. We pressed our foreheads together and looked at each other, smiling.

He said, "That wasn't an appetizer."

We dressed and turned our attention to wine and food...the feeling of him still inside me. Our earlier sexual encounter stayed with me well into the night...sexually full...I wrapped myself around Garrett while we watched television.

Sleep is all I desire now.

THURSDAY, NOVEMBER 25, 1999: Dear Friend,

Caitlyn here.

The holidays always remind me that I'm alone. I don't even have anyone to send good wishes to. So what am I thankful for? Not much other than I'm not with Cal.

Since I wasn't celebrating the holiday with anyone, I decided to go to that woman's house and then I followed her and the teenager to a restaurant. I asked to be seated in a booth diagonally from them. The teenager pulled the chair out for the woman before sitting down. He spoke with such confidence and maturity that I questioned his age. My back was to them, but I took small opportunities to look at the boy. He had grown in height over the past year, and his face was losing its baby cushion. Although thin, he had an appetite like a samurai.

The woman commented on how nice it was to go out instead of cooking for just the two of them. I smiled to myself, thinking the same thing so I could (in a roundabout way) celebrate with them.

The woman asked the teenager, "How is school coming along?"

"Great. I have all A's, except for math. I got a B in the class. I don't think the teacher likes me very much."

She reached over, squeezed his hand, and said, "Wonderful! I'm so proud of you. I doubt the teacher dislikes you…math simply isn't your strong subject." The woman took a sip of her coffee and asked, "Have you started looking into colleges? You know this is the time to do it."

"Yes. I've filled out some of the information on the application forms. I'll have to redo them, but I'll already have most of the information."

She patted his hand, and said, "Oh that's good, son. You'll get in anywhere you choose. They'll be lucky to have you as a student…and you'll go far as a psychiatrist."

I ate in silence, listening to their conversation…such positivity. Before paying my bill, I waited until the teenager and woman made their way to the parking lot. I got up from the booth, paid my tab and hurried to my car, where I stood by the driver's side watching as they pulled away and disappeared from view.

Why are you wasting your time following them?

What does it matter to you?

It was nice (sighs). Maybe someday I'll actually get to make a Thanksgiving dinner for a tableful of people. Then I'll be thankful.

Time to say good night. I appreciate you listening to me.

FRIDAY, NOVEMBER 28, 2008: Oh Friends,

The other shoe dropped. I should have known when things were going good that something bad was going to happen.

You can't keep thinking that way.

Why not? Every time I find happiness, or things are good, it takes a turn for the worst.

I got a call from Officer Callahan telling me he received the information from the Chicago Police Department, checked it out and was ready for me to come in to tell my story again. This was great news. Something will finally start happening as far as protection goes. Garrett wanted to go with me, but I told him it was best that I go alone. He dropped me off at the station and told me to call him when I was done.

The police station seemed more active than the last time I was there. I approached the front desk, asking to speak to Callahan. Before the officer could answer, a few cops with a guy in handcuffs came barging through the door, adding to the fast-paced environment.

"What have we here?" asked the front desk officer.

One of the cops accompanying the guy in handcuffs responded, "We caught this one behind the new restaurant having sex with a prostitute. She's being brought in, too."

"Fuck you! I wasn't having sex with her," said the guy in handcuffs.

The cop's expression was priceless when he asked, "Really? Did you slip and fall into her?"

Laughter erupted in the station as they hauled him into a private room.

The front desk officer returned to what he was doing when I arrived, forgetting I was even there. Again, I approached the front desk asking to speak to Officer Callahan.

"Officer Callahan? And you would be?"

"Ashley Powell. He called this morning telling me he received the reports from the Chicago Police Department and asked if I could come in to file my complaint."

He eyed me up and down, told me to have a seat and went to the desk of another officer. They both turned, not hiding the fact they were talking about me, whispered some more and then the original cop returned to the front desk.

"Can you come here, please?"

He started walking away and saw I wasn't following so he stopped.

"Is there a problem?"

"Yeah, there is a problem. Callahan has been in the hospital since Tuesday night."

My mouth hung loose—my mind was racing, although I still had the ability to ask what happened.

"Car accident. He's been in intensive care since, so please fill me in on how you could have received a call from him when he's been unconscious?"

Interesting. Who DID call me?

My eyes scanned the police station, not knowing what I was looking for. Everyone continued on with their work, except for the officer the front desk cop had talked to—who was staring at me—his eyes familiar and somewhat menacing. I felt my skin weep. I clamped my hands together to cover the trembling.

What about him is familiar? How do I know him? Did he call me pretending to be Callahan?

He smiled at me as if he knew what I was thinking.

I turned away, folded my arms, and approached the front desk officer and asked, "Can you tell me who that—"

"Excuse me, but you haven't answered my question."

"No, I—"

"How did you get a phone call from Officer Callahan when he's been in intensive care?"

I was confused and scared, whispering, "I don't know. It sounded like him."

"Did he leave you a message and identify himself as Callahan? Did you actually talk to him?"

With a glimmer of hope, my eyes widened then shrunk when I realized I had already deleted the message.

"No…I mean, he left a message, but I just remembered, I deleted it," I said, cowering. "Wait!"

I took my phone out, looked at my recently received calls to show him the number.

The officer looked at it and said, "Yeah, so? It's our main number. Anyone could have called you."

"But why would anyone call me from here if they didn't know me."

The cop dropped his pen, put his hands on the desk and leaned forward, glaring down at me. "Listen, lady, I don't have time for guessing games. What's this about anyway?"

"I'm being stalked. I explained to Callahan that I think someone has been in my apartment and told him the entire story, starting from when I lived in Chicago. He called to tell me the police report information arrived."

"There haven't been any Chicago Police Reports at the fax machine."

"Maybe they arrived another day," I offered up.

His voice began to rise as he said, "I've worked every day this week, and I check the fax machine. I can tell you first hand there weren't any reports from Chicago."

I sighed.

In a nonchalant response, the front desk cop asked, "Why don't you explain it to someone else?"

"No! Officer Callahan knows everything about it and was expecting the reports from Chicago to verify my story so I could file my complaint."

"I don't know anything about it," the officer said.

"Can you recheck to see—"

"Miss, I have a million things to do and I don't have time to look for some paperwork you claim Callahan was going to receive. I told you, you can talk to another officer. Otherwise, you'll have to wait until Callahan returns—if he returns."

I was about to leave, and then turned back to the officer and asked, "Excuse me?"

The officer groaned before responding, "Yes?"

I pointed to the officer who had smiled (and stared) at me earlier and asked, "Could you just tell me the name of that officer?"

"Officer Atticus."

I looked back at Officer Atticus, watching him talk on the phone as he searched for something on his desk. He caught me staring. His smile seemed wicked so I left.

Instead of calling Garrett, I walked part of the way so I could think about what I should do next.

It's too much of a coincidence that Callahan got into an accident the night I saw him. Something isn't right...and if it isn't a coincidence, then I'm jeopardizing Garrett's safety as well.

Officer Atticus is a little off. He's eerily familiar, though. His eyes remind me of Arcane's with that threatening slant he would assume when he wanted terror to anesthetize me. Other than that, Officer Atticus looked nothing like Arcane. I dragged my feet home, filled with hopelessness similar to how I feel being unable to escape Arcane. The repeated intrusions are putting my nerves on alert, second-guessing everyone in my new life. Sydney never really became Ashley because the stalker is only a few steps behind.

Garrett wasn't home when I arrived, so I went into my own apartment. I walked around. It felt foreign to me, but I searched for anything to prove Arcane has been here. The place isn't as daunting in the daytime. Nothing was disturbed in my living room or the kitchen, but I only walked around without moving anything. I went down the hallway, first looking in the washroom then the bedroom. Standing in the doorway of the bedroom, my body pulled itself up completely straight.

Someone had tucked in the sheets around the bed and placed the pillows at the head.

Has he been sleeping here?

Inching my way to the bed, I pulled the sheets back and found them completely stained with what looked like bodily fluids. I dropped the sheet, walked backward out of the room and ran from the apartment.

Just as I closed the door, Garrett came down the hallway.

"What's going on? Why are you here…and why didn't you call me to pick you up?"

"He's been here. Garrett, I know he's been in my apartment."

Garrett dropped the bag he was hugging in his arm and walked toward my apartment, asking, "How do you know? Let me see."

"The bed. It looks like he had sex or masturbated all over it. My bed wasn't dirty."

"If he did then they could run DNA tests on the sheets. Let me check it out."

Garrett was right. We might have him.

"Who could run the tests?"

"Callahan. Didn't you talk to him? " I shook my head 'no' and he stopped.

"Callahan was in an auto accident Tuesday night and is in the hospital."

"We saw him on Tuesday." Garrett started.

"I know."

I let it sink in. "Let's go in your apartment and talk."

Garrett picked up the bag and we disappeared from the hallway. I told him what happened with Callahan, about the Chicago reports not arriving, and that I would need to talk to someone else. I also told him about Atticus.

"There was this Officer Atticus watching me. There's something wrong with him."

"How do you know there's something wrong with him?"

"Well...I don't know exactly, I mean...if he has mental problems, but he looks threatening. He smiled at me a few times like he knew me and what I was doing there."

"Are you sure you're not just saying that because you're freaked out? Could it be that you're a little paranoid—understandably, of course?"

"I'm sure, Garrett. The way he looked at me was like looking into the face of Arcane, except he looks nothing like him. I know it sounds messed up, but my gut feeling tells me he's trouble."

"What kind of trouble? You're running away from Arcane. I don't doubt you, but you can't accuse every guy who makes you uncomfortable. "

I looked down at my hands, "I'm just saying I don't want to talk to *him*."

You'll have to talk to him at some point.

You're being spooked.

Better calm your nerves before you let Arcane get the best of you.

We sat for a few minutes before I started up again. "I'm scared, Garrett. I'm scared for both of us."

He pulled me close to him on the couch, and said, "I won't let anything happen to you, Ashley." He kissed me. "He won't touch you."

I shifted to see his face and asked, "What about you? What if he does something to you?"

He pressed my head against his shoulder, sighed and said, "Let's not worry about it now."

But I felt his heartbeat speed up.

I feel guilt along with fear.

Arcane might have added Garrett to his prey list. I can't exactly break it off with Garrett—I have nowhere else to go except back to Chicago and that isn't an option. Besides, I rely on Garrett as a friend, lover and for safety. The world is starting to become very small to me. No place is safe.

I knew this was going to happen…just when my life was picking up. At least I can count on you.

Right?

FRIDAY, APRIL 21, 1995: Dear Friend,

It's Caitlyn, and I gotta tell ya, Seattle is wonderful! I feel free to do whatever I want whenever I want—no Cal abusing me. Shortly after arriving, I got a job at the Kings Inn in downtown Seattle. The money is all right, but not enough for my newfound freedom. I started…well, let's say I started entertaining some gentlemen friends for extra money. Sometimes they even take me out for drinks to the Alibi Room to prepare for a night full of good times. As long as they're nice, and don't hit, I'm open to anything they want.

One night I met a guy by the name of Ed Atticus. He immediately took a liking to me and gave me things. I think it was his way of getting me to like him. Of course I accepted his gifts, but I breathed a lot easier when he left for the night. He has cold, dark eyes—menacing, although he's never raised his voice or a hand to me. Ed gave me flowers, took me out to dinner, and gave me presents, such as a necklace and bracelet. I tried to overlook his weirdness—to enjoy the little treats he gave me; however, I eventually had to break it off. His creepiness canceled out all the nice things he did for me…and there was no…I mean NO attraction toward him.

Ed didn't take the break up well, and followed me when I was out with other men. I couldn't believe it. It was creating a problem with other 'friends'. I wanted the stalking to stop, so I had one of my clients threaten him. After a few months, he must have gotten tired of me because I haven't seen him since.

I still wear one of the pieces of jewelry he gave me—a pendant necklace to put pictures in. I love the gold heart shape.

You didn't have a problem taking and keeping Ed's gifts.

I know…I tried to like him…but not enough to keep getting showered with gifts.

One day, when you least expect it, he may find you and get you back for breaking up with him.

I deserve the gifts after all the abuse I've put up with over the years. They belong to me.

I'm free in Seattle and free of Ed. The nightlife here is great. Until next time…

MONDAY, DECEMBER 1, 2008: Friends,

The weekend was devoid of surprises. BUT, it's only a sign that something else is about to happen.

I had the afternoon shift, so Garrett had the washroom all to himself this morning. While he was showering I started to wake up, scooting farther under the covers into the warmth he left behind. Garrett came into the bedroom, naked, opening the closet to find something to wear. I propped my head up on the pillow with my arm to get a better look at his body—especially the part that makes mine come alive. He grabbed a shirt off the hanger and turned around to find me staring at him.

Tilting his head to the side, he smiled and said, "What are you doing up?"

"I heard this hot guy getting ready for work and I had to get a look at him."

Garrett shook his head, blushing.

He slipped his feet into his jeans, jumped in them and came to the side of the bed. Garrett bent down to give me a kiss. This simple gesture made my body cry out for him, so I wrapped my fingers around the back of his neck and pulled him in.

He laughed and said, "Miss Ashley, you are a little nympho."

It was my turn to blush. I answered with a deep kiss that stopped him from moving away. He came closer to me, his hands moved over my body, working their way under my pajamas resting his hand on the bed for stability. Then he stopped.

"Babe." He pressed his forehead against mine. "I can't do this now. I have to get to work. I have so many cases waiting for me and there are a few in dire need of attention. Only one day and I fell behind."

My hands slipped away from his neck lying limp in my lap.

"Because of me...you lost that day because of me...so many people count on you. I won't ask you to do that again."

"Yes, they count on me that's why my job is called social work." He playfully touched my nose and continued. "And y*ou* didn't ask me. I volunteered, remember? Anyways, you are important to me."

I LOVE GARRETT

His finger tickled my nose and then moved to my breast lightly tracing my nipple. "God, I want to make love to you now, you know I do..."

I sat back, saying, "I know, Garrett. I shouldn't have done that."

"So, you're not mad?"

I shook my head from side to side and said, "How can I get mad at you for being responsible? Your clients rely on you, and there are plenty of them."

He brushed the hair from my face and said, "How did I get so lucky?"

I traced his lips with my finger, and then pointed to the ceiling. "You? I think someone up there was on *my* side when I met you. I should be home around 8:00 or 9:00...maybe we can show each other how lucky we are then?"

Garrett pulled me up into a hug and said, "Not maybe. I'm excited now and will be thinking about you all day. I'll make sure to have dinner ready...and take care of you...all night if I have to."

I looked into his eyes, and said, "I can't even begin to describe to you how you make me feel."

Garrett took my chin in his hands and said, "I love you so much."

HE. LOVES. ME! Did you hear that world?!

My hand cupped the side of his face as my thumb stroked his cheek.

"I love you too, Garrett."

***

I was preoccupied at work thinking about what Garrett said and all he has done for me. Whenever I look into his eyes, I see the person I always wanted to resemble—a caring, trusting person to share my life with and give to whole-heartedly. Garrett gives without ever expecting anything in return. He has an innocent quality that allows him to trust—in me—in us. He doesn't close himself off, unless provoked.

At the coffee shop today, I wrote on a piece of paper.

Ashley ♡ Garrett

Later when there weren't any new customers, I wrote on that same piece of paper that I left by the coffee machine:

Ashley Hart

And then several times…

Mrs. Garrett Hart

I definitely did not expect him to say he loves me. For quite a while, I believe we both curled those words around our tongues—practicing without letting them escape. Garrett stood for several things in my life; a life preserver, a blanket, a hand and another voice.

Sooner or later Arcane will get you.

How will you protect Garrett? You need to think about what you'd do if something happened to him.

Forget that! Worry about how he'll torture Garrett. He'll probably make you watch.

Don't do that…you shouldn't think about things like that.

You might as well be prepared. He'll make Garrett suffer before finally getting rid of you. But first, he'll have fun with you…fuck you with everything he's got right after he kills Garrett. He'll rip you apart before death gets a chance to save you.

I pressed my elbow on the hot coffee machine to get rid of my painful thoughts until I couldn't handle the burning anymore.

We love each other. If I lost him, it would destroy all that's left of me.

Garrett must have been busy because I didn't hear from him. In a sense, I feel like I was his entire life since he rarely spoke of family, and when he did there was a sad undertone. As the night wore on my mood darkened with thoughts of Garrett tiring of me and my problems; mixed with feelings that something might have happened to him. I'm always waiting for the other shoe to drop instead of living in the moment. Every time the doorbell jingled, my head popped up to see if Garrett wanted some coffee or just to see me—my body slouched when it wasn't him.

I took my time walking home trying to relinquish my fears and insecurities. I am warmed by thoughts of Garrett's love, yet shiver from Arcane's invisible presence—a cold draft by a fire.

Garrett and I kept forgetting to get another key made for our places, so I knocked on the door. I knocked again then put my ear to the door, but I didn't hear anything inside. I turned the doorknob to test it and it opened.

Garrett always locks the door.

I pushed the door open. My legs inched their way into the living room…then the kitchen, a few times stopping to listen for sounds. I went back to the door, kicked it shut and then my unsteady hand locked it. I closed my eyes, praying Garrett just stepped out and forgot to lock the door—that nothing happened to him. It smelled like he had been cooking. I walked toward the bedroom with my head moving from side to side—eyes darting everywhere. Halfway there, someone knocked on the front door and I jumped, lost my balance, and fell on my back. I stared at the ceiling, clenching my hands into fists and praying whoever it was would go away. The knocking turned to pounding. I got to my feet, ran to the door and threw the chain on as I looked out the peephole. No one was there. My apartment door is ajar.

I backed up—into someone's arms. They wrapped around me from behind.

I kicked and screamed, "Let me go!" as I continued to buck my body.

"Whoa! What's wrong with you?" said Garrett from behind me.

I swung around staring at him, fuming.

"What were you doing?! Why didn't you answer the door when I knocked?"

He raised his hands in surrender, saying, "Ashley, I fell asleep. I didn't hear you knocking. What is wrong with you?"

I covered my eyes with my hands to keep myself from looking at the walls that felt like they were breathing—large expanding and contracting movements. Garrett pulled me into his chest. I hugged him and he let me find my stability again, whispering, "What's wrong, babe? Tell me. What happened to make you this shaken up?"

I moved away, wiping my face with the back of my hand.

"The door was unlocked, Garrett."

"You're confused. You just asked me why I didn't answer the door."

"I assumed the door was locked, so I knocked first. Then I tried the doorknob. It turned and opened. I didn't have the key, you did!"

He shook his head as if trying to wake himself up, walked to the door to check it, shrugged and jiggled the chain.

"Don't shrug and act like this isn't a big deal! I put the chain on the door! When I was walking to the bedroom someone started knocking…then pounding on the door. I ran back to put the chain on and looked through the peephole."

"Okay, Ashley, calm down. I don't remember leaving the door unlocked. It's always been a habit to check it a few times."

"Well you didn't this time. Think! Has it been unlocked since you got home?"

Garrett recounted what he did when he got home to see if he could remember whether or not he locked the door.

He put his hands on his hips, frowned and said, "I guess…I mean…I don't remember if I double-checked it or not."

"You can't do that. He might have been here while you were sleeping. Something could have happened to you!"

"Ash, quit yelling. Calm down."

"Don't tell me to calm down! You know how out of hand things have been getting. You left this door open while you slept, letting anyone walk in and hurt you. He could have come in after being in my apartment."

"What do you mean after being in your apartment?"

"When I looked out the peephole to see who was knocking I saw my apartment door was open."

Garrett walked to the door, slid the chain off and was about to open it, but I grabbed his hand— my other hand pushing the door closed.

"No, don't go out there." My panic had hit an all time high.

"Ashley, stop this now. I want to see if your—"

I grabbed him by the arms, tears pooling in my eyes, pleading, "Please don't open it, Garrett. For me…don't go out there."

I could feel an attack about to come…calm. Deep breath in…Deep breath out through the mouth.

He looked down at me with concern and said, "Ashley. We're going to have to leave here some time. You don't know if it's him. Kids could have been knocking on doors, running up and down the hall. Maybe you forgot to lock your door."

I shook my head 'no' when I said, "There aren't any kids and you know it. We'd hear them. And I didn't forget to lock my door."

We stood for a moment in silence—then he tried to come up with other explanations, but I disputed them all. Finally, he turned and grabbed his keys, took me by the hand and opened the door.

He stuck his head out into the hallway. "No one's out here. Let's go."

Still holding his hand, I followed him out. He closed the door behind us, checked the lock and pulled me across the hall, pushing my door open with the toe of his shoe.

I tugged on his hand, pulling him back. "He might be in there. Let's just call the police."

"You said you didn't like that Atticus guy and he might be the one they send. Callahan was the only one who seemed willing to help. And honestly, I don't think the psycho is in here."

He turned his focus to my apartment and went in, pulling me along. Kicking the door shut, we stood for a moment looking around. Garrett opened the front closet—nothing appeared different. I squeezed his hand as he began to move around the apartment. He looked at me, unlocked our hands, shook his own to restart the circulation and then took my hand again. I made an attempt at making a 'sorry' face, but my heart was racing and I kept checking over my shoulder to make sure Arcane wasn't behind us. The bedroom door was closed, so Garrett moved it with the tip of his shoe.

I whispered, "I never closed this door."

As if he didn't hear me, he walked into the room and stood next to the bed. There was something bunched up under the sheets. Garrett grabbed the sheet and pulled it back. In the middle of the bed lay three pairs of women's underwear. The top pair had the crotch cut out, the second had "Slut" written on it and the third had a birth control pill on top of it.

I said, "I told you he's here. He did this!"

"We're calling the police."

Garrett grabbed my hand and we went back to his apartment and made the phone call.

I stayed in Garrett's apartment while he met the police over at mine.

I'm so glad he took care of things.

You know he'll always be doing that.

It's how I've lasted this long.

An hour passed before he returned. He climbed into bed with me, scooted his body behind mine and embraced me.

After so much crying, my words were strained when I spoke. "What did they say?"

"They'll look into it."

I turned toward him with the intention of asking more questions, but he pressed his lips against mine, ending the rest of the discussion—or any other talk for the night.

I woke in the middle of the night and couldn't fall back to sleep. That's why I'm writing to you, in the silence of the night to settle my anxiousness. As you can see, Arcane's close and has picked up the pace of the game. Let's hope they link him to the underwear.

SATURDAY, DECEMBER 6, 2008: Hey Friends,

What a long ass week! It dragged as we waited to hear what the police were doing about what's happened so far. When I'd ask Garrett if he heard from them, he'd brush over it with a short response then change the subject. I called him on it, asking why he wouldn't talk about it, and he claimed he wasn't avoiding the subject. They were probably still processing tests and searching for fingerprints.

He doesn't tell you everything because of how you react.

I need to at least know what's going on.

He's protected you up to this point, so why are you questioning his motives?

On top of all of this we had another day I referred to as an 'Arcane's Day'. His efforts are claiming so many these days. The day started out all right. By the evening, it turned nasty, leaving both of us rattled and uptight.

The sun peeked through the sides of the blinds. I rolled on top of Garrett, put my chin on my hand as it rested on his chest, and gazed at him. Memorizing his features makes me feel at ease…like wanting to embed it in my mind. His fingers glided along my exposed skin and he watched me with a devilish grin.

"What are you smiling about?" I asked.

"Oh, I was just thinking about last night and how I reacted to my little sex pistol."

He pulled me up toward him, hastily kissing me. Other parts of him started to wake, which in turn stirred me. Our mouths grabbed at one another as we rolled around on the bed until I was back on top. He reached for my vibrator on the bedside table. Garrett lifted my left thigh, pulling it to one side. I parted my legs further and dropped my right knee to his other side—straddling him as I sat up. He pushed the vibrator inside me while I took him in my hand and stroked him. Our breathing heated the room.

His fingers moved between my thighs, parting me and rolling my clit between his fingers. I moaned louder when he rubbed the tip of his cock on my clit, causing him to join in. Moving up and down produced enough lubrication that he pulled out and pushed the vibrator back in. I took a deep breath, whispering his name as I allowed the air to escape my mouth. Garrett began working his cock inside me with the vibrator. My head fell back. My thighs were soaked. I was caught up in the moment when he slipped the vibrator out and unexpectedly moved it up to my anus and pressed against it. I jumped away from him and fell off the bed, breathing hard and trying to cover myself with the sheets.

He looked over the side of the bed, smirking and asked, "Are you all right? I take it you don't like that."

Looking up at him, I yelled, "I'm fine!"

I grabbed the rest of the sheet, wrapped it around me and went into the washroom. Turning the faucet on, I wet my face to cool down before I sat on the toilet to collect myself.

He never did that before. I realize accidents happen…but he was smiling.

You're making a big deal out of it.

Garrett tapped on the door, "Ashley, are you all right? Babe, I'm sorry."

I used the sheet to wipe my face off and opened the door.

I walked passed him then stopped and said, "Don't ever do that again."

"Ash, why are you so mad? I said I'm sorry."

"You know what *he* did to me. The damage he caused to my body. There isn't anything funny about what you did."

He looked defeated when he responded, "Damn, Ashley, I totally forgot. I would have never done that. Shit!"

Look at his face—he didn't mean it.

I didn't think he meant to do it…I was surprised, that's all.

You have to forgive him. It was an accident.

"It's okay. I realize you didn't mean it. I'm sorry too."

Garrett made up for his mistake in bed and with breakfast afterward. Full and clean, we decided to take a little drive to an artsy town several miles away to walk around and do some shopping on this beautiful day. I packed a little cooler in case we got thirsty on the road. As we drove, I took pictures of the scenery and when I got bored I stared at Garrett's profile and held his hand with the unexpected warmth of the generous December sun beating on my face.

We pulled into a Norman Rockwell town—it couldn't have come at a better time in my life. Its oldness mixed with virtue and beauty conjured up sweet memories of childhood. Open shop doors and booths lined the sidewalks selling everything from paintings and books to clothes and furniture. The buildings all had small yards tucked on the sides that were filled with Christmas decorations. Firs and the scent of evergreens adorned the inside of the stores. Everyone was hospitable with a helping hand and a nice word to say.

An old woman sat in one of the booths rocking back and forth. A younger woman stood beside her selling Elephant Ears—fried dough sprinkled with powdered sugar. The old woman looked into dead space, only moving her head when the younger woman touched her shoulder.

We walked up to the booth and the younger woman said, "Hello Garrett. It's been a long time." She seemed to have no expectation of a return greeting or further conversation.

He just nodded, ordered and with his hand on my lower back guided us to another booth. When I looked back, the old woman was watching us. I looked at Garrett, but he ignored my glance by talking to someone at another booth.

Fresh apple cider and curry fries were a few of the foods offered, along with pastries and ice cream. I walked alongside Garrett, proud and happy to be enjoying the day with him—even though I kept thinking about the women.

Who are they?

He'd tell you if it was important.

It's so out of character for him to not respond.

Leave it alone. Stop looking for something that's not there.

I used my camera as my eyes, snapping at everything until Garrett took it away and told me to enjoy it firsthand. We walked with arms around each other's waists and our breath swirling in the frigid air, clouding our vision. I tested Garrett's patience by going into every store and stopping at every booth to either browse or buy. He didn't complain, only smiled or steered me away when I spent too much time in one place. Occasionally, he took me in his arms, kissed me and told me he loved me. I ate up his touches and attention feeling as though I was floating.

I Love Garrett

At the end of the street, surrounded by a lake, was a seafood restaurant covered with Christmas decorations. Garrett joked about the fish being eaten so close to home. It was a sad thought, but not sad enough to detour me from checking out the place. We went down to the restaurant to find the place decked out with an electric train that ran around the entire perimeter. No area was left naked of the holiday season. After eating our way through the day, we only had enough space for a few drinks, so we sat in the bar area by a window that overlooked the lake. The place buzzed with conversations and laughter.

We were enjoying our drinks when I felt a need to tell Garrett how I was feeling. I reached across the table, took his hands in mine and said, "I love this place. I love you. Thank you for bringing me here."

He lifted my hands to his mouth, kissed them and responded, "I love you, too, and you're welcome."

We turned back to the lake and I asked, "Do you come here often?"

"Kinda. I grew up here."

My head shifted back to him, stunned by his nonchalance.

"You grew up here? In this quaint town? Why didn't you tell me before we came? Is your—"

He looked at me and said, "Yes," turning his attention back to the lake and adding, "My mom still lives here."

I sat slack-jawed—amazed that he brought me close to his upbringing, yet kept me in the dark from the details.

I slowly released his hands, folded them in front of me, and asked, "Why, Garrett? Why would you bring me here? It's obvious you don't want me to meet your family."

"That isn't true, Ash. I brought you here because it's the perfect place for us to relax, and I wanted you to meet my mom."

"You wanted? You changed your mind?"

His face fell in pain.

"You already did...sort of...the old woman sitting at the booth selling Elephant Ears."

My mouth cracked open. I unfolded my arms and brought his hands to my lips and kissed them.

I took one hand in both of mine and quietly asked, "Babe, why didn't you introduce us? I'd love to meet the woman who raised the wonderful man I love."

He let a slight smile appear and then it disappeared. Garrett's voice broke when he said, "Because she doesn't know me, and it would have only confused her more. She has Alzheimer's. It's why I stopped coming back home."

I put my hand on his forearm, massaging it and said, "I'm so sorry, Garrett. It's probably very hard for you to see her. Honey, why did you say you wanted me to meet her if you knew her condition?"

The light caught a tear as it ran down his cheek. I reached over, wiped it away and rubbed the side of his face.

"I'm not a good son. I haven't kept up on my mother's progress, so it wasn't until I saw her today that I realized just how severe her decline has been. She looked right at me, but had no idea who I was. I saw the distance in her eyes and heart. I love my mom...I really wanted you to meet her...but my mom is gone. The mother I knew is locked in her own body."

"Garrett, whether or not she remembers you—locked in her own body—she has the memories and her love for you to carry with her."

His face crumpled and his body slumped forward. I let him silently cry and deal with coming to terms with his mother's decline.

"I love you, Garrett. Even though I didn't get to formally meet your mother, I want to thank you for bringing me here and sharing this part of your life with me."

As he composed himself, I asked, "If you don't mind me asking, who was the young woman with her?"

He spoke down at the table. "A woman from the facility she lives at. Her name is Beth. She took a liking to my mother even though there's not much left to take a liking to."

I cleared my throat and said, "Let's come back here in a few weeks to see her. We can go to the facility and sit with her."

Garrett's eyes begged for understanding as he said, "I don't think so. This is about as close as you're going to get to her, because it's too much for me to deal with. I know that sounds mean, but I can't handle her looking at me like I'm a stranger—as if she's never seen me before. Sitting here weekly or monthly with my mom won't bring her back to me. It won't jog her memory. My mom was already forgetting who I was when I'd visit before. Each time it took longer and longer for her to remember who I was, and each time I got more depressed."

"I can only imagine how horrible that must make you feel."

"Can we talk about something else? I wanted to see her again and wanted her to meet you, even if she doesn't know us. She's past the point of knowing who is around her. I got to see her—she saw you—so let's move on to another subject."

"Okay," I said, changing the subject. "This is a small town. Why didn't anyone come up to talk to you? Isn't there anyone else here you know?"

He let out a slight laugh. "Well, after high school, I only came to town to visit my mom—never staying long enough to visit anyone else. I look a little different from my high school years with the help of an auto accident about four years ago. The scar on my right temple is a gift from the accident. I had some plastic surgery done in noticeable areas, like my left cheek and eye, but decided against any additional surgeries."

"An auto accident! Did anyone die?"

"Nope. It was a one-man show. I got distracted and ran my car into a tree."

I outlined the scar on his right temple with my forefinger.

We finished our drinks and then decided to get on the road before it got too late. When we were walking across the parking lot, we saw people gathering around a car. We realized it was Garrett's and picked up the pace. He pushed his way through the crowd to see what they were looking at.

"Abandon the Bitch" was spray-painted on the hood of his car. A Barbie doll was propped up on the hood, bent over with something sticking out. Garrett punched the top of the car, glaring at everyone standing around.

He kicked the car, yelling, "Did anyone bother to call the fucking cops? Did anyone see who did this to my fucking car?"

They looked from Garrett to me to the doll and then at each other. I felt dirty just looking at it, so I turned away. I couldn't believe this was happening after such a beautiful day spent with Garrett.

The police arrived and Garrett told them someone has been stalking me. They took a report, pictures and confiscated the doll for fingerprinting, saying they'd "take it from here" and call us when the results came back. Garrett took a copy of the report and without further conversation got into the car, ordering me to get in.

I remained quiet, knowing he was too upset to talk. It was too much for him—first seeing his mom and then his car damaged by the psycho following me. My elbow rested on the side door with my chin on my fist. Images of the horrors I went through because of Arcane whizzed past me. Garrett's hands gripped the steering wheel with fury, straightening his arms as if putting the car into high gear. We gave in to self-pity, paying little attention to the other.

When we arrived home there was a voice mail message from the Seattle police department stating they'd like us both to come in tomorrow. Garrett pounded his fist on the table, telling me to take off work. Before I could respond he went into the washroom and slammed the door. I knew he shouldn't be taking off work, but arguing with him now was futile.

What is this about? Why do they want us both down there?

I bet they found Arcane.

How? They don't even fucking know who he is.

Maybe they got the report?

And so I wave good-bye to another Arcane Day.

I HATE ARCANE!!

WEDNESDAY, AUGUST 30, 2006: Dear Friend,

It's Caitlyn. It's been a while.

I've been feeling restless...have always struggled with being alone. Sometimes I wonder if I should have stayed with Ed. He liked me enough for the both of us (sighs). My days in Seattle have come to a close. The gentlemen friends faded away as the clientele changed. I was too old for the younger crowd that invaded the Kings Inn. I lost my nightlife … evenings out … dinner … gifts … company … even if it was only for the night.

Staying home all the time only makes it worse. Today the sun beat down hard pushing everyone out of their homes. I was no exception. It was time to get out of town for some fresh air.

I followed him (sighs. He's no longer a teenager) to a quaint little town that reminded me of another time—years before I had been born. The scent of evergreens adorned the town as I walked at an undetected distance. It had been a long time since I had seen him, and at the distance I followed, I wasn't able to get a close look. It was frustrating. I wanted to see his face...hear his voice...watch his gentle mannerisms.

He walked into a building and disappeared. Kicking the ground, I turned away and saw a large tree (good enough to hide by) near a window. I sneaked around the side, crouched down near the tree and peeked through the window. There he was (I smiled so BIG). He was in a private room with some woman. There was a cocktail table and big leather chairs. I still couldn't get a good look at his face, either because the woman was blocking it, or he walked into shadows.

He hugged the woman and they swayed from side to side, both humming something I couldn't make out. I wanted to run in there and get that woman away from him. He shouldn't be doing that to her—it should be me! I moved closer to the building so the woman wouldn't see me when she turned to the window to stare out. He moved to one of the leather chairs and sat down.

It was tough hearing what they were saying all I could hear was the woman say, "They have no sympathy for me and I didn't do anything to them." Then she turned toward him smothering the rest of the words.

The woman moved toward him and nestled herself on his lap. I didn't want to see anymore, so I scooted out from under the tree and walked around the grounds looking at the Christmas decorations.

SUNDAY, DECEMBER 7, 2008: Dear Friends,

I wasn't quite sure how the day would turn out. So far, every time I think the police have something on Arcane, something happens and I'm back to where I was in Chicago.

The '60s couple wanted me to come in to work when I was done at the police station. I had gotten up before Garrett to take a shower and by the time he woke, the coffee had finished brewing and I was sitting in the living room reading the paper. He mumbled a 'good morning' then carried on with getting ready. When he finally made his way into the kitchen for coffee, I could see that all of this was taking a toll on him. He wants out—yet doesn't know how to tell me. I want to cling to the romantic notion he'd do anything, even risk his life, not to lose me. In reality, Arcane has started to break him, too. I made a decision. I'll start moving my things back to my apartment. I will gradually cut things off with Garrett. It is tough to watch him suffer and unfair to keep him in this mess just so I'll have someone by my side. I began this turmoil with Arcane by letting him into my life in the first place, so I have to try to escape it alone. But the thought of not having Garrett in my life is hard to swallow. He is the first man to stand by me.

Garrett asked, "Are you ready?"

A few police officers sat at their desks while others talked in the halls or slammed doors behind them. Once more, the front desk officer didn't look too happy to see me.

Garrett said, "I received a call from an Officer Quinn asking us to come down here."

The officer eyed both of us as if we got him into trouble and responded, "Yeah, he told me. Have a seat and I'll let him know you're here."

A big man in his fifties walked out of a back office with a disgruntled look and a determination to fix whatever problem arose. He put out a large, calloused hand to shake Garrett's and said, "I'm Officer Quinn."

His demeanor was opposite of my first impression—it was better than most of the others I had dealt with at the Seattle Police Department. We followed him into his office...or what someone might describe as a hazard zone. Quinn lifted some files from one of the chairs and moved them to the floor. I was stunned to see a policeman working in this kind of chaotic environment.

"Have a seat. Do you want any coffee? It's not Peace, Love & Latte, but chewing on it might wake you up."

Garrett and I laughed.

Quinn got right down to business.

"I've been going over some of Callahan's reports and came across yours."

I asked, "How is Officer Callahan?"

"He's improving each day, but still in intensive care. Thanks for asking. Anyway, it shows here he ordered copies of police reports you filed in Chicago. Do you know if he received them?"

"No. He left us a message stating he did and wanted us to come in. When I came in, I was told Callahan got in a car accident the day we saw him and the front desk officer kept asking me how he could have called me when he was in the hospital."

Quinn didn't bother discussing the other officer's comment. The old "Boys Club" has to stick together.

"Yeah, I noticed he was in the accident the same day. The problem is we can't seem to find the reports, but the Chicago Police claim they faxed them the following day. Not like things never get lost here, as you can see, except we requested the reports again—and again we can't find them. Would you by chance have copies?" Quinn asked.

"I wish I had. The things that happened in Chicago forced me to act fast. I threw them away when I decided to start a new life. As for Seattle, the police took the underwear found in my room and were going to test them. We never heard back about the findings. We also filed another police report yesterday in another town because of another stalking incident."

Quinn looked at both of us like he was drowning in information.

"What underwear? What happened yesterday?"

We all looked at each other and then I spoke.

"Officer Quinn, I believe my stalker followed me here. Things have shown up in my apartment. I found discharge all over the sheets on my bed and three pairs of women's underwear. The officers said they would test the underwear and sheets. Yesterday someone vandalized Garrett's car and left a Barbie doll on top in an obscene position. The police took that for testing also."

"Excuse me for—"

There was a knock on the door followed by Officer Atticus sticking his head in, stating, "Sorry to bother you, but your witness for the O'Reilly case is here." He looked at me and I turned away before I could see his reaction. Garrett turned around to see what he looked like and turned back to me.

Quinn said to us, "I apologize to the both of you, but I have to talk to this witness. Could you wait until I'm done and I'll try to straighten this out?"

"Do you want me to take over anything here?" Atticus asked.

Garrett answered before anyone else. "No, that's fine. We'll wait for Officer Quinn."

Quinn left and Atticus asked, "Could I get you anything to drink?"

I kept my back to him, responding, "No thanks."

"Suit yourself," Atticus said, closing the door.

"See what I mean?" I said.

We both grew quiet. I turned my head to the window in Quinn's office and abruptly broke the ice.

"I decided it's time for me to move out. You don't need me around making your life difficult. You didn't sign—"

"What the hell do you mean you're moving out? Did it ever occur to you to maybe let me know how you feel and what your plans are?"

"I just decided this morning."

"You decided. What the hell, Ash?! I've given you everything I could and you make a decision like this without even asking how I feel about it?"

I looked at him and said, "I'm sorry, Garrett. It's just that…my life is affecting your life in a negative way. It hurts like hell to see you suffer because of my past, and I couldn't bear it if something happened to you. Last night—"

"Don't even use last night as an excuse, Ash. Yeah, I was pissed because of my car and what was done to you, but I've never said that I wanted us to end things."

"You don't have to tell me, I see it in your face. Garrett, I love you so much. You don't deserve what happened yesterday or anything bad that might happen in the future. I couldn't live with myself if I knew you've been hurt because of me."

"So you're making up my mind for me because *you* feel a certain way? Deciding what's best for me because *you* can't handle future possibilities? Thanks, Ash. I totally appreciate your disregard for my feelings."

He got up and left the office. I sat for a moment before getting up and walking to the window to try and see the front door or parking lot from there. The office faced the opposite direction.

I turned around to find Atticus right behind me.

Startled, I jumped back, angrily saying, "What are you doing?! I didn't hear you come in."

He looked at me like he could see right through me and said, "I came to see if you were all right. I saw your boyfriend leave."

My expression let him know that I didn't appreciate his intrusion and I responded with a curt, "I'm fine."

"It's a shame we can't find the Chicago Police Reports. We could at least keep our eyes open for the guy you described in them. Then again we could have asked you for the description."

When I didn't respond he looked me up and down then left the room just as Garrett returned with a couple of Pepsi's.

"What the hell did *he* want?"

"To see if I was all right. Apparently he was concerned when he saw my boyfriend leave the office." I looked at the Pepsis in his hands and said, "I thought you left."

"How does he know I'm your boyfriend? I could be your brother."

"I have no idea, but he is also concerned about the…"

My face went rigid like the yellowish walls as I slowly sat down and leaned back in my chair, staring at the desk.

Garrett put the Pepsi's on Quinn's desk, sat in the chair next to mine and asked, "Ash, what's wrong?"

"…Chicago Police Department reports. He said it's too bad they can't find them."

"Yeah, so?"

I looked at Garrett. "Then he said it's too bad they couldn't keep an eye out for the guy I described in them."

"Yeah?"

"How does he know I described the guy in the reports?"

Garrett froze in the wake of my words.

"DID you describe him in your reports?"

"Well, yes. I met him on the internet and didn't have any other information to give them. The only thing I could do was describe what he looked like."

"Do you think he saw the reports and hid them?"

"That or he knows Arcane. I'm telling you, Garrett, there's something wrong with him. The way he looks at me…talks…it's eerie and he seems too anxious to help."

"Should we mention it to Quinn?"

"Mention what? That he's creepy?"

"No! The comment about describing the guy in the reports."

"I'd like to, but what if he doesn't believe me. It's my word against Atticus's and I can't afford to make an enemy out of Quinn. I have enough barriers without losing another person who could help."

"Fine. Let me handle it. I'll ask some questions to get a feel of how well he knows Atticus and then if I get the feeling they're not buddies, I'll mention it."

I nodded in agreement. He handed me the other Pepsi, but I was too nervous to drink it. Instead, without looking at him, I said, "Garrett, I know I should have told you earlier about my decision to move out."

He was about to respond when Quinn came in closing the door behind him.

"Sorry about that," he said, walking behind his desk and sitting down. "Now where were we?"

Garrett said, "Talking about the Chicago Police reports. You've misplaced them twice and we told you about the incidents at Ashley's apartment and what happened yesterday."

"Oh yeah, thanks. May I ask how long you two have known each other?"

"A few months, why?"

"Just curious."

He turned his attention to me and asked, "Do you know which officer helped you with the incident at your apartment?"

Garrett responded, "Miller."

Quinn looked at Garrett and asked, "*You* talked to them about her apartment? Why?"

"Ashley was too upset over the incident. She's been afraid to do anything—convinced her stalker is somewhere in this town— neither the Chicago Police nor the Seattle Police seem to be able to help her."

"Excuse me, Garrett, but we're on overload and we don't have the reports from Chicago. It was an oversight and we were more concerned about Callahan. I'm trying to get the information so I can help Ashley out. I deserve some respect from you."

I put my hand on Garrett's arm and said, "Officer Quinn. Garrett's been my only lifesaver here—and after yesterday—he's a little wound up."

"Remind me again…what happened yesterday?"

I nodded to Garrett and he proceeded to explain the incident to Quinn. When he finished, Quinn sat back, rubbed his eyes and said, "I'll need to get that report, too."

Garrett pulled his copy of the report out of his pocket. Surprised, Quinn thanked Garrett and left the room to personally make a copy. We gave Quinn a few minutes to read it over before saying anything.

When he finished, he leaned back in his chair, put his hands behind his head and asked, "Hypothetically speaking, if this *is* your stalker, do you know why he did this?"

Garrett was about to say something, but Quinn spoke first."I don't mean to sound rude, but I'd like to hear from Ashley."

Garrett sat back and they both waited for me.

"Since you don't have the reports, I'll tell you a few things about Arcane and our relationship. I met him in a chat room and before I knew it we were involved. It was a little over a month, but in that time he spent a lot of time at my place. His last name and address were an afterthought. How I went about the relationship was stupid on my part, and every minute since I wish I could do it all over again. Arcane played with my mind, taking over my life and I let him…until he raped and sodomized me. I had a few reports made out against him, but like everyone has told me, there is nothing they can do until something actually happens—meaning they catch him in the act. For some reason, I've become his prey. He got into my apartment in Chicago, hurt an employer of mine, then followed me out of town one weekend and used a lug wrench on me, causing permanent damage to my internal organs. It's been hell. I left my friends and family, moved halfway across the country to get away from him and here I am in the same situation."

I knew my voice was getting louder by the sentence so I stopped talking for a moment to regain my composure.

"I'm sorry I raised my voice," I continued, "but my patience is breaking. Garrett's frustration pales in comparison to mine. I'm tired of being afraid. Tired of looking over my shoulder, wondering if he's watching and tired of hearing there's nothing anyone can do."

Quinn didn't know how to respond and Garrett looked stunned as if he was hearing it all for the first time.

"To answer your question, Officer Quinn, yes, I know why he did it. He wants me to know he's here and wants Garrett to get out of the way. 'Abandon the Bitch' was his message. The doll … well … that's to let us know he's watching very closely. By the way, my name isn't Ashley, it's Sydney, Sydney Hayes."

Quinn looked surprised. "Um…that's an important fact with the reports."

"I know I just realized it. But I did let Callahan know, so he should have requested the reports with the correct name."

Garrett sat forward, saying, "What do you mean 'watching us very closely'?"

"The more I think about the doll and what happened in the bedroom—the other day—it leads me to believe he got in your apartment and planted a camera."

Quinn said, "What happened in the bedroom?"

I explained with as little detail as possible, and then he asked, "But how do you know it didn't have anything to do with the trip you made when you were still living in Chicago?"

"Because his message was to Garrett. He used the doll to prove to us he's watching."

Quinn got on the phone with the Chicago Police Department to have the reports faxed over. He got them while we were still there and then told us he'd get the other reports regarding my apartment. Garrett and I stood to leave and shook hands with Quinn. When I was about to open the door, Quinn stopped me, saying, "I'd like you to only deal with me regarding this stalker issue. I think too many involved can cause things to get lost and confused."

"I like your thinking and completely agree," I said, "Thank you for your time."

Quinn said, "Your thinking sounds like it's spot on. Thanks for helping us out."

He turned to Garrett and said, "Since Sydney feels there might be a recorder somewhere in your apartment, I'd like to send someone over there to check it out. It's fine for you to stay there tonight, but I want to get someone over there as soon as possible."

Garrett said, "Sure. It will make me feel better knowing it's been searched and cleared of anything."

Before leaving Quinn's office, I said, "Please call me Ashley...for safety reasons."

Quinn agreed.

On our way out of the police station, Atticus came running to tell us he'd be out tomorrow to check out Garrett's apartment.

My luck. The day wasn't a total waste. At least now I feel like I'm getting somewhere. We'll see where this leads.

MONDAY, DECEMBER 8, 2008: Friends,

Officer Quinn is willing to help, which is a relief and a BIG reason Garrett and I didn't want to complain to him about Atticus without any proof. Instead, we accepted the fact that Atticus was searching the place. Garrett stayed home and I went to work, but not before arguing that he shouldn't take another day off because of my issues. Garrett rebutted by saying they were *our* issues, and after we left the police station, he picked up some case files from work to stop me from nagging him. He promised his job was okay with it. Someone was covering for him and he would call me once Atticus showed up.

It was hard for me to concentrate at work fearing something might happen. I already regretted not letting Quinn know how I felt about Atticus.

What if Atticus plants something in the apartment? Or hurts Garrett?

Quit being paranoid!

I have every right to be. It seems every time I let my guard down another bad thing happens to us.

Don't forget, you're the one who caused all of this. If you had kept your mouth shut instead of spreading your legs for this guy, his life wouldn't be in danger.

I pressed my forehead against the wall to crush these thoughts. The police department knew Atticus went to Garrett's apartment.

The '60s couple weren't too happy that I didn't make it in yesterday. The wife wouldn't look at me, and the husband was constantly reprimanding me for the smallest things. "Make sure you put the milk on the left, not right." "Wipe off the counter if anything drips on it." If I wasn't so close to the store, and hadn't helped them out in the past, I think they would have fired me already. They rarely talk to me anymore, which is fine since I prefer spending time torturing myself with thoughts of 'what ifs'.

I kept my cell phone on vibrate in my jeans pocket so I would know when Garrett called. In the middle of a rush I finally heard from Garrett. Atticus had arrived and was in the process of checking out the bedroom. I wanted to stay on the phone with him, but the '60s couple frowned at me, looking at the crowd then back at me. I cut Garrett off in mid-sentence, telling him I'd call back later.

An hour passed before I had time to call him, and by then Atticus had left. With my back toward the rest of the room, I told Garrett how much I loved him.

"Did he claim he didn't find anything?"

"Yep! But I tore everything apart in our bedroom after he left, so don't freak out."

I laughed and said, "I won't. Did you stay in the room with him while he looked around?"

"Other than stepping out to call you, yeah, I stayed in the room the whole time. And you're right, there's something not right with him."

"Why? What did he do?"

"It's not so much what he did as it is how he acts. He tilts his head down, so when he looks at you it's threatening. I don't recall him doing that at the police station. He also has what I'd call a confrontational walk—ready to pounce on his prey. And when he talks I just want to crawl under the bed and hide."

"He did leave a lasting impression. I told you something is weird about him and I can't believe they made him a cop. Garrett, I don't want him working on this case with Quinn. I honestly don't want him anywhere near us."

"I agree, Ash. We'll have to think of something to tell Quinn. Saying he's creepy won't score us points—we need something more substantial."

The '60s couple cleared their throats and I felt them glaring at me from the corner of my eye.

"I'm going to have to let you go," I told Garrett, "We'll think of something."

I hung up and turned around to find Atticus standing there. My face crumpled then straightened out to hide my true emotions.

Did he hear what I said?

"Hi, Ashley."

I swallowed hard and said, "Hello, Officer Atticus."

"Atticus is fine—no need for formalities."

I didn't respond, but my fingers grabbed underneath the counter, tightening my grip until my knuckles whitened.

"Everything checked out fine at your place."

"I heard—thanks."

"How's my coffee coming along?"

"Let me get it for you."

I prepared his coffee while he stared at me the entire time. When I went to set it on the counter, he wrapped his hand around mine, which was still holding his coffee. My eyes narrowed at his gripping stare until he let my hand go and I snatched it back.

"Have a nice day, Ashley."

He walked out the door without looking back.

I waited until I got home to tell Garrett about what happened.

"When I hung up with you, he was standing right behind me. He had to have heard."

"Let me give Quinn a call and see what's up. Maybe I can mention something that won't sound like we're being rude."

Garrett picked up the phone, dialed Quinn and stood by the windows in the living room as I clung to his arm. I watched Garrett awkwardly phrase his request to Quinn.

"Well...no..." Garrett said to Quinn, "it's based more on how he makes us feel—by the way he looks and acts."

Garrett frowned.

I mouthed, 'What?'

"I'm not asking you to," Garrett responded to Quinn. "All we're asking is if you could assign another officer to do any additional things on our case. You told us to only work with you, so we're asking a favor, too."

"I see," Garrett said, shrugging at me. "Sure, I understand. I apologize. This is awkward. I didn't mean to insult you in any way."

More silence as Garrett shook his head and rolled his eyes at me.

Garrett hung up, letting out a long breath.

"He's his cousin."

Laughing at the thought, he rephrased it, saying, "Atticus is Quinn's cousin."

"What?! That's what he told you?"

Garrett looked at me and said, "Yeah. He plans on using Atticus for investigations concerning your case."

My arms dropped to my sides. We both stared outside— dumbfounded.

I said to no one in particular, "I'm never going to get my life back. I'll be running for the rest of my life."

"Then I guess I'll be running with you."

Garrett and I are in this together. He doesn't want me to leave and I don't either. We'll just have to ignore the fact that Atticus is on the case. I finally got people to take notice to what's been happening to me. There's no point in ruining it. Talk to you later.

FRIDAY, DECEMBER 12, 2008: Friends!

I am so ecstatic. Like they say, "when one door closes, another one opens".

Garrett and I went on with our daily routines, trying to pretend everything was normal. When I came home today, I found the door to my apartment open—again. I could hear someone inside moving things around in the living room. My heart fought inside my chest as I cautiously opened the door to find Garrett putting things in boxes.

"What are you doing?"

He came to me and put his arm around me, raising my chin with the other hand and giving me one of the most loving kisses I have ever experienced. His eyes opened, looking down at me. Garrett stopped kissing me, brushing his lips from side to side against mine then applying more pressure. Only for a second did he pull away—his breath warming my face—before he opened my mouth with his curious tongue and heated lips. My arms wrapped around him, enjoying the salt from his lips and the tenderness of his mouth. Any anger I felt when I first saw him rummaging through my things dripped on the floor and evaporated.

When he finally allowed our lips to breathe, tingling from the cool air, he asked, "Move in with me?"

"Nothing would make me happier, but—"

"No buts. Move in with me."

His eyes lost me in their pool of tenderness as his hand stroked my cheek.

The offer isn't absurd at all. I've already been in his apartment for almost a month. Besides, we love each other and I feel much safer being with him. This apartment is no longer home to me.

"I'd love to."

We got down to the business of throwing insignificant things out or bringing items over to Garrett's apartment. I called the landlord to see if I could get out of the lease. The landlord said I would still be responsible for the remaining months until he could rent it. It didn't take long to clean out the belongings I brought from Chicago. By Saturday night I hope to have the place echoing from lack of furnishings.

I locked the door and we crossed the hall to 'our' home.

What I brought over didn't exactly fit into the closets, so we piled the items in the spare bedroom until further evaluation. It feels good knowing we'll be living together. While I worked at getting organized, the smell of freshly baked bread drifted throughout the rooms. Garrett found a need to bake this first night of moving in. He wanted it to feel like home for the both of us. While he found the time to warm the apartment with cooking, I spent my time folding and straightening up the clutter. My things managed to push their way off dressers, spill out of drawers and fall along walkways as I searched to make the small space work. It will take time to toss additional baggage and claim parts of the apartment as my own.

A door opened wide for our relationship. This is a huge step for both of us. I'm so glad I met Garrett. It appears he is turning things around for me.

SUNDAY, DECEMBER 14, 2008: Dear Friends,

Why aren't roller coasters only found in amusement parks? It's exactly how my life is going. When one door closes, another door opens, and each one you step through is a ride.

Garrett got up early, but before he could leave the room I made sure I let him know how much I loved living with him. I took control—dominated our lovemaking—something he devoured. What I set out to do for an hour went longer. We were both amazed by our stamina. I wanted to feel that way forever; to keep the happiness flowing so it would drown any bad karma about to flow my way. I laid on his right side with my right leg across his legs, my head on his shoulder and my hand rubbing his chest. Deep breathing sang in the room—an a cappella performance expressing our love.

His fingers walked up and down my spine.

"This is good," he whispered.

I moved my head just enough to see the contentment on his face and said, "It sure is. Did you enjoy it?"

"Yes I did, my little sex pistol. Couldn't you tell?"

I pulled the covers over my shoulders. Even though part of me was warmed by his arms—the room's air snapped at my exposed skin.

He rolled on top kissing me before getting up.

"I take that as a sign you don't want any more of this…" and with that I threw the covers to the side—lying naked.

"I always want that, but my guy needs to take a nap and we need to eat." He tilted his head, grinned and said, "I'll make the breakfast if you make the coffee. I love the way you make it. It's like it chisels away at my stomach."

"Hey! There's nothing wrong with my coffee."

"I know there isn't. There's something wrong with me that I like it." I threw a pillow at him and he ducked into the washroom.

As I put on a pair of pajama bottoms and a long underwear shirt, I accidentally hit the lamp on the nightstand and knocked it over with other items on the stand. I started picking things up and noticed something shiny in the corner, so I bent down to pick it up and found a very small, silver object. My hand followed a pencil thin wire that ran from what looked like a microphone down to a flat video recorder that was tucked inside a book.

I pulled it into full view and heard, "You found me."

Laughter came from the speaker. I stumbled back, screaming when I heard his voice. I fell and hit my head on the iron bed frame. Stunned, I lifted my hand to my head and wiped at the warmth oozing down my face into my eye.

It was blood.

Garrett came bolting into the room when he heard me scream. He fell to his knees, asking, "What happened, Ash? You're bleeding."

He scanned me, trying to take it all in. My lips were shaking and tears and blood dripped onto my shirt. I pointed to the microphone and recorder as he helped me up. Swearing under his breath, he went to get a towel. He pressed the towel against my head and then turned his attention to the microphone and recorder.

Garrett pulled so hard on the wire that the whole thing came flying past us and hit the floor. He stomped several times on the mic and recorder, crushing them until parts spilled out everywhere.

"Come on, we're going to the hospital," he said.

He finished dressing and he helped me put on some decent clothes. We went outside to where he parked his car, but it wasn't there.

"Fuck! Are you fucking kidding me?"

I started to cry, out of feeling Garrett's pain and knowing Arcane was getting closer...we were dissolving. I pressed the blood soaked towel against my head and dropped to the curb, sobbing from all that has happened and all that was to come. I couldn't even offer my car because I sold it a month ago so I could have more money.

"I'm sorry," I said to him.

He kissed me and removed the towel to check my head. The wound was still bleeding.

"It's okay, we'll get there," Garrett reassured me.

Atticus pulled up.

"Is there a problem?"

"I have to take Ashley to the hospital, but someone stole my car."

"I'll drive you to the hospital and fill out the police report."

Garrett looked at me to see if it was all right, but I just continued crying. He helped me to my feet and into Atticus's car.

I leaned on Garrett as he held the towel to my head.

"What happened to her?"

"She hit her head on the bed frame."

"Too wild, huh?"

Garrett didn't answer; instead he turned to look out the window.

While we waited in the emergency room, Atticus took down the information regarding Garrett's car. He finally left, allowing me to relax. I started to fall asleep, but Garrett kept patting my face to keep me up.

"Come on, Ashley, you have to stay up in case you have a concussion. Talk to me, okay?"

My words came out gurgled and hoarse. "Am I still bleeding?"

Garrett moved the towel and responded, "A little, yes. I will call Quinn to let him know about the camera and my car. Also, if a police report isn't made out then he'll at least know it's Atticus's fault."

As I listened to him, I felt my eyes grow heavier and I wanted to close them, but Garrett kept moving my head so I wouldn't fall asleep.

"I want to sleep, Garrett. Let me sleep."

He kissed me saying, "You can't babe. Please. Stay awake for me."

I opened my eyes and watched him dial his phone. While he talked to Quinn, he kept me awake by pinching my leg, arm or moving my head.

"What did he say?"

"He said you need to stop being a little sex pistol."

I laughed, then in a slow drawl said, "No-o. Really. What did he say?"

The nurse called my name.

It was a tar-coated sky by the time we got home—hungry and tired. I don't have a concussion, but the nurse told Garrett to at least watch me for the night. He called for pizza delivery while I went into the washroom to clean my hands and face. A shower sounded great, but I was too tired to avoid getting my ten stitches wet, so the sink would have to do. I went into the bedroom to get a change of clothes and realized we forgot about the microphone and camera. Garrett was bent over the counter reading the paper when I put my hand on his arm, leading him into the bedroom. He waved me out of the room.

After changing in the washroom, I came out and overheard Garrett talking to Quinn. Garrett was in our room describing what the microphone and recorder looked like and where they had been located. Quinn must have told him to put gloves or socks on his hands and disconnect it, because Garrett was explaining that he had crushed them with his foot and he didn't think he had to worry about putting fingerprints on them. Quinn must have insisted because Garrett slipped socks over his hands and gathered the parts.

We had had enough entertainment for the day, so Garrett asked Quinn if someone could come on by tomorrow evening for a report and to pick up the devices.

Next time I could end up in the hospital with a serious injury…or maybe it will happen to Garrett. I can't think about that now. My eyes can barely stay open. Talk to you later.

WEDNESDAY, DECEMBER 17, 2008: Dear Friends,

It has been a while since I spoke to my mother and sister, so I called to inform them about my moving in with Garrett. I could feel their apprehension in wishing me well…I mean…who could blame them after my encounter with Arcane? My mother asked every possible question about Garrett and I answered without offense. She lost her daughter to a monster, so there was no way I could, should or would take offense at her interrogation. I asked what she had planned for Christmas. She said she was getting together with Carolyn.

"Sydney, is he good to you?" Mom asked.

I paused for a moment, reflecting on my real name.

"He's very good to me, Mom. I know I screwed up before and it's hard not to think I jumped into the arms of the next guy who showed the slightest bit of kindness, but please know I'm happy. Garrett makes me laugh, smile, and most of all, makes me feel safe. On our first date, he bought me gloves because it was cold and I forgot mine. There hasn't been a time where he's treated me bad or made me fear him. Mom, I love him so much. I do want you and Carolyn to meet him."

"I can hear the happiness in your voice. I just worry about you, Syd. You're so far away and if something were to happen…" She started to cry.

"Don't cry, Mom. Nothing will happen. It's been tough being away from you two, but we're all safer this way."

My mom regained control and said, "Are *you* safe? Has anything happened while you've been out there?"

I hesitated for a slight second and then said, "No, it's been fine."

"Do you know when we'll see you next? I was kind of hoping to see you for Christmas, but I understand it's hard to travel."

"Maybe I can get away from work for a few days in March."

"March? Sydney, that's so far away."

"I'll see if I can get out there in January or February, okay?" I said in an effort to pacify her.

"That would be great. I love you, Sydney. Please take care of yourself."

We hung up, wishing one another well and vowing to be together soon.

When Garrett got home from work, I was sitting on the couch with the television off, just staring into space.

He kissed me on the cheek, patted my arm and asked, "What's wrong? Why isn't anything on?"

I sighed and said, "There's really nothing on television and I wanted to relax."

"How's your head feeling?"

"Fine."

I could feel him watching me from behind as he put his lunch containers in the dishwasher and poured something to drink.

He plopped down next to me, rubbing my foot, which stuck out from underneath me.

"Did you finally talk to your mom?"

"How did you know that?"

"Because I know you, and you haven't been this quiet without something happening. And since you're too calm to have had anything bad happen, I guessed you might have talked to your mom—you have a nostalgic look in your eyes."

"Yes, we talked. She's worried about me and started crying."

I pulled at the bottom of my sweater.

"Why don't you go home and visit?"

"Um…because I have a job…you…and not a whole heck of a lot of money to be able to take off when I want to. Besides, I don't want to take a chance now with the weather."

The apartment went quiet. Garrett continued to massage my foot and I played with my sweater.

"What else is wrong?"

"Nothing."

"Come on, Ash. I know you by now and something's bothering you."

"Well, Christmas is almost here and we haven't really discussed anything."

"If you haven't noticed, we've been a bit preoccupied."

I gave a weak smile and said, "I know. Were you planning on going somewhere or having anyone over?"

"I plan on spending Christmas with my new love, my sex pistol. And I hope it's an easy day. We've been through a lot over the past month. I think it's time we relax by not doing much."

"Sounds good to me."

"Hey!"

I looked at him and he proceeded. "Did you want to do

something?"

"Not necessarily. I guess I was wondering about gifts. I haven't gotten you anything."

"You already gave me a gift."

"No, I didn't." I paused then asked, "What? What did I give you?"

"You, Ashley—I only need you. But if it will make you feel better you can put a big, red bow around yourself."

I rested my head on the couch and said, "You're right. I don't know why I'm getting all weird about this holiday. Maybe talking to my mom brought it on. Not to change the subject, but have you heard from Quinn regarding the microphone and recorder? Did they get a fingerprint?"

"He'll probably call you about it. Don't you remember? He wasn't too keen on me answering his questions?"

"It didn't have anything to do with you talking. I think he wanted my version, that's all."

Garrett pointed his finger at me and said, "Exactly! Your stalker— your situation. He's going to call you if and when something comes up. If not, you call him to see what's up."

"I guess I'm a little embarrassed about Atticus being his cousin. We complained he's creepy and then the guy drives us to the hospital."

"Yeah…well…he's still creepy."

I took Garrett's hand and asked, "Would you mind if we went to church on Christmas? I think I need to pray or ask God for forgiveness to get rid of Arcane."

"Whatever you need," he said warmly.

I'm looking forward to Christmas. It's my favorite holiday. The decorations, music and spirit will help me forget about Arcane for the day.

THURSDAY, DECEMBER 25, 2008: Dear Friends,

The police still haven't found Garrett's car, so we walked to church to attend midnight mass. We got there an hour early and sat toward the front on the left side where the choir sang. They practiced with the organist while we sat holding hands, listening to the beauty of the words and music. Christmas decorations hung around the church and a large manger sat on the altar. I began to cry—maybe from a combination of all that's happened and my gratitude for having Garrett in my life. Without making a big deal about it, Garrett passed me some Kleenex he had in his pocket, put his arm around me and rested his head on top of mine. Even though I cried, it was peaceful sitting there listening to the choir, wrapped in his arm. People came down the aisle, filling our pew, moving their eyes from us to the choir then settling down for a long hour.

By midnight we had been squeezed into the pew from both sides until we wound up in the middle with strangers all around us, hugging their spouses or children. The scene and ambience uplifted me—singing the hymns that filled my heart on this wonderful night. Throughout, Garrett seemed to be inventing new ways to touch, as if wanting to make sure I was still next to him. His pinky finger would wrap around mine, or he'd cross his legs to touch my legs. They were sweet gestures. Most of the time my hand rested on his leg with his hand on top of mine. When it came to the hand-shaking portion of the service, people hugged instead and wished each other a Merry Christmas.

The woman next to me didn't hesitate to put her arms around me, saying, "May God Bless You." Words I desperately needed to hear, but didn't realize it until spoken.

I turned to Garrett, wrapped my arms around him and said, "I thank God for giving you to me." We pulled away and he dried my cheeks.

When mass ended, we stayed until the choir finished singing and the majority of people had poured out of the church. The weather was calling for freezing rain, but it hadn't arrived yet so we walked to the park a few blocks away.

I ran to a swing, sat down and pushed off with my feet. My hands gripped the swing chains pulling back as I kicked my feet forward then tucked them under the swing to build momentum.

"Wasn't mass beautiful?" I said to Garrett.

Garrett watched me swing for a few moments before sitting down on the swing to the right of me. "It was nice. It put me in the holiday mood."

He leaned on the chain, staring at my childlike enjoyment.

I looked down at him as I sailed by and said, "Did I tell you, you look handsome tonight? Not that you don't look handsome every day, but tonight especially."

"Thanks. And you look gorgeous as ever."

"WOW! I have brainwashed you," I shouted as I whisked by him again.

He put his swing in motion and staggered it with his foot, scraping the ground until we were moving together. We listened to the sounds of the night and the music in the distance.

After a while Garrett slowed his swing, got off and stopped mine, saying, "Let's go home. I want to give you a few bedroom gifts."

In the vestibule our mailboxes were brimming with what looked like Christmas cards, so we scooped them up as we passed. It had been a few days since we last checked our mail. Inside our apartment, the Christmas lights warmly lit the room. We fell onto the couch, still in our coats, and started opening the cards.

Garrett read a card, tossed it across the room and then grabbed mine. He shook his head 'no', and said, "Don't read it."

"Why? It's from him, isn't it?"

"Yes. It isn't worth ruining your Christmas. He just wrote some dumb shit."

I could tell Garrett downplayed what Arcane wrote in the card, so I asked, "What did yours say?"

"Ashley, we should burn them. There's no sense in bothering with this crap, especially when we're enjoying the holiday."

I got up to get his card and he wrapped his arms around my waist and pulled me onto his lap.

"Garrett! We can't burn them. What if the police could use them? What if they have fingerprints on them?"

"I doubt he's that stupid to put them in the envelope without wearing gloves."

"They're sealed shut—maybe he licked them and his DNA is on it."

"Uh…yeah, stop watching CSI."

"Don't be so negative. They might be able to get something from them," I said, annoyed by his disregard.

"Fine, but don't read them. Promise me you won't? I want to enjoy the rest of the holiday without sharing it with Arcane."

I promised not to read the cards, so Garrett put them in a large envelope, sealed it and tossed it by the door. We sat a while longer watching lights dance on the walls and ceilings—a flickering of the street lights. After half an hour, we went to the bedroom to get some sleep so we could wake early enough for a nice, big breakfast.

When we went to bed, Garrett and I made love with such an

extreme intensity—a desire to delve deeper into each other's souls. I don't know if it was going to church or an 'in your face' to Arcane that brought us to a higher level. Our emotions simmered on our skin; every touch, breath and word uttered pushed us further into a world where only we existed. We opened up with feelings and actions that left no doubt about how we felt.

MRS. GARRETT HART

FRIDAY (night), DECEMBER 26, 2008: Dear Friends,

It didn't matter that I went to church and prayed...prayers went unanswered...a reflection of my life.

Christmas morning I found Garrett standing by the windows looking out at the soft, melting snow. He was sexy standing there with the white velvet flakes behind him, taking their time to drift to the ground, disintegrating as soon as they touched. My arms went around him and I rested against his side.

He handed me his cup of coffee and I took a sip, handing it back as he kissed me on the forehead, asking, "Would you like a cup, beautiful?"

"I would, my love."

We shared a morning kiss—fresh and intimate—before Garrett made his way into the kitchen to pour me a big cup of coffee. It felt like a perfect day. I was in *our* warm apartment with Garrett looking out onto a calm, frosty day. He came up behind me, handed me my cup and put his arm around me. We watched the quiet town we live in start to wake. We huddled together in the window as people wiped off their cars still in pajamas or wearing their Christmas gifts with the tags still on. This moment brought back the after effects of last night and my heart ached with love.

"Garrett, what are we going to do today?"

He started to slowly rock back and forth as we continued to look out the window and drink our coffee.

"Whatever we want to, but first I'm going to make us a big breakfast."

"Mmm...you know how to spoil me."

"Well, you did earn it for some of the things you did to me last night."

I turned around, beaming red and letting out a small giggle, saying, "I didn't do anything you haven't had done to you before."

"Yes, but they weren't done by you."

"You are a bad boy. Who would have thought the sweet, nice man who wanted a coffee before the rest of the town woke up could be so naughty?"

His laugh made my body tingle; his words adding a twinge when he said, "What can I say? You bring out the naughty in me."

Garrett made enough breakfast to feed the entire apartment complex and we ate as much as our stomachs could expand. We took showers, got dressed and left the apartment to walk off some of the food.

When we stepped out into the hallway, my apartment door was open—for the twentieth time. We looked at each other and then Garrett bounded toward the door and kicked it with his foot. It swung open and hit someone in the head causing the intruder to stumble and fall backward. When Garrett realized who it was, he ran in and tried to help Atticus to his knees.

"What the hell is wrong with you? You don't go walking around kicking in doors." Atticus jerked away from Garrett, looking at us like we were crazy.

"Nice try. What the hell are you doing in her apartment?" Garrett asked.

"We received a call from the tenant below stating something was dripping into her apartment. When I got here, the door wasn't locked, so I came inside."

Garrett retorted, "Really. Why would the police investigate instead of the tenant calling the owner? And why wouldn't you contact Ashley? You have her number and you know where she's staying."

Atticus's cold, dark eyes made me move closer to Garrett when he said, "Because it's Christmas, the owner isn't around and I thought I'd check it out first before bothering either of you."

Garrett, not backing down, said, "Did you find anything?"

"Not yet. I just got here and had a door kicked into my head, so I haven't had time."

They stared each other down, neither one willing to retreat.

Finally, Garrett said, "Then let's see if anything is dripping."

He walked into the kitchen. The faucet wasn't on and nothing was dripping underneath. Atticus and Garrett walked down the hallway to the washroom.

I heard gasps and then, "What the fuck?"

I started moving toward the washroom to make sure nothing had happened to Garrett. Instead, he walked out, ghost white, and put up a hand, indicating for me to stop.

"Go to our apartment."

My heart was racing.

"What's wrong, Garrett? I don't want to leave you alone with him," I said in a loud whisper.

"I am asking you to go to the apartment. I'll be there soon."

"What is it, Garrett? You're scaring me. I can't—"

"Ash, please!"

The grave look on his face told me to listen, so I returned to the apartment and waited until he came back. Half an hour passed before he came back with Atticus behind him. I didn't conceal my surprise to see Atticus.

"What's happened?"

Atticus said, "Someone has been in your apartment...and left the bathtub faucet running."

"And? There's more to that story than just running water," I retorted, scowling at him.

Atticus looked at Garrett to see if he was going to answer, but he didn't.

"And there were a few...dead animals...in the tub." Atticus continued, pleading with Garrett to take over the conversation.

I lowered myself to the couch.

He's sick. Arcane hit a new low, killing animals for the sake of frightening me?

"What else? There's something else you haven't told me."

Again, Atticus looked to Garrett for a reprieve, but didn't get it.

"They left a message...in blood...for you."

Blood rushed through my veins and the pounding of my heart drowned out everything around me. The apartment air felt thick.

Do I want to know it?

I took a deep breath, looked at Garrett and asked, "What's the message?"

Garrett's eyes were filled with pain when he said, "The message says, "Your sister's blood was redder."

The air put a choke hold on me as I stood and backed up to get away. I tripped over the table and fell on my back, letting out a chilling scream. Garrett threw himself on top of me, trying to calm me down.

"Ashley, listen to me. It's…"

My eyes clouded with tears diminishing all the images around me. The screams and crying only stopped when I held my breath until my lungs gave out. I shivered from shock—unable to take in air steadily. Garrett could only hold me—words failed him.

Atticus left us to deal with our own fear and agony. For the rest of the day, Garrett took care of me like I was an infant. I was incapable of doing anything for myself. The nothingness of space kept me company. I found relief in the darkness, sleeping as long as possible until Garrett woke me for my next feeding. I know I ate, but the Christmas breakfast was the last big meal I actually remember eating.

I heard phones ringing, people coming into the apartment, but no one and nothing broke my relationship with the emptiness.

WEDNESDAY, DECEMBER 22, 2006: Dear Friend,

It's me, Caitlyn.

I went to the library to use one of their computers. The loneliness at home and being away from Chicago is getting to me. It's been a long time, so I thought I'd read up on the news and see if there's anything about him. I scrolled through the local news and found the article. After several complaints, police went to the Chatham neighborhood where they found the body of a twenty-five-year-old woman who was murdered. She has yet to be identified, but police say someone broke into her home on Tuesday morning and stabbed her repeatedly with a knife.

My body began to shake. I gripped the keyboard to cauterize my internal sorrow. Damn her! Carolyn was responsible for him. I had looked up to her—admired her. If she had cared about him, he wouldn't be in this mess. I couldn't read anymore. I didn't care if Christmas Eve was only a few days away, I had to get back to Chicago.

When I arrived, I paid a visit to Carolyn Baker—the woman who betrayed me. I counted on her…trusted her to do the right thing…but Carolyn failed me. I had no choice. She neglected my boy.

I drove to Carolyn's condo, rang the buzzer and slipped into the back area where I waited for her. When she arrived, I confronted Carolyn she acted like she had no idea what I was talking about. I stepped in front of her when she tried to go into her condo. Again I asked her why but she just shook her head and started to giggle. She laughed! This was nothing to laugh about. Before I knew what I had done, I was putting Carolyn's bloody corpse in the trunk of her own car. I drove her car to the airport, left it in some parking lot and flew back home.

It's a waiting game to see if they figure out it was me. I doubt they will…I've been invisible to society. Ignored and abused. It's time someone pays the price for neglect.

If you don't hear from me for a while, it's probably because they found me. Take care, friend.

SATURDAY, DECEMBER 27, 2008: Dear Friends,

The following days were like a misty forest of dense thoughts curling around emotions. We found out Arcane had called my sister pretending to be Garrett, saying I was in the hospital and that Carolyn needed to come to Seattle. Carolyn told my mother she'd send for money if it was needed.

My sister never made it out of the Chicago airport.

After the Seattle police contacted the Chicago police, they searched and found Carolyn's car—her body was in the trunk. Her eyes were frozen open, as if she had watched him repeatedly stab her before slitting her throat.

Garrett called the Wilsons to let them know what happened and made arrangements for us to go to Chicago. I have said very little in the past few days and Garrett doesn't push it.

As we waited for our flight, he talked about insignificant things and I alternated between looking at him and drifting in and out of the past.

Carolyn and I were so different, but we grew up respecting our differences. As much as I thought I was timid, Carolyn had a much harder time meeting people. I used to think what a boring, quiet life she led, but Carolyn seemed happy.

I closed my eyes and tears leaked onto my face at thoughts about the lack of time I spent with her. We were not 'hanging out' sisters. It wasn't that we didn't want to—we had to think about something we'd both like to do. The effort to find common ground was too much, so we let each other live the way each knew how. We called when we needed something or to coordinate holiday ideas, but confiding wasn't our style. Instead, we masked our words with purple prose, often hiding the unflattering. Our lives were simple sketches—outlines—absent of color.

Garrett feels helpless, offering his hand or wrapping an arm around my shoulder. I feared for *our* safety, yet never really thought in depth about Carolyn or my mom's.

How self-absorbed am I? Do I not love my mother and sister as much as I love Garrett? Why didn't I warn them?

You forgot about them.

I didn't think Carolyn and my mother's lives would be in jeopardy.

That's right, you didn't think, like you didn't think about opening up to others.

Why must I be punished for mistakes others make as well?

You're not like everyone else. You're unique.

Garrett put a tissue in my hand and I opened my eyes, pressing and wiping the tears. I finally turned my attention to him. His left ankle crossed his right knee, balancing a book on his lap with a hand on my leg. For a few moments I felt safe sitting next to him in the busy airport.

"Do you want me to get you something before we get on the plane?" Garrett asked.

In my hazed state, I responded with a strained 'no' and slipped back into my thoughts of Carolyn. Her timid nature came off as frail—an injured bird. When we were young I remember sticking up for Carolyn, but she didn't necessarily need it. Any verbal assaults shot at her simply blew away. She refrained from giving them power, as if she laughed off the attempts to harm her. It was late at night—in the darkness—where Carolyn buried her sorrow. Night played a consoling companion from the spotlight of daytime ordeals. The darkness hid the tears, muffled the cries and then disappeared.

Garrett pulled me gently from my seat, slipped the boarding pass into my hand and guided me to the ramp. It felt like we walked into a dream without an invitation and no one really saw us or cared about us being there. We sat toward the back, me by the window and Garrett in the middle. He held my hand caressing fingertips. Later, I watched him sleep. I didn't have to talk or explain myself; just watched how peaceful he looked sleeping. Garrett's body finally decided to take a hiatus from responsibility. I sighed, placing my head on his shoulder and intertwining my fingers with his. He stayed that way until we arrived in Chicago.

On the cab ride to my mother's house I shook off my own hell and worried about what condition she might be in. Garrett worried about meeting her under such awful circumstances. My mother lived for Carolyn and me, so I imagined there was a part of her cut and discarded forever.

Mom opened the door and fell into my arms, holding on for dear life until I had the presence of mind to break the embrace and introduce her to Garrett.

He held out his hand and said, "I'm sorry for your loss and that we're meeting for the first time under these conditions."

I knew my mother wasn't up for being on guard. She was in no condition to size him up and wonder about what kind of person he was. She wrapped her arms around him and cried. He let her hang on to him until she found the stability to stand on her own.

We walked my mother back into the house, sat her on the couch next to me and I wrapped around her like a shawl. Garrett brought our luggage in and left it by the door.

The awkward silence stretched across the room until my mother's head rose and she said to Garrett, "It's nice to finally meet you. Sydney has told us so…"

She started to cry again, realizing 'us' meant her and Carolyn. For the first time for as far back as I can remember, my mother and I shared an emotional moment caring for each other. We dealt with our pain individually and together. Garrett retrieved a blanket from the back of the couch, covered us and left the room to take a look around my childhood home.

Several hours later, I found Garrett in the basement with a stack of photo albums on each side of him.

I sat next to him and asked, "What are you doing?"

Indicating the stack to his right, he said, "I already looked through those."

He put his hand on the back of my neck and began massaging. Still browsing the pictures, he asked, "How's your mom?"

I picked up a pile of pictures and shuffled through them as I responded, "Not good. She's in her room sleeping."

My mother saved every picture she ever took, no matter how distorted it was. Carolyn and I each had baby albums, school picture albums, and vacation and play time albums. I picked up one and came to a picture of the two of us on a swing. I was on Carolyn's lap and she was holding me...and it made me wonder...who let go first?

Did she let go of me years ago when she got her own place...started her first job? Or did I—when I was too busy partying in my twenties to call her?

Maybe we held on until Arcane entered the picture and I started treating her as if she didn't matter. Maybe it happened then.

My finger outlined our bodies, individually and together.

Whoever let go first...why didn't the other one say something? Didn't it matter to us?

A tear dropped on the page magnifying our faces.

Garrett put an album partially on my lap and asked, "Is this you?"

I looked at it and nodded 'yes'.

He accepted that short response, turning his attention back to the picture and then finally closing the album. Though I'm sure he knew these books would reveal things about me, right then I think Garrett wasn't sure he wanted to learn more.

"Are we sleeping at your mom's house?"

"Yes. She wouldn't even think about having us stay at a hotel. Besides, she needs me here."

"That's fine. I wanted to take the suitcases out of the living room, but I wasn't sure what room we would stay in."

"I'll sleep in my old room and you can sleep in Carolyn's. If that feels too weird for you, you could sleep on the couch. I know my mother wouldn't like us sleeping in the same room."

"I'll sleep in Carolyn's room."

"Hers is the first room on the left and my old room is next to it. I think I'll finish going through these pictures. I need to find a few of Carolyn to display at the wake."

I sat for some time, tracing the tear-stained image of Carolyn and me, reminiscing on a time in our lives without responsibilities or regret.

My body won't cooperate anymore. Good night, friends. Give me strength tomorrow.

SUNDAY, DECEMBER 28, 2008: Friends,

I wouldn't wish a day like today on anyone...except Arcane.

Die!

I hate Arcane!!

The wake is tomorrow and the burial is Tuesday. The holiday season put a rush on this agonizing time for us.

My mother and I went to the funeral home and then to Carolyn's condo to get an outfit. I decided to venture around the condo while my mother went into the living room, sitting on the couch and staring blankly at the opposite wall. On the kitchen counter I found a note Carolyn had written that said, "Syd in trouble. Needs my help." My fingers touched every letter as if they were a newborn's fingers and toes—each letter delicate and breakable.

She was going to help me. Why wasn't I there for her?

I leaned on the counter, tensing my body as I screamed inside. My eyes and jaws clenched. She cared about me, yet I ignored the possibility of Carolyn getting hurt.

I let go...it was me...something I'll have to live with.

There are several things you'll have to live with.

When will you learn you can't brush everything under the rug? You have to confront your life...your choices...who you have become.

You wear many faces.

I lifted my head and then bounced it off the kitchen cabinet to silence blame.

My mom turned and looked at me when I walked out of the

kitchen, but her eyes were empty of emotion.

I went into Carolyn's bedroom; walking around and touching her bed, dresser and opening closets. In the corner was Carolyn's vanity. I sat down and started opening drawers. In the top drawer there were several pictures of a baby—dark, wide eyes smiling up at something and another picture with an almost identical face, but with a serious expression. I shuffled from one to the other, looking on the back for a name. There were a few more pictures of two toddler boys at the park sitting on swings. One of the boys was looking down at his feet while the other was looking at someone in the distance—with the same dark eyes.

Whose children are these? Was Carolyn a Godmother? If so, why didn't I know? I'll ask my mom.

I put the pictures back in the drawer and chose a dress and shoes I hoped Carolyn would have approved of.

***

The funeral director conducted everything like a business transaction; as if sympathy and emotion were one of the piles on his desk. He calmly asked a list of questions: Is she to be cremated or buried? Would we like an oak or brass casket? Open or closed? I handled the decisions; my mother cried at each casket, moaning 'I don't know'.

I asked, "Has her body been brought here yet?"

"Yes, this morning."

"I'd like to see her."

My mother looked at me, took my hand and said, "Oh, yes. Can we please see her?"

"Of course you can. Please follow me."

We walked behind him, holding each other for fear of what we might find. He opened a door and there she lay—on a table—ready for preparation for her journey into her other life.

The funeral director motioned in Carolyn's direction, saying, "Take your time."

My mother and I inched our way to the table, hoping we wouldn't find death markings. When we got to her side, we saw a sleeping Carolyn with stitches across her neck. I started to wish I hadn't come.

I'll never be able to extract this vision from memory, and I'll know Arcane ended her life by slitting her throat. My sister—the one willing to help me—yet I failed her.

I touched her cold, smooth face, whispering, "I'm sorry, Carolyn. I'm so, so, sorry. Please forgive me."

My mother released her earlier-muffled cries into the funeral home. I had to half carry her out of the room and sit her down before we could leave. Her body shook nonstop. Garrett had chauffeured us to the funeral home and sat outside waiting. When he saw me practically carrying my mother he came to my rescue.

It was the worst day of my life. I took advantage of my sister and time…assuming tomorrow would come and mistakes would be forgotten. Arcane took her from me. I will find him.

Die! Die! Die!

MONDAY, DECEMBER 29, 2008: Dear Friends,

Today I listened (with a stranger's ears) to stories about my sister. It's amazing how much you learn about a family member after they're dead.

So many people turned out for the wake, offering condolences and telling my mom and me stories about Carolyn. I thought I knew everything about her, but I only knew the icing on Carolyn's life and not the contents that made her who she was. At work, people loved her for her honest, hard work. Every month Carolyn got together with a group of friends, each taking a turn picking the place. Last month was Carolyn's choice. She wanted to have dinner at this little Italian restaurant called *Bertucci's,* because Carolyn told them it was my favorite place. I started to cry again— just when I thought there were no more tears left.

What about the timid Carolyn? Or the introvert? She remembered my favorite restaurant. What was her favorite? Did my sister seem so different that I didn't want to bother keeping up with who she was?

The line at the funeral home was like a chain link pulley—moving in a circle without an end. My mother and I took turns sitting down, alternating between resting and greeting people. As I listened to them, I found myself wishing I could have recorded all their words to play back over and over so I wouldn't forget her, since I had forgotten her in life.

When did she accumulate all these friends?

A tall man with dark hair and an even complexion—strong features—walked up to the casket and bowed in a silent prayer. Most people searched Carolyn's body, whispering curiosities about her death, but this man was different. He gazed at her face, lost in thought, swallowed hard and headed over to where my mother sat. Bending down, he took her hands in his, said something and then sat a few rows back. Whenever I looked at him, he was either looking at Carolyn or me.

When my mom got up to take her turn at receiving mourners, Garrett brought me to the back room where he had sandwiches, snacks and desserts set up. He wouldn't let me leave until I ate a small portion of a sandwich.

Rubbing my back he asked, "How are you holding up?"

"Okay. I'm amazed at how many people knew Carolyn. And the stories they've told me proved what little I knew of her. This is very hard on my mom. I'm worried about her."

"This morning several neighbors brought food over and left freezer and refrigerator instructions. At least she won't have to cook for a while."

I turned back in the direction of where Carolyn was laid out and then back at Garrett.

"I haven't thanked you for everything. You've been a big help and I don't think we could have done this without you," I said.

"I'm here for you, Sydney—to talk or just sit."

I took his hand and said, 'I know you are. You've been great. You haven't complained about anything."

"There's nothing for me to complain about outside of dealing with the Arcane bullshit. And even then, I know it's not—"

My voice came out louder than expected, saying, "Don't speak his name! His name doesn't deserve to be uttered. Call him asshole, Satan, Lucifer, but don't call him by that name."

Garrett stayed calm, in spite of my outburst, saying, "Well anyway, the police will probably want to talk to us."

"I know, but I can't think about it now."

I returned to the main room and found the man still sitting, staring straight ahead at Carolyn's casket. I walked down the row of seats and sat next to him.

He turned, offered his hand and said, "You're Sydney."

"Yes. And you're… "

"Nick."

Up close, his average-width nose balanced above his thin lips, blending well with his defined features and chocolate-colored eyes. He was extremely handsome.

"How do you know who I am?"

He smiled and said, "Carolyn talked a lot about you."

"I'm sorry, but she never mentioned you. How did you know her?"

"She hired me—a long time ago. I've known her for a good twenty-five years."

"Forgive me, but what did she hire you for?"

"That's between me and Carolyn."

"Well, yes, except she's dead and I'm sure she wouldn't mind you telling me—especially since she talked about me a lot."

He looked deep into my eyes and said, "Sydney, no offense, but I'm not going to tell you what she hired me for. I knew Carolyn for many years. I didn't betray her trust in life and I'm not about to in death."

I knew my impatience showed when I said, "Nick. See all these people here. They're here to say good-bye to Carolyn—to tell my mother and I what she meant to them and how they knew her. If you didn't want me asking, why did you say she hired you?"

"To let you know everyone has secrets."

"It seems like you're taunting me."

"On the contrary. I came to say good-bye to an old friend and express my condolences to the two people she always spoke highly of. Your sister hired me and asked that I keep it a secret forever. I promised her I would."

He took my hand, opened my fist and placed a pendant necklace in it.

"Your sister wore this necklace up until a few years ago. She gave it to me for safekeeping and asked that I give it to you if anything ever happened to her."

"Why only up to a few years ago? And why not leave it with the rest of her jewelry?"

"She had her reasons to stop wearing it, and it meant too much to her to just leave it in her house."

I turned and faced forward, opening the pendant. The pictures were dark and faded. I could only make out that they were pictures of babies. *Is this a picture of Carolyn and me?*

Without looking at him I asked, "Why didn't she tell *me* her secrets? I was her only sister. Didn't that give me the right to know her secrets?"

He sighed, got up and started walking away. I turned to watch him and he stopped, turning back to me.

"You do know the secret. You were part of it."

He disappeared. I was left with another puzzle—an enormous overload of information and more questions that need answers. But I can't think anymore. Exhaustion wins.

WEDNESDAY, DECEMBER 27, 2006: Dear Friend,

Psst…It's Caitlyn.

They (the cops) got me…a day after I arrived in Seattle. I don't know how they figured it out…no one cared about me…I've been invisible for so long. When did I become noticeable?

The cops thought they'd get me to admit it. HA! Delusional. They have no idea who they're dealing with. Like I'm going to help them?! Where were they for me when I needed them? But I begged for my journal, and under constant watch, I got it back. This is how it went.

I was brought into a room, looked around at the pale walls and then rested my eyes on a guy in a suit and a woman. He indicated for me to take a seat, but I decided to stand instead, bringing my right arm across my body and hooking my hand around my left elbow.

"Caitlyn. My name is Officer Katie Flannigan and this is Officer Mike O'Connor. We'd like to talk to you about Carolyn Baker. Please have a seat."

O'Connor thought he could intimidate me by standing with his arms folded over his wide chest, legs spread shoulder width. If anything, I wanted to laugh at his tactics…or maybe he really did think he was a tough guy.

He sighed and said, "We're going to be here for a while so you might want to get comfortable."

I glared at him and then turned away, my hair covering part of my face.

I made no attempt to move so he got up, pulled the chair out, and guided me by the arm into the chair. I sat with my head forward, staring at the nothingness of the walls…like the nothingness I have in me.

Officer Flannigan softly asked, "Caitlyn? Do you know a Carolyn Baker?"

Stone–faced was all they got. Question after question—our breaths loud and obnoxious against the simmering silence. Finally they decided to call it quits for the time being.

After some time listening to me cry and beg for my journal, a cop slipped it through the bars.

I'll let you know more tomorrow.

SATURDAY, JANUARY 3, 2009: Dear Friends,

On Tuesday I said good-bye to my sister for the last time, leaving my mom in good hands with plenty of neighbors willing to check in on her. I told my mother I'd be back around spring to help her go through Carolyn's things. My mother had always demonstrated such strength in raising us alone, which is why her frailty now pushed me further into a restless state. The optimistic road she walked now lay like a muddy path. Carolyn and I were her world, and having Carolyn nearby helped my mother cope with the distance Arcane created between us. Now, she has to cope with losing one daughter to death and another geographically. I just can't go back and live in Chicago—too many bad memories. And Garrett isn't there. As much as I worry about something happening to my mother, I'm sure Arcane has already done his destruction and is back in Seattle, waiting to circle his prey again.

We finally made it back home. Both spent—we were looking forward to a relaxing few days. Unfortunately, we have to deal with more police and stories.

The work schedule has already been made out for the coming week, so I'm not on the schedule until Monday. This gives me time to blend back into my life and gather my thoughts before returning the phone calls from the Seattle Police Department. Another day won't change anything.

I wasn't in the mood to discuss tragedy. It feels like months since I have had time to myself and I am looking forward to when Garrett returns to work. I know he can't wait to relieve himself of drama...for the time being anyway.

He brought the luggage in and dumped the clothes by the washer and dryer. He was quiet during our trip back, but my own thoughts consumed me and I didn't really care what he was feeling. Garrett's silence stretched longer and today we offered each other nothing more than short responses.

While he was emptying the luggage, I asked, "Do you want me to make something to eat?"

"I don't care."

"What do you want?"

"I said I don't care."

I walked over to him.

"What's wrong?"

"Nothing, Ash. I'm tired. Can't *I* be a little exhausted and crabby for once?"

"Fine. I just thought something was wrong."

He threw some clothes into the washing machine, adding, "You can make eggs. I think we have a carton."

That was the extent of our conversation for the rest of the night. We kept company with our own feelings, letting our minds linger on things that nagged us...like Nick. I can't get his words out of my mind.

How was I a part of Carolyn's secret without knowing I was in on a secret? Does it have anything to do with the pictures I found in her drawer of the two babies and then boys...along with the others I brought home? Who are they? She has known Nick for a long time. Why hadn't I ever met him?

I rubbed Carolyn's pendant between my fingers. Earlier in the evening, I had put the pendant on, silently vowing to wear it every day in her memory.

My sister's death raises plenty of questions I hadn't planned to resolve. I decided not to ask my mom about the pictures I found in Carolyn's drawer, it would only upset her more.

I spent the day trying to think of how Carolyn knew Nick—what their relationship was about and how the boys might fit into the picture. I am as clueless as when I first started.

When Garrett and I went to bed we kept our closeness to cuddling. Neither one of us wanted to start a conversation about any of the things that had occupied our thoughts today or any day in the past.

THURSDAY, JANUARY 8, 2009: Friends,

I'm tired … frayed from thinking … anxious from the unknown … cracking from pressure. Nothing feels right, inside or out. And nothing is working out either. My brittle existence is losing the game.

Garrett left for work while I was cleaning myself up and getting ready to go to the police station. I told him I'd go it alone this time. The station was sending a squad car to pick me up.

I put the pendant back on and went downstairs to wait.

A young officer I haven't seen before picked me up. I was relieved it wasn't Atticus. What a blessing. The officer never tried to make small talk with me and I was eternally grateful.

Officer Quinn sat behind his desk, running his hands through his hair. When I came into his office, he got up to shake my hand and offer his condolences.

"Ashley, I'm sorry to hear about your sister."

I looked down at our hands and said, "Thank you."

"Please have a seat. Can I get you something to drink?"

"No thanks."

He tried relaxing before proceeding by sitting in a chair next to me, reclining and taking a sip out of the water bottle he was fidgeting with. I was getting nervous. He got up scraping the chair a bit and returned to the chair behind his desk, leaned forward and said, "I called you in here to let you know we'll get him. The police reports from Chicago, along with the ones you made here, are in your file. DNA from the sheets hasn't come back yet, but we're hopeful to get something from them."

Atticus knocked on the door and Quinn gestured for him to enter.

Atticus looked defeated when he sighed and said, "I'm sorry about your sister, Ashley."

"Thanks, Atticus. I received your voice message letting me know you took care of the mess in my apartment. I appreciate it."

He nodded his head. Before closing the door, he said, "That's all I wanted to say. I'll let you two get back to what you were doing."

Quinn said to me, "We have the movie ticket you gave us, and we wiped the kitchen from top to bottom without luck."

With my fingers intertwined on my lap, my eyes pleading for hope, I let out a frustrated sigh and asked, "Do you think the discharge on the sheets is his? He wore gloves while doing everything else to keep his identity safe, so why would he take a chance and do that to the sheets?"

"I don't know. Maybe his anger got the best of him and he got careless. They *all* get careless over time."

I clung to desperation since I had wanted to hear some kind of substantial information—thinking they already had proof it was Arcane.

"If we don't get anything from the sheets, then what do we do? It leaves everyone I love in danger…my mother…Garrett. He could harm them…and they're all I have left."

Oh, now you're going to care about your mother.

I've always cared about her.

They'll never catch him. You know that, right?

At some time Arcane will screw up.

I closed my eyes, gripped the armrests and then I shook my head. When I opened my eyes, Quinn was looking down, as if trying to come up with the right thing to say to ease my mind.

"I know," he finally said, "but because of recent events we *are* planning on providing you and Garrett and your mother some protection. I've contacted the Chicago police regarding your mother and they've agreed to help…and I'm placing a car by your apartment and the coffee shop when you're at work."

"Thank you. I appreciate it, but the car should stay at the apartment. He's not going to harm me at work. Someone needs to watch for him there…especially if Garrett's home…I can't have anything happen to him…"

"We will," Officer Quinn promised. "Although, I want an officer keeping an eye on things when you're at work, too. We need to protect you *and* the public in case he decides to come into the store and cause further trouble."

"Will the police keep track of my mom? I want her protected at all times."

"They could only promise they'll do their best to keep an eye on her. She hasn't been threatened, so there's only so much they can do."

I scoffed at the comment, turning my head toward the window.

The son of a bitch is out there enjoying all he inflicts on me and everyone I love. How can someone go undetected for so long? How can his friends and family not know something is wrong with him?

I turned my attention back to Quinn when I heard him speak my name.

"I read through the police reports, but wondered if I could ask you more questions?"

"Yes, I wish you would. Those reports only explain the instances as to why the police came. Callahan knew the rest."

"That's the problem with protection—we can only work with what's been reported. We can't take action, even if it's connected to your present circumstance, without a report. Even though Callahan is out of the hospital, he has his own concerns to worry about, which is why I haven't visited him to inquire about you."

"I couldn't report anything without probable cause—based on a hunch. The reports are only of incidences that occurred *with* proof. It was hard to even prove Arcane had ever been there and I wasn't insane…although even the proof I thought existed was questionable at times. And I understand about Callahan. I'm glad he's out of the hospital and home recuperating."

"I don't blame you for not reporting everything," Quinn said. "I blame the system. This is why I'd like to know more about what's happened."

Without waiting for his questions, I said, "I told you how I met Arcane, what he did to me, and you have the police reports of the times he was on my property. One thing I didn't tell you was about my old employer. I worked at a law firm where an attorney and I were working late on a big case, sometimes eating dinner at the office. One night after we had left each other's company, someone brutally attacked him. The police never found who did it and assumed it was a random act of violence, but I know Arcane was the attacker. It couldn't be a coincidence."

"What makes you think Arcane did it? I'm not ruling it out; however, coincidences happen more often than you'd think. There are times the police pursue a good lead only to find out later it was a simple act of wrong place, wrong time. Since it was a law firm, it could have been a disgruntled client."

"Because Richard told the police that the only thing the guy said before throwing acid on him was something about 'Newbies lie'. Newbie was the name I used when I entered the chat room—the name Arcane toyed with before I gave him my real name."

"That makes it plausible for Arcane to be the culprit, but to most looking in on this case it's not enough. It still could have been someone not wanting him to continue with that trial."

"True, except the last time I saw Arcane I told him to stay away from me. He came by my condo wanting to go up and talk, but I wouldn't let him. When I asked him to leave, the look he gave me indicated I hadn't seen the last of him. Every time things settle— and I think Arcane is gone for good—he does something else to disrupt my life. The act against Richard was a violent act and seemed intentional. When I think of a random act, I think of a stabbing or shooting. And just as you question my assumption, back then the police did the same thing due to Richard's line of work. But I know Arcane's twisted mind and I KNOW he is responsible for Richard's injuries. I know it!"

"In this report it states you claimed someone was in your condo, based on a scribbling of 'change locks' found on a notepad? The police didn't think the writing looked any different from the other writing on the page—your writing."

I sat up straight in my seat and said, "I don't mean to attack anyone, but one of the officers acted like he was put out by having to be there. They took the notepad, so it should be in the file. You could look at it yourself or get a handwriting expert to look at it, right?"

"I'll see if they can fax a copy of the notepad," Quinn said, continuing on. "After what Arcane did to you when you attempted to go away for the weekend, you decided to move to Seattle, right? What made you pick Seattle?"

I looked out the window, smiled and responded as if miles away.

"Carolyn … my sister. She knew I was looking to move out of state … she gave me some information on Seattle."

Quinn shifted in his chair, which brought me back to the present, then asked, "Had your sister been to Seattle? I mean, what would make her choose Seattle as a good place for you to relocate?"

"No, that's what was weird about it…though at the time I didn't ask her. I had my own physical and mental problems to deal with and didn't think to question her about it."

"Do you think there is a reason why she had information about Seattle?"

"I don't know. Like I said—"

"Yes, I know, but I'm asking do *you* have a gut feeling she directed you here?"

"I do. Carolyn always thought things through. She was organized, meticulous and didn't do anything spontaneous. Everything was analyzed—pros and cons—before she made a decision. I definitely feel like she gave me the information for a reason, if that's what you mean."

"But you have no idea what it could be?"

"No, but…" I thought about Nick and his comment about me being a part of her secret.

Quinn waited while I finished my thought.

"At my sister's wake, a man by the name of Nick gave his condolences to my mother and then sat in a back row. He was alone and I found it odd the way he looked at Carolyn in the casket—sitting there looking straight ahead—so I went up to him. He knew who I was and gave me this pendant."

I pulled the pendant out from underneath my shirt and held it in my palm.

"Supposedly Carolyn hired him for some reason, but he wouldn't tell me what he did or why she hired him. I told him she wouldn't have kept a dark secret from me and he said I knew the secret because I was part of it...but I haven't figured out my connection to the secret."

Quinn stood to get a better look at the pendant and then scrunched his face when he said, "Weird. Can I have the necklace for a better look?"

I took it off and handed it to him. He opened it, squinted to see the pictures and then walked to the window for more light.

"It looks like a picture of two babies. Did your sister have children?"

"No. My sister always kept to herself. Although—after her wake— I'm guessing I didn't know as much about her as I should have. She did so many things I wasn't aware of."

"Did anyone in the family lose a child?"

Hmmm...why didn't I make the connection?

I reached over for the pendant, opened it and concentrated on the pictures.

You've searched for a long time.

But I didn't know what happened to them. If I didn't know, how could Carolyn know so much?

Face it, you didn't care enough.

I pressed the ball of my palm against my forehead.

"Ashley? Any other children? Are you all right?" Quinn asked, stirring me from my thoughts.

I looked up at him, cleared my throat and said, "Yes. Mine."

He fell noisily back into his chair, exhaled and said, "Children?

You've never mentioned children before."

I blurted out, "I got pregnant at sixteen years old with twin boys and gave them up for adoption."

I can't believe I told him.

You shouldn't have opened up your mouth. What the hell is wrong with you?

Calm down. It's no big deal.

Quinn seemed miles away—like I was detached—watching this scene unfold from a corner of the room.

My sons. What kind of mother was I to give them up? It sounds so unemotional...harsh to discard and forget so easily. If these are my sons, it shows how caring Carolyn was and how selfish I am.

I rubbed my eyes and used my hands to wipe the excess dread off my face. Quinn waited until I came back to him.

"If these are my sons how did she get the pictures and why? Carolyn was a couple years older than me. When I got pregnant, she wouldn't talk to me for weeks. When she found out I was giving them up for adoption, she stopped talking to me for months after they were born. I was still in high school and living at home; she was away at college. She wouldn't even talk to me when she called home—not even to see how I was doing."

"That's a pretty harsh reaction."

"I was just happy when she started talking to me again."

"Ashley ... do you know where your children are? Do you know who adopted them?"

They have better lives than I did.

"No…No. I gave them up and moved on."

My head started hurting. Words began to seep out without my control.

"I don't care."

I could feel Quinn staring at me, confused when he asked, "Excuse me … what? You don't care?"

Of course you care … I didn't mean to … I mean …

No you didn't! You threw them away like garbage!

You did the best you could under the circumstances.

I saw my chest rise and fall fast—guilt swirling around in the air.

"They're not my children! I gave them up long ago. I have no rights."

I walked to the window and looked outside for an answer.

I'm confused. I need to think. No—I DON'T need to think. Those boys were better off without me. I did the right thing.

Did I?

Yes you did.

I'm not going to relive this.

"Did you date the father?" Quinn broke in.

I took a deep breath and moved back to my seat, buying myself a few seconds to regroup.

"For a short time—a high school romance that lasted about as long as an ice cream cone. He pressured me into having sex with him, saying everyone else was doing it. I'm not blaming him for my own stupidity. I believed him when he told me he loved me, so I slept with him one time and got pregnant. When he found out, he claimed it wasn't his. Needless to say, I kept a low profile for the rest of high school after giving them up."

"Do you know how you can contact him?" Quinn asked, as if he hadn't heard a single thing I said.

"How I can contact *who*?"

"How *we* might contact the father, I mean. Maybe he knows their whereabouts and—"

"I'm not here to search for my long lost children. I'm here because I have someone stalking me and my sister is dead because of it."

Stop yelling! Control yourself.

Quinn leaned back as if he feared my eyes might pop out of their sockets. "I understand, but don't—"

"I don't want to know anything about him *or* them."

I felt a lot of internal commotion and needed to end this right now.

"My sister is dead. Dead because of some sicko out there doing everything in his power to break me—to take away all those I love. So I'm not concerned, nor do I care, about two boys I gave up for adoption when I was sixteen. I'm sure that sounds cold to you, but I want all energies put into finding this asshole. If he—"

"Okay, Ashley—I get it—calm down."

My skin heated up as I sprang to my feet, opening and closing my hands as I spoke.

"No, I don't think you get it. I don't think *any* of you get it. Try walking around constantly looking over your shoulder to see if someone is following you. Or entering your home with caution—searching to make sure no one broke in. Or how about praying every day he won't find you—only to receive a call telling you someone murdered your sister and all evidence points to the monster you've been hiding from. So please don't tell me you get it. Tell me you got *him*."

I walked to the chair, picked up my purse and headed out the door.

"Ashley. I will get him."

I shot him a skeptical look, saying, "Don't say it—do it."

FRIDAY, JANUARY 16, 2009: Dear Friends,

What did I do to deserve all of this? My relationship with Garrett is strained, and today turned out to be another horrible day…equal to finding out about Carolyn. I can't take this much longer. Maybe I should have killed myself years ago then I would have never met Arcane, Garrett would be happy and Carolyn still alive.

I HATE ARCANE!!

Die! ARCANE!!

We spent last weekend at home lying around watching television. Garrett held me when my thoughts and sorrow got the best of me. Food was a toss-up between ordering out or running to the store for a few things.

Last Saturday the police station called to let Garrett know they found his car—stripped inside and out. There was nothing left behind and no word of who stole the vehicle. Since Garrett doesn't have insurance, and until we can save up money, our modes of transportation will be public or walking.

My apartment has yellow police tape going up and down and across the door. I sometimes look out the peephole to see if it had been moved or torn. When I get really bored I stand at the door until Garrett tells me to sit down or go to bed. We don't fight—we let the silence do the brooding for us.

I lost my job. The looks on the Wilson's faces when I told them everything resembled that of someone who had taken too many hits off a bong. They listened and then relieved me of my duties, offering the excuse of needing someone more reliable. They gave their condolences about my sister's death, but had a vacation planned and couldn't risk leaving their business in the hands of someone who has danger following her. Confinement to the apartment started to drive me nuts, but I worried too much about Arcane to walk around the city alone. Sometimes Garrett expresses his frustration by yelling at me to look for another job or at least clean the apartment, but for the most part he lets things go.

I looked in the paper for any possibilities. When Garrett is home he occasionally walks with me to fill out job applications. My heart wasn't into anything—going through the motions knowing I have to do something. It was driving me crazy sitting around thinking about my sister and all the things that have happened over the past year, so today, out of frustration and desperation, I ventured out to the deli around the corner from Peace, Love & Latte to fill out a job application and have something to eat.

The deli is surrounded by windows so I took a seat in a corner, eating my turkey sandwich and answering the questions on the application. I saw someone coming toward me from the corner of my eye.

It was Atticus.

"Hi, Ashley. Do you mind if I have a seat?"

I minded, but I just shrugged as if I didn't care and went back to filling out the form.

"How are you doing?"

Without looking at him, I said, "All right, thanks. How are you?"

"Fine. You're looking for a job?"

I continued to work on the application, saying, "Yep! It seems I wasn't reliable enough for Peace, Love & Latte."

"Sorry about that. You can try the florist shop—they're usually looking for someone."

He paused then asked, "Did you talk to Quinn yet?"

This got my attention. I stopped writing, looked up at him and said, "No. Why? Is he looking for me?"

"Yeah, I guess the DNA results came in."

My mouth went dry just thinking about what might be in the results. I stared at him, hoping he'd tell me more, but he didn't look like he was about to share any more information. I pulled out my cell phone. There were messages from Quinn.

"Damn it! My phone was on vibrate!" I said. "Do you know the results?"

"No. Quinn won't share the information with anyone. He locked them in his drawer until he could talk to you about them."

I stuffed the application in my purse, stood and asked, "Are you heading back to the station? Can you give me a ride?"

"Yeah, but I can't drive you back home."

"That's okay. I can cab it."

I arrived at the police station hoping Quinn was ready and waiting. The police officer stationed at the desk said he had stepped out and hadn't indicated a return time.

"Sorry. You can sit over there and wait," the officer said.

I walked around the permitted area, torturing myself over what the results might reveal. A group of police officers came in with a recent arrest and I listened to them rattle off what the offender had done. A burglar found in the Hutchinson's house was standing in their kitchen with a bag of stolen goods making a sandwich. The cop berated the burglar, commenting on how stupid it was of him to make himself at home. Another cop brought in a guy who had just robbed a convenience store. He pushed the guy down in a chair a few seats away from me and handcuffed him to the arm of the chair. The guy looked over at me, licking his lips and calling me 'baby'.

The officer barked, "Shut the hell up! If I hear one more thing from you, you'll be sharing a cell with someone who will be calling *you* baby."

"Fuck you man, I didn't do anything. This is against the law."

"Yeah, you didn't do anything. Someone put the gun in your hand and made you point it at the cashier, demanding money. And that someone was also stupid enough to do it with a cop in the place."

The robber spit on the floor in front of the cop. The officer uncuffed the offender from the chair, letting the guy push him back and try to make a run for it. Another officer put out his foot, tripping the guy and cuffing him behind his back. The guy cried out, saying they were hurting him, as they pulled him to his feet and pushed him out a door.

I watched as cops struggled with dirty and/or violent people until I lost interest and let my eyes rest.

Quinn gently touched my arm and said my name. Quinn asked, "How long have you been here?"

I rubbed my eyes, looked at the clock and said, "A couple of hours … I guess."

"Why didn't you call first? At least you would have known I wasn't in the office."

"I missed your messages. Atticus told me you were looking for me."

This made him tense up and he told me to follow him.

When we were safely behind closed doors, he asked, "Did Atticus say anything else?"

"No. Now you're freaking me out."

"I want to make sure no one knew anything about the results. When they came in, I kept it quiet, put them in my drawer and contacted you. I'm surprised Atticus knew the results came in at all."

"Were they sent by mail?"

He shook his head 'yes' and said, "The envelope wasn't opened."

"Maybe he guessed those were the results."

"Probably, probably," he said, as though if he repeated it, it might make it true.

Concern creased his face.

"Have a seat, Ashley."

Why is he acting this way? Did the results come back inconclusive? Do I want to hear it after all that's happened?

He unlocked the drawer and took out the results, looking at them before saying, "The results came back with a match to the discharge on the sheets. Um … they found a few hairs on the sheets, so they decided to run them through analysis, too. They weren't sure if it was your hair or his."

He paused, choosing his words carefully before continuing.

"Once they received the results, they contacted me requesting a hair from you to run it against the one they found. I got it when you came in the last time; there was a hair on your pendant. Fortunately, it had the root intact. I sent it to the lab."

"I don't understand why you're telling me about my own DNA."

He leaned back in his chair, clearly exhausted. I could tell he put in long hours at this place; whether or not it was on my case, it was too much time.

"When they got the DNA from the discharge they ran it through a National DNA database and it came up with a match—a repeat offender for assault and sexual assault. It matches Arcane's DNA."

Even though I expected to hear this about Arcane, every pore on my body opened and I watched my chest rise and fall like an anchored ship in turbulent waters as the weight of his words poured over me.

It was him. I'm not crazy.

I finally managed to say, "I hope you're about to tell me he's been arrested."

"It seems he lived a tough life."

My right eyebrow lifted when I said, "I'm supposed to feel bad he had it tough? That excuses him for the despicable things he did to me and others? When did the assaults start and when was the first sexual assault?"

Quinn's head fell in defeat, clearly regretting his comment.

Instead of apologizing, he answered, "When he was fifteen years old, he pulled a knife on a foster father he'd lived with for seven years. His first sexual assault happened in the same house—he assaulted his foster sister. His offenses got more violent over time."

"Yet our society allows someone like that to walk free, terrorizing and ruining more lives."

"His attorney convinced the jury that the last violent act was the result of sexual abuse at the hands of his foster father. His sentence was reduced—tremendously. The last assault happened two and a half years ago. I'm sure the state hoped he'd changed."

"Yeah, he changed his direction to me. He took out his anger on me."

Hearing this guy was a repeat offender—still free—pissed me off. I looked away from Quinn and swallowed hard. New tears filled my eyes.

This man got out of jail because of pity, stalked me and killed my sister, yet they can't do anything about it.

My body trembled with rage.

You're as much to blame for this guy running free as the police.

Why? Because I overlooked finding out his name and address.

The blame doesn't start there.

I gripped the armrests to tame the beast that started to grow inside me—clenching my jaw to prevent the screams from escaping.

In a dead stare, I asked, "Now that you know who he is, are you going to arrest him?"

He quietly said, "There's more."

I turned to him, asking, "Do I need to know any more?"

The door opened and Garrett came in and sat in the chair next to me. If there was ever a time I was ecstatic to see him, this was it.

Quinn said, "I asked Garrett to come down when he finished work. I hope you don't mind."

Garrett took my hand, smiled and said to Quinn, "We're ready."

Ready for what?

I looked from one to the other searching for a hint. Garrett looked straight ahead at Quinn, and Quinn took on a poker face.

"I'm not going to go over everything I already discussed with

Ashley since she doesn't need to hear it again. She can fill you in later."

We both nodded, and I found myself holding my breath until Quinn spoke again.

"The DNA matched a man named Arcane Dresner. He was tossed from foster home to foster home until he was locked up at fifteen for three years for sexual assault. When he got out, he continued to commit more crimes."

I asked, "Were his other crimes related to his foster care?"

"Yes. All his crimes had to do with people he knew."

"Except me," I pointed out.

"Well ... no," Quinn said. "He knew you, too."

My mouth began to water as his eyes moved to my pendant.

I clutched the pendant as though it might silence Quinn's words. Instead, they choked me.

"He's your son, Ashley."

The words screamed in my ears, but my mind couldn't comprehend them.

"What? He's not! Why would a son stalk a mother? Why would he want to physically harm me? The sex ... oh my God!"

Bile coated my throat. I grabbed for the garbage can next to the desk and began throwing up. Garrett and Quinn had both moved to the window to give me privacy. My moans and agonizing screams echoed in the garbage as I continued to empty my stomach.

Garrett, help me. Help me. You know I can't handle this alone. Stop the lies.

Moments later Garrett pulled his chair closer to mine, rubbing my back with one hand and holding my hair with the other. I stopped vomiting, but continued to cry and moan—occasionally asking, "Why?"

We have to get him. Stop him from ruining our lives...from telling more lies.

Quinn put a box of tissues by me. Garrett wiped my mouth with the tissues like a helpless child. As my body started to become unresponsive, Garrett lifted my head up and sat me back. I heard them calling my name, but I found myself detached again— looking from the outside in. Garrett and Quinn whispered something to each other and Garrett tugged gently at my arm until I became part of the conversation again.

Quinn offered to give us a ride home. With both of them supporting me, we walked out of the station. The frigid air hit my face, freezing the existing tears and creating more.

Back at home, Garrett tucked me into bed and Quinn filled Garrett in on the rest of the details.

The police department posted a cop at my apartment, outside our building and notified the Chicago police to step up protection for my mother. They didn't want him getting away this time. Quinn asked Garrett to keep me in the apartment as much as possible until they could find Arcane.

Quinn left and Garrett slid under the covers, taking me in his arms and whispering that everything-was going to be fine. But I knew it wouldn't be fine. My son slept with me, killed his loving aunt and is determined to kill me.

How did I bear such a child?

It was my fault that violence had consumed Arcane, instead of love. I gave him up for adoption where he endured his own abuse.

This is a mistake I will have to learn to live with or it will kill me before Arcane does.

I considered giving myself to Arcane, but my mother didn't deserve the loss of another child.

I was a bad mother. I don't need to add bad daughter to the list. In my heart I know I did the right thing. I was sixteen...

I only hope my other son is a ray of sunshine.

I had to get up and tell you about what happened—the horror movie I'm living in. Garrett helps as much as possible, but the realization that my son hates me cuts deep. I'm sure I'll have more misery to share with you tomorrow—it's a way of life now.

WEDNESDAY, FEBRUARY 4, 2009: Friends,

He's going to leave me, I know he is. I think I've pushed Garrett to his breaking point.

In recent weeks, I have sat inside looking out the window, crying and screaming—refusing to talk. I wrap my sorrows into bed, hug the pillows and wish that when I wake up Carolyn will be back and Arcane gone forever. This cycle continues. Garrett's frustration is growing and he now goes out for walks to escape. I've tried to get a handle on my feelings for his sake, but every time I think about Carolyn, sex with Arcane and knowing he is my son, it drives me right back into a downward spiral.

Finally, the call came that we both had been waiting for.

They caught him.

I rolled those words around and around in my head.

He was in a holding cell at the jail until he could be transferred back to Chicago to await trial for my sister's murder—along with other charges. I told Garrett I wanted to see him and he responded with a resounding 'no'.

"What good would it do? Do you really think he'll be sorry for what he did to you?"

"I need to see him, Garrett. A part of me hates him and hopes he dies, yet another part feels guilt—like it's my fault."

"Your fault? How can what he did be your fault?"

"Because I gave him up for adoption. If I had kept him—*them*—he wouldn't have been abused, which is probably why he committed the crimes."

"Bullshit, Ashley! I've been here watching you throw up from thoughts of what he did, and cry over the loss of your sister. Don't give him that power. You giving him up for adoption has nothing to do with what he did. He is the only one accountable for his crimes. There are plenty of people out there with hard lives, but they're not raping and killing people."

I looked at my hands, focusing on the cracks I had accumulated over time, before I responded. "Then I at least need to know why he killed my sister. Did she ever visit him? Maybe he knows something about her—why she had the pictures and wore the pendant."

Garrett's anger did not subside as I continued to list my reasons for seeing Arcane.

"You're not going to get any answers from him, Ash! All you're going to do is feel dejected again by the lack of information and come back here depressed about how you'll never know."

My eyes caught his as I said, "Why are you being like this? I'm sorry I've been a burden to you. You know I didn't want any of this and was even willing to move back to my own apartment. Don't make me feel like shit for ignoring your needs."

He got up, went into the bedroom and slammed the door behind him. I ran my fingers through my hair, thinking about what I should do.

If I don't at least try to see him, I'll wonder for the rest of my life if he might have told me something I needed to know.

But I also knew Garrett was right. I would react exactly as he had said if I wasn't able to get information from Arcane.

I went into the bedroom.

Garrett lay on his back with his left arm over his eyes. My feelings had been churning for so many days that I was unaware—until now—how much I needed a release. I went to him and grabbed at him in the way one might hunger for a blanket to rid their bones of a chill. My hands seemed almost independent of my arms, unbuttoning and unzipping his pants with fervor. At first he resisted, restraining my hands and trying to calm me.

"Ashley…you don't have anything to prove to me—"

"Stop talking…" I said.

In one fell swoop I pulled his pants and underwear down and I took him in my mouth. The sound of his moans increased my excitement and I touched, prodded and sucked to get him to want me just as much as I wanted him. Having captured his full attention, I took my pants off and straddled him, pushing him deep inside. I closed my eyes—moving up and down—taking in short breaths as his hands cupped my breasts. Garrett saw the tears and I sensed he knew they were washing away some of the pain—not tears caused by him. He rolled me onto my back, putting my legs over his shoulders and thrusting in fast and hard. We needed the pleasure that went with it. Anything intimate or needy was left out. Concentration was on the act of gratification. Garrett's thrusts came on harder, but I enjoyed the roughness of it.

When we finished hitting our heights, we laid on our backs waiting for our normal breathing rhythms.

Turning our backs to each other, we fell asleep and didn't wake until the morning. Sex didn't resolve our frustrations. Our emotions ran too deep for that.

THURSDAY, FEBRUARY 5, 2009: Friends,

I made my decision—I went to see Arcane. Everyone thought I was insane, nothing would come of it, but I felt I had to try.

Garrett went to work without asking what I had planned for the day, although he did kiss me on the cheek before leaving. By now he didn't count on me to do anything around the place; no expectations, no disappointments. I called Quinn to let him know I wanted to go to the jail to see Arcane. Like Garrett, he argued about what good it would do, but in the end he granted my request. I grabbed whatever change we had around the apartment and hopped on the bus. I had limited experience in taking public transportation and I found it refreshing to be able to kick back and watch the town go by. Rain washed away strings and streamers left over from Christmas by those reluctant to depart from the holiday cheer. Peoples' faces were stuck in a scowl at the abundance of rain. I imagined that they all anticipated a much needed warm up and for the city to come alive again, as I did; longing to go out without coats.

The bus stopped across the street from the police station. I tried running to avoid getting soaked, but I still managed to get drenched. Quinn was in his office drinking coffee and reading something when I walked in. I shook the rain off my jacket and stomped my feet on the entry mat.

Quinn approached the front desk, asking, "Are you sure you want to do this, Ashley?"

"It's more about need than want."

"I'll be in the room while you talk to him. He'll be handcuffed and a glass plate will separate you."

We walked down the stairs through several secured gates. The door opened to reveal booth after booth with phones and chairs on each side of the glass. I froze at the scene—afraid I was making the wrong decision. Quinn looked at me, I nodded and he led me to the third booth. There weren't any other visitors or inmates and they hadn't brought Arcane out yet.

Quinn gestured for me to sit and said, "We usually let visitors get used to the surroundings before bringing out the prisoner. I'll be by the door. Remember—he can't touch you."

I was too scared to cry outwardly. Inwardly, blood rushed through my veins at great speeds.

"Ashley, are you sure you're ready to see him?"

"I can't take the chance they'll move him to Chicago before I get to talk to him. I might not get anything new from him, but at least I won't beat myself up over wondering if I should have seen him or not."

Quinn handed me a handkerchief and said, "Keep in mind that you won. Prison or death is what awaits him. It should help when he starts to antagonize you."

"Antagonize me? Will he do that?"

"I'm guessing he will. He doesn't have any remorse for anything he's done, and will probably say some pretty painful things."

He watched for my reaction and continued. "We can postpone this for another day if you'd like."

I cleared my throat, took a deep breath and said, "No. I'm ready. I need to get this over with and put an end to it."

He shook his head and said, "I'll give the okay to bring him in then. Again, I'll be ten feet away if you need me for anything."

My eyes followed Quinn as he walked to the door. I looked down at my hands, twisting the handkerchief and trying to think of Garrett.

Don't start crying when he comes in. He is pure evil—whether he's your son or not. He damaged you from ever having children, deformed Richard and killed your sister. There isn't anything left for him to do now that he is behind bars. He may even be executed.

But he's my son—should I be all right with an execution verdict?

It's not up to you. It's up to a jury.

The door opened. My head came up as I placed my hands on my knees, giving them a light squeeze. He walked into the room, saw me and smirked. It was the same look I had seen on the highway. The guard pushed him down in the chair and we sat staring at one another. Looking at him now, I could see some of his father in him. The dark mystery in his eyes, his carefree hair and flirtatious smile reminded me briefly of the qualities that made me fall for his father all those years ago. Along with his father's looks, he had apparently inherited some of the same character flaws. Neither of them cared about anyone else; only what they could gain for themselves. Narcissists. The anger began to rumble inside so I picked up the phone, indicating to him to do the same. With his wrists handcuffed together, he picked up the receiver with his left hand, resting it on his shoulder.

For a few moments the only sound was of us breathing. I realized I wasn't sure how to start things out. I glanced over at Quinn to see if a question would pop into my head—when I heard him whisper my name.

I turned back to him, scrunched my eyebrows and said, "Arcane?"

"Yes, Sydney."

"Why?"

"Why what, babe? You were lonely, enjoyed me fucking you. Then you threw me aside like before."

It took everything I had not to let him see me cringe at his words.

"Arcane, you realize I'm your mother, right?"

A faint, sinister laugh escaped him and then he said, "Are you?"

The way he responded sent chills up and down my spine.

I gripped the phone tighter and said, "I might not have raised you, but I did give birth—"

"Ah, yes, you are my biological mother. Tell me, *mother*, did you ever lose even one good night's sleep thinking about how you got rid of us."

"I was sixteen years old—it wasn't an easy decision."

"No, I'm sure it was tough," he said mockingly.

"Arcane, I couldn't raise two sons at—"

"I kinda realized that when we were bounced around from one place to the other until we were split up."

"Why would you do what you did to me?" I started—then anger poured out and I began to yell.

"You had sex with your own mother! I can't have anymore children because of you."

My voice rose with every point.

"Richard had nothing to do with any of this and you destroyed him. You killed my sister, you son of a bitch!"

Quinn walked over, put his hand on my shoulder and gently guided me back into my seat. I was oblivious to the fact that I had risen in the heat of the moment. He gave Arcane a deep, hard look and walked back to the door.

I struggled to regain my composure, hoping a few of my words would get through to him. Looking at his blank stare only confirmed the evil residing in him.

His jaw gritted when he responded with, "Having sex with you was no big deal. My old man had sex with me every night from eight to fifteen years old. And you don't deserve to have children. You didn't deserve us."

"You did all of this because you had a tough life? That justifies rape and murder? What kind of a monster are you?"

I couldn't begin to match the menacing look he returned; his head slightly tilted down, eyes looking up and staring straight on.

Garrett and Quinn were right. I won't get anywhere with him. He's too far gone to have a morsel of humanity—an ounce of forgiveness.

He bit back.

"You didn't think I was such a monster when I was fucking your brains out, you whore. I don't recall you saying 'no', you pathetic bitch. You were looking for a young stud to fuck you until you were blue and that's exactly what you got, so what are you complaining about? It's exactly what you were looking for in that chat room."

Tears soaked my face as I shook my head and yelled, "It was YOU looking for me!"

That's it, Sydney. Let him know you know the truth. Giving him up for adoption has nothing to do with what he did. There are plenty of people out there with hard lives.

I slightly tilted my head down, eyes looking up and staring straight on. "Talk about pathetic. You're a sick fuck who wasted his life just to get back at me. You're just like your father!"

He jumped up, yelling back, "Fuck you, bitch! You abandoned us!

What gave you the right to do that? To give us to abusers so you can live a happy life. You were responsible for us!"

The security guard rushed over to him, pushing him back in his seat.

"No, Arcane! You are responsible for yourself. I'm sorry for what happened to you. I gave you to the adoption agency. It was their job to put you in a good home, but no one wanted an evil child."

"You bitch! I hope you never forget what you did to us and what I did to you and know it was *your fault* for what happened to Richard and your sister. Your sister at least showed some interest in our future."

Nick! That's how he knew Carolyn.

"Then why? Why would you kill her? She hired someone to look for you two. She has pictures, and you knew she found you, so why?"

"At first I didn't want to do it. I mean … sex with her was good. She hadn't had it in such a long time."

My mouth dropped opened as he continued. "Oh yeah, I did her about two years before getting to you. She got me excited with her screams as I screwed her—all the while calling her 'auntie'. I see you're wearing the pendant she had on … cute picture of us. Poor thing couldn't have kids."

Listening to his disgusting words made me want to jump through the glass and kill him. He had just resolved any difficulty I had with him possibly being executed. Hell yes, I want him dead! If there was ever any good in him, it was gone now. As much as I knew he was provoking me, I also knew he meant everything he said, which stabbed me every time he spoke.

What he did to Carolyn is probably the reason she stopped wearing the pendant. She hired Nick to find her nephews. What did he mean she couldn't have kids?

His maniacal laugh seared through me. I slapped the glass with my hand. Quinn came running over, taking my hand off the glass and asking me not to do that. The other guards were on edge and irritated by my actions.

I shouted into the phone, "I can't wait until they kill you."

"That's impossible. You already did that."

He slammed the phone down. Our eyes connected and for the first time I saw a damaged boy. My damaged boy. He called the guard to come and get him as I robotically put the phone back in its holster.

I watched them take him away.

For the rest of my life I will pay for a decision I made twenty-six years ago.

As I sat, other questions came to mind.

Where is my other son? Did he suffer the same abuse? Is he seeking revenge, too?

The visit answered my questions about Arcane, yet left so many dangling like a cigarette between my lips. It took courage...now I need to find out the rest of the puzzle. Once that happens, I can fix my relationship with Garrett. He'll just have to understand.

SATURDAY, JULY 16, 1994: Dear Friend,

It's Caitlyn. I can't believe what I saw today. *shakes head*

The thought still makes me gag. If I had known what he would become, I would have stopped caring and release the guilt. Abandonment is best. I've had too much despair in my life...too much for one person to bear.

It's been ten years today. Ever since I found him, I'd periodically go to the park where he plays, watch him for a while before joining him. On his birthdays, I give him his gift and we talk a while...well, I talk. He's always been a boy of few words—silent and brooding. I guess that's to be expected. His demeanor would change once I'd hand him his gift. Instead of offering me a smile, I'd get a somber look and a whispered, "Thanks."

He was different when I first met him. Time seemed to have skipped over good days each year I saw the sadness spread like weeds. Today, I watched from a distance with a bag in my lap that had a little wrapped box with a blue bow. He sat by himself on a bench while the other children stayed away; his arms folded tight, grimacing at anyone who came close to him. He made sure they kept their distance. Loneliness must have become a comfort. His eyes seared into the other children as they played.

There must have been something moving on the ground next to a nearby tree. He got up to see what it was. When he picked it up, I saw that it was a bird. I smiled watching him hold it. But then...he began picking at the wings and plucking the feathers off. My hand shot to my mouth as I watched him dangle the bird by its leg, twirl it and then fling it at the tree. I ran away, afraid to witness any more.

On my way home, I tossed the bag into a dumpster. I threw up a few times when I got home and then scrubbed my hands until they were red. Sadness doesn't exist in him—only malice.

You would have been just as repulsed as I was if you saw him.

I pray someone comes to rescue him…saves him from himself.

Let's both pray he finds his way.

MONDAY, FEBRUARY 9, 2009: Friends,

It took me a few days to recover after seeing Arcane. My body trembles when I think about what he said and did, and my stomach flips when I think about bringing him into this world. He didn't appreciate life and didn't have any regard for anyone else's. Because of a decision I made years ago, he wreaked havoc on my life, taking an important person away from me forever. The anger and sadness simmer most of the time, on occasion rise to a boil. I didn't discuss what happened with Garrett or how I felt about meeting Arcane. He already voiced his opinion about the visit and I had gone against it. He had either become too exhausted to listen to my pains or he had his own emotions to deal with. Either way, he withdrew. We love one another, but our relationship has so much drama. Garrett protected me from a monster and helped me learn to trust again. That's a lot to put on a twenty-six year old.

I finally contacted my mom to ask her about Nick. She went to my sister's house and was able to find a number for someone named Nick in Carolyn's telephone book. It turned out to be the man at the wake. I called Nick and told him about Arcane and asked if he could help me find my other son. I explained that I didn't have much money, but he said he'd do it for Carolyn's sake.

"I lost track of your other son years ago."

"So, you found Arcane and told Carolyn where?"

I sensed some sort of guilt when he said, "Since he remained in Chicago, I could follow him easier than your other son. When Arcane turned twenty-four, Carolyn thought it would be nice to meet him and give him a birthday gift. That was about the same time she started feeling ill and was worried she didn't have much time left. I contacted Arcane and set up a meeting. Afterwards, Carolyn demanded I stop following Arcane and look for your other son. I didn't question her. It was her money."

I said this more to myself than Nick, "Ill? I didn't know she was ill. What from?"

"She had breast cancer and had already undergone chemotherapy and radiation. It spread to her lymph nodes. Time was limited, so she decided to meet at least one of her nephews."

I felt angry and hurt.

"Breast cancer? I can't believe she never told me. Why did she keep so many secrets from me? Did she not trust me enough to tell me? I mean…sisters tell one another everything."

"I don't know, Sydney. Your sister kept many things private. Your personalities are very different, so maybe she didn't know how you'd react. Maybe she felt she needed to protect you and your mother."

"We might have been different, but we were blood and blood—"

"Carolyn was adopted."

I couldn't find the words to express how deceived I felt by my mother and hurt by Carolyn.

Adopted?! Why wasn't I told? This at least explains Carolyn's need to look for her nephews.

He decided to cut through the thick silence, saying, "I take it you didn't know."

I whispered, "No," and shook my head in disbelief.

"Do you know why my parents adopted?"

"It's my understanding your mom couldn't get pregnant so they adopted Carolyn—then a few years later, got pregnant with you."

"This explains a lot about our childhood and why she wanted to find my sons. Do you by chance know my other son's name?"

"The name Aaron is on his birth certificate, although it might have been changed like Arcane's."

"What happened? Why were the boys separated?"

"The system. They were adopted as infants, but the parents died in a car accident when the twins were one and a half years old. The money left over after paying debtors went into a savings account for the boys. Then a gay couple adopted them, but their relationship ended and neither wanted to raise children alone so they went back into the system. By this time they were older—not many people want to adopt older children. Arcane and Aaron were moved from one foster family to another until somehow—and I'm not quite sure how it happened—an older couple adopted Aaron, leaving Arcane behind. They wanted to adopt a boy because their real son had died of leukemia, yet they couldn't handle two. The split happened around the age of eight. Talking with the social workers and foster families, Arcane tended to be unruly whereas Aaron was a quiet boy. That's probably why the older couple decided to take him."

My heart ached for their separation at such a young age. I abandoned them and then "the system" failed them.

"Will it be difficult for you to find Aaron, or whatever his name is now?"

"I don't think so. I still have his social security number, so if it hasn't been changed I should have something for you in a couple of weeks. It shouldn't take that long, but I have another commitment to attend to first."

So, I'm waiting to have my unanswered questions answered. In the meantime, I'm going to try to make things better with Garrett. I love him.

THURSDAY, FEBRUARY 19, 2009: Dear Friends,

I thought it was going to be a good day for our relationship to start growing again.

On Monday, it was President's Day and Garrett had the day off, so to celebrate my unspoken freedom we decided to go out for the day. Our relationship had become stale—this was an opportunity to bring it back to life again. A friend of Garrett's sold him one of his cars for $600, so we went back to his hometown to visit his mother. I think after all he had seen and heard between *this* mother and son, he felt it was the least he could do for his own.

The sun dodged in and out of the sky every now and then, drying what leaves remained on the ground. Neither of us could wait for the weather to warm up again.

Tucked into a quiet area of town stood the brick and stone building where his mother lived. Trees huddled around the exterior. The window faced south, offering a promise of a serene view of flowers in the spring. The sound of heels could be heard echoing in the halls and periodic shouts coming from other rooms. Garrett called ahead to let them know we'd be visiting, so they already had his mother sitting in a wheelchair by a large window with couches and chairs, forming a semi-circle.

The nurse whispered to Ms. Hart that her son and his girlfriend were there for a visit. She squinted her eyes at us, absent of recognition. The horrible disease takes the most precious thing we all live for and hope to rely on in old age—memories—any memories of good times and bad simply wiped away. It upset Garrett to see her uncertainty and distance—not knowing her own son. I indicated for him to sit across from her in a chair and I sat on the couch next to his chair.

"Hi, Mom."

"Who are you? Did you bring me anything?"

He let out a light laugh and said, "I brought you some chocolates. Your favorite—turtles."

He extended his arm to her. She watched him as she took the box from him. Taking the lid off the box, her hand hovered over the chocolates until she picked one and pushed it in her mouth. While she chewed the chocolate—brown saliva leaking out—she looked over the other chocolates to see which one she would eat next.

Garrett said, "You're looking good today."

"I don't know who you are. What do you want?"

"I'm your son, Garrett."

"I don't have a son. Couldn't have children. We lived happily without children."

Garrett flinched at her words. He looked at me and sighed in frustration. I held his hand and kissed the top of it.

"In her heart, Garrett, she knows and loves you—that's all that matters," I whispered to him.

He looked down at our hands and asked, "In your heart, did you love your sons? Ever miss them?"

My eyes narrowed at his question. I withdrew my hands and snapped, "Of course I missed them! Why would you ask such a thing? Do you honestly think I'm that cold of a person?"

Garrett looked at his mother and then back at me, annoyed. "No. I didn't ask because I think of you that way. I was curious, that's all."

"Yes, I did. When I first gave them up I thought about them a lot, but I knew I couldn't take care of them. I thought I did the best thing for them. There were plenty of nights I laid in bed crying, wondering if I made the right choice and if I'd think about them every day of my life. And I did think about them, but not as often as I originally did. I tried to forget them for my own selfish heart. Then as I got older, and my friends started having children, I saw their faces in other babies. My heart began to ache again. For a while, thinking of them was a daily thing."

Pointing at me, Garrett's mother asked, "Who are you?"

"I'm your son's friend."

She leaned forward and said, "I told you I don't have a son."

She grabbed at another turtle and shoved it in her mouth.

Chocolate outlined her lips, accumulating in the corners of her mouth. Garrett took a Kleenex from the table and went to wipe her mouth, but she hit his hand out of the way. Feeling rejected, he returned to his seat and looked out the window. We sat for a while longer watching her eat. Periodically, she would ask who we were. I was sad for Garrett.

We had a quiet ride home. I knew Garrett felt alone in this world, and I found myself wishing I could convince him he wasn't. Besides me, his mom was all he had. His father died when he was in his teens and he didn't have any siblings.

We got something to eat and went back home to relax. I felt confused after meeting Arcane; and now Garrett's mother. It all swirled in my head.

Later, as I rested on the couch, I became aware that Garrett was staring at me from the kitchen.

"What's wrong?" I asked.

His eyes dug into me as he clenched his hands, opening and closing into fists. I got up from the couch, keeping the coffee table between us.

"Garrett, what's wrong?"

His eyes didn't divert from me and he continued gripping his hands.

"Garrett, you're scaring me. Stop it!"

He walked into the kitchen and returned with a small knife. I took in a quick breath, held it and slowly let it out, hoping I'd stop time.

"Garrett—"

He began to laugh just as my cell phone rang. My phone was closer to him so I was afraid to go for it. The knife plunged into the couch as he pushed it in, shredding the top of it. It was almost as if the ringing phone was the catalyst for his anger. When the phone stopped…so did he. I had moved over to the windows, my back against them, trying to get as far away from him as possible.

Garrett started toward me and I scrambled to get away. He grabbed my hair, threw me back on the couch and straddled me. My legs flailed and my hands punched and scratched at him.

"Please Garrett, don't do this."

He smiled at my plea and opened the top of my shirt, baring my chest.

I screamed until he hit me so hard I blacked out.

MONDAY, AUGUST 30, 2010: Chicago State Hospital

Caitlyn strolls into the visiting area to find me sitting there waiting. When she sees me, her eyes widen and she hurries over and I stand up to put my arms around her. It makes her feel good to know she matters to someone. A psychiatrist leads us into a private room furnished with a cocktail table and two big leather chairs. The window faces south, offering a serene view of flowers in full bloom. Trees huddled around the exterior. The sound of heels can be heard echoing in the halls and periodic shouts come from other rooms.

Taking Caitlyn's hand, I say, "It's good to see you."

She runs her hands along mine, kissing the tops of them.

"I always love seeing you. When you told me you were coming, I made sure the nurses helped me clean up my room and I dressed so I could look beautiful for you."

"You do look beautiful Caitlyn—and I appreciate you taking the time to do it."

"Did you bring my journal with you? Did you finish it? I'll need it to prove to these doctors that I'm not insane."

"I did finish reading it and have it with me."

"Now do you understand what I've been through? Do you see that I don't belong here, Nick?"

She looks into my eyes and her body slinks forward. Her hand moves up to my face and she lightly rubs my cheek.

"You look so sad, Nick. Do you miss me?"

Pulling her back into my arms, I say, "Of course I miss you."

Her body is deteriorating from her refusal to eat. All of her spare time is spent divulging her pain into a journal toward the possibility of release. The thing is—they can't release her. She is still a danger to herself and others.

We sway from side to side, the motion melting her in my arms as she closes her eyes. I rest my head on hers and we hum our favorite song, *Angel,* by Sarah McLachlan. I often call her an angel. It took a long time for me to earn her trust, and now I have to be honest with her. I need to ease her into it—placate her to prevent an outburst.

"Caitlyn? Do you remember what happened to Garrett?"

She sighs, not wanting to think about it. Her fingers play with mine, intermingling them.

She finally asks, "Do we have to talk about it?"

I take my right hand from hers, pull the journal from my coat pocket and say, "I think it's important that we talk about your journal. You gave it to me and said you wanted to present it to the doctors. There are a few things we need to discuss first, ok?"

Caitlyn eyes the journal. She wants to please, so she cooperates, saying, "No, I don't know what happened to Garrett. The last time I saw him he was with an older woman. I followed him to a beautiful place where she must live."

The way she's talking is like she's far away, talking to no one in particular—melancholy. If she only knew...

I move to the chair to sit down, anticipating that she will follow my lead. Instead, she continues to look out onto the warm summer day.

"Was that the last time you saw him?"

Caitlyn turns and looks at me as if I had lost my mind.

"I said it was the last time."

"I know, but in your journal you talk about when he came after you with a knife."

She came toward me, grabbing a clump of hair and running her fingers down it. She repeats this motion with the other hand and alternates the motion between hands as she starts to pace. I can tell she's thinking about what I said.

She stops playing with her hair, and shakes her head no, as she says, "That's not in my journal. You must have read it somewhere else."

I reached over for the journal, turned to entry date, February 19, 2009, and began reading: "He walked into the kitchen and returned with a small knife. I took in a quick breath, held it and slowly let it out, hoping I'd stop time."

Caitlyn grabs the journal from my hands, but I don't try to take it back. I let her have it. Her breathing changes along with her voice taking on a deeper pitch.

"What the hell are you doing? You have no business reading my journal?"

"Sydney?"

"Who else? I'm the only one smart enough not to bother with psychiatrists. All you want is to drug me up and charge me enormous fees."

I remain seated, and say, "I'm not a psychiatrist, Sydney. I'm a friend. Don't you recognize me?"

Sydney tilts her head, looks long and hard at me and I realize she makes the connection.

"Nick. You're the one who helped Carolyn find my sons."

"I am … and now I'm here to help you get out of here, but we need to go over a few things in your journal."

She smiles and says, "You're going to help me get out of here?! Then ask away!"

"Can you tell me what happened to Garrett, Sydney."

"Since you read my journal, you already know he carved his initials into my chest and knocked me out."

She stops in front of my chair, unbuttons the first two buttons of her dress to show me the initials and presses her hand against her chest for emphasis.

While buttoning her dress back up, Sydney continues, "He found the pictures I brought back from Carolyn's. It turns out Garrett was my other son. He hates me as much as Arcane does."

She turns and looks out the window, numbed by the thought. As always, I observe Caitlyn's sadness and understand that she believes what she says. Her imagination distorts reality due to the blocks of time she loses and she can't even tell the difference.

I go over to her, take the strand of hair that has fallen from her barrette and tuck it behind her ear, asking, "Is that when you ended up here?"

"I must have flipped out for a minute. I just couldn't deal with another tragedy in my life. When I finally collected myself, the doctors refused to let me go. I don't understand their reasoning or why they treat me as if I'm crazy—like the rest."

She turns to look at me—her eyes pleading for understanding and her voice is higher when she speaks. I've become accustomed to figuring out who is talking, Caitlyn or Sydney/Ashley. Caitlyn is more vulnerable and scared.

"They have no sympathy for me and I didn't do anything to them.

When I get out, could you help me find out who put me in here? I'd like to talk to them and ask them why they would do such a thing."

I return to my chair and she follows, nestling herself on my lap.

"Do you know who I am, Caitlyn?"

"Of course—you're my friend, Nick."

I am all Caitlyn has. My heart can't find her despicable for her crimes after knowing all she has been through.

I gesture for her to move to the chair next to mine. She complies.

I pull some pictures from my coat pocket and lay them on the table.

"Do you know who these people are, Caitlyn?"

She moves closer to them and shakes her head.

"You don't know who these boys are?"

"I've never seen them before in my life."

With a soothing tone, I say, "They're your sons, Caitlyn."

Her eyes pop wide open, as she pushes off the chair, grabs the pictures and with a deeper voice, she says, "OMG! Where did you get these pictures of Arcane and Garrett?"

"Is that who you see, Sydney? Do you see Arcane and Garrett?"

She looks at me as if I have gone mad. It *is* a picture of her sons at the age of ten.

The pitch of her voice climbs as she responds, "What do you mean is *that* what I see? It's Arcane and Garrett. Why are you questioning my answer?"

"Sydney, I'm not yelling at you, so I'd appreciate it if you didn't yell at me."

"But you're questioning me like I'm crazy."

"Our discussions are always like this, Sydney, and you know it. We need to respect one another in order to understand what the other person is saying. Do you respect me?"

Her mannerisms change again...Caitlyn is coming back. She scoots back in her chair, hunches her shoulders, and she says, "I do, Nick...you know I do."

I lift her chin up, brush the hair from her face and encourage her to relax.

"All right, I'd like you to take another look at the pictures and tell me again who you see."

She releases her breath, leans forward and moves the pictures closer to her.

After a few seconds, she whispers, "I haven't seen them in a long time."

"Can I tell you a story?"

She smiles at me, slides back in her chair and pulls her knees up to her chest.

"Oh, Nick, I love stories. Please tell me."

I nod and respond, "Okay, I'm going to begin. Years ago there was this little girl named Caitlyn."

She lights up when she says, "That's me! You're going to tell a story about me?"

"I am, but you must pay close attention to the story. Promise me you will."

"You have my full attention, Nick. I want to hear about me."

I clear my throat and continue.

"This girl, Caitlyn, lived with her single mother, who drank too much and loved too little. Instead of taking care of little Caitlyn, her mother went out until all hours of the night looking for a man to love her—no man did. Sometimes she brought them home and maybe they'd get too drunk and a fight would break out. Or sometimes the man would sneak out of her mother's room into Caitlyn's to make her play with things she didn't like."

"Stop, Nick! I don't want to hear a sad story about me. I thought this would be a fairy tale."

"Fairy tales are sometimes sad, aren't they?"

She looks down and says, "Sometimes...but can't you make it a sweet fairy tale?"

"I'm telling the story and you promised to listen."

Barely above a whisper, she says, "Okay."

"When Caitlyn turned nine, her beauty captivated everyone, especially her mother's lovers. She hadn't gotten her period yet, so her mother took advantage of this time in her young, defenseless daughter's life. At night, her mother would dress her up, put makeup on her and bring her around to local establishments. For a hundred dollars men could have sex with Caitlyn and for two hundred dollars they could have anything they liked."

I pause to offer Caitlyn a tissue. Her body shakes as she looks out the window, tears pouring down her pale cheeks.

"Why are you crying, Caitlyn?"

Without looking at me she says, "Because sometimes I remember … things."

"Do you think any of it was your fault?"

She continues to stare out the window as she says, "No."

"You're right. It was your mother's fault and all the men who abused you. What they did to you deserves punishment. They're guilty and you're innocent. Am I right, Caitlyn?"

She nods. My body stiffens a bit watching this beautiful woman crumble from the events of a wretched childhood. It sickens me that a mother could do such a thing to her daughter. I take a deep breath before going on.

"Caitlyn's mother continued to pass her around until she turned sixteen years old and ran away, but it was too late. Caitlyn was pregnant. She returned home to get help from her mother. The terrible men didn't have a problem with Caitlyn's condition. They continued to pay for her services."

I pause a moment to choose my words carefully.

"One hot and humid summer night on a mattress in the basement, Caitlyn gave birth to twin boys. Her mother wrapped them in newspaper as Caitlyn cried, wanting to hold them—"

Caitlyn sits up straight and turns her head toward me.

"I *did* want to hold them! I *did,* Nick! I wanted to keep them and take care of them. They were perfect—my little angels. You believe that I wanted them, don't you?"

"Of course I do, Caitlyn…may I continue?"

She moves back in her chair, hanging her head and staring at her feet.

"Her mother left the babies in an alley. When she returned home, Caitlyn had passed out and blood was still dripping out of her. Thinking about all the money she'd lose if her daughter didn't get back to servicing, her terrible mother packed Caitlyn with dirty rags. When the men came by the next day to find her disoriented, they left without paying."

By this time, Caitlyn's tears are a constant. I stop talking and watch her struggle with the story—remembering bits and pieces—attempting to tuck the rest of the horrid events deep into her soul. I reach over and take her hand in mine. She doesn't reject it, only increases pressure.

"Will you look at me for a moment, Caitlyn?"

She reluctantly looks up at me—her face smeared with mucus and tears. I give her hand a slight squeeze and let go.

I look into her eyes and say, "Your mother is an awful person, Caitlyn, and she's in prison for what she did to you. I just wish they could have caught every man who wronged you, too. Do you still agree with me that you're not to blame?"

She nods 'yes' and wipes her face with a tissue.

"I'm going to continue with the story, but I'd like you to look at me so I know I have your attention."

In a broken voice she says, "You have my attention, Nick."

I nod and proceed.

"The twin boys were found, starving but safe and put up for adoption. Caitlyn wound up in the hospital with an infection. The doctors performed a hysterectomy in order to stop the infection from spreading. When released, she went to the adoption agency to report what her mother did. This brought on an investigation and the prosecution against her mother. By the time the trial ended—and her mother was in prison—Caitlyn was seventeen and alone.

She fought to get her children, but they denied her request because of lack of shelter and money. She returned to her mother's home in search of something that proved her mother cared about her, but all she could find were pictures of her mother in sexually explicit positions. Feeling the years of being unloved and the rejection coming down on her, Caitlyn started down a physical and mental road of self-destruction.

"The only one willing to help her was an old boyfriend of her mother's, Cal Birch. At twenty-eight years old, he agreed to put a roof over Caitlyn's head and food on the table as long as she became his slave. For the next five years, Caitlyn was beaten, tied up and taken against her will. She thought this was the only way she could survive and possibly get her children back."

I stop and say, "Are you all right to hear more?"

"No. I don't like this story, Nick. Can't you change it?"

"I would love to change it into a fairy tale, but we both know it wouldn't be true."

Under her breath, she says, "We can pretend it's the truth," while she cowers even lower in her chair.

"We can, Caitlyn, but I'm here about the journal—your freedom."

"So, you *are* going to help me?" She perks back up.

"Let's continue with the story, okay?"

She looks at me, out the window then back at me and sighs, "I'll try."

"I guess that's all I can ask."

I let the silence coddle her a bit before proceeding. "In order to get through these horrible ordeals, Caitlyn's mind began to make up multiple personalities to withstand her abuser. Certain situations triggered her switching from one persona to the next. The strongest personality, Arcane, dealt with the blows—even fighting back once in a while. Her other personality, Garrett, licked the wounds and comforted her afterward. She—"

"What?! No! No! That's ridiculous."

It's Sydney. She jumps off the chair, patting her ears, screaming at me with a blotched face and lines of dried tears. I remain seated so as not to challenge her.

"No! You're trying to trick me into thinking Arcane and Garrett don't exist. I know they do and you read the journal, so you know, too. Look!"

Again, she pulls the top of her dress apart to reveal the initials carved in her chest then closes her dress, shaking her head 'no' and covering her face with her hands. I come to her rescue and take her in my arms and let her cry.

"Arcane and Garrett did exist. They existed in order for you to survive. You used them as a protective shield against the nightmare you lived in. But, Sydney…"

She lifts her head, confused but waiting for me to finish my thought.

"You don't need them anymore. You have me."

Her dirty face distorts with pain, begs me to stop. I kiss her forehead, sit down and pull her onto my lap.

Finding her voice, she says, "If Arcane is someone I conjured up, why did I end up in the hospital? What about the police report that he broke into my place?"

"After Arcane fought against your abuser and you escaped, he became your nemesis and no one was safe. The situation became really dangerous when you tried to escape Arcane's grip. He's the personality you accuse of using a lug wrench on you."

She jumps off my lap and shouts at me, "Accuse? You don't believe me?! *You're* the one who's crazy!" She jabs her finger in my direction.

"It wasn't a lug wrench, Sydney. You got an infection, which led to your hysterectomy. There was never an incident with a lug wrench."

"Like I said, *you're* crazy! I suppose the next thing you'll tell me is the writing on the notepad was mine."

I'm sure she sees the agony on my face.

"Same writing—different personality. Do you understand, Sydney? Just like the journal—different personalities."

She leans over to take a look at the journal, rubs her chin with her shoulder and moves to the window. Sydney's body is shaking uncontrollably and she begins to pace. I might have pushed her too far. I decide to take a break from the story and sit in silence for over a half an hour before she finally surrenders into her chair, glaring at me and saying, "I trusted you. You were the only person I trusted with my journal and now I have no one."

"Sydney, you do have me. I'm here to help you. I've read your journal and believe that *you* believe everything you wrote. I'm not arguing with you about the things you wrote in your journal."

I offer my hand to her.

She looks away.

"No, you're just saying *I* did them—telling me it's all in my head when I know it isn't. You're trying to cover up the fact that you can't find Arcane. It's easier for you to say I'm crazy than to try to find him. He escaped from prison and now you can't find him."

Instead of irritating her more, I turn my attention to the window, sigh and say, "You know I wouldn't do that. Arcane is a dangerous character. I'd be out there looking for him myself and you know that."

"Don't lie to me! You played me. You have no intention on helping me get out of here. You're worse than those here. At least they're honest about their intentions."

She freezes for several seconds and then shouts, "Aha!" It looks like a sudden realization comes to her as she points at me and says, "The picture! What about the picture of Garrett in front of the waterfall? It's in my journal."

I shuffle through her journal until I come upon the picture. I remove it and place it on the table asking, "This picture?

At first, she jumps at the sight and then watchfully moves toward the picture with her eyes narrowing.

"What do you see in this picture, Sydney?"

"No! He was in that picture. You're messing with me. Someone replaced my picture with this one of just the waterfall. I took lots of pictures, especially when we went into Garrett's hometown. What about all of those?"

"All the pictures are simply of the town. I have no doubt you were in that town. As a matter of fact, I know that you went there to watch over Garrett. You wanted to make sure he was okay, and that's when you saw his mother."

She moves to the window and runs her forearm across her eyes, smearing what little makeup she has on.

A slight crack in her voice indicates Sydney is leaving, and Caitlyn asks, "What about Carolyn? Please don't tell me I made her up, too?"

I want to spare her some truth, so I decide to only tell a portion of it.

"You never had a sister, Caitlyn. When you were younger, you somehow got the address of the people who adopted one of your sons. For some time, you would stop at the condo where he lived and watched a woman named Carolyn. Unfortunately, you were watching the wrong person; she wasn't the one who adopted your son. I believe that what you wrote about her and how you felt about her came from a deep desire to have a sister. She was someone you *aspired* to be. Carolyn became another personality when you couldn't bear the loneliness anymore."

She flattens her hands against the window, looking exhausted. All Caitlyn ever wanted was a normal family, and now she's being told that this normal family is all in her head.

In a low, monotone voice she asks, "What about Garrett's mother? Are you saying he doesn't have a mother?"

"No, I'm not."

She turns to me, obviously confused.

I speak before she does. "You didn't let me finish the story."

"I don't know if you should finish it. You're only going to keep claiming I'm crazy."

"Caitlyn, sit down and let me finish...please?"

She gives me an irritated look and falls into her chair, staring down at the table.

"You came up with those names because you found out those were the names of your twin sons. The other personalities are your protectors—except Arcane turned from protector to predator. He's the one who ultimately brought you here. And now you're fighting to get out, just like you fought to get your sons back, Caitlyn."

"Shut up! Who the hell do you think you are calling me dangerous? I'll fucking kill you, too."

"Hello, Arcane," I say calmly.

"Fuck you. Don't even try to use your psycho-babble bullshit on me! Quit putting crazy thoughts in Caitlyn's head. I'm still her protector. All you've done is betray her. I can't fucking believe you're calling me evil when you've been playing poor Caitlyn."

"Okay, Arcane, you tell me what happened then."

"Why should I fucking bother talking to you? You'll just turn everything around and blame me anyway."

"I'll listen to you, Arcane. I'll listen if you want to give your side of the story."

"It isn't *my* side of the story, Nick. It's the way things are."

"Okay, then tell me the way things really are. What happened to Richard?"

"Caitlyn started having feelings for him. She can't help opening her legs for anyone. Her mom turned her into a little whore. Richard didn't have the same feelings, so Caitlyn went after him. Garrett and I tried to stop her, but she already threw the acid on him."

Arcane draws me in with his story and I bob my head in acknowledgment.

Her expression changes.

She puts her weight on her right leg, leans to that side and shakes her head. In a more feminine voice she says, "She didn't. Arcane hurt him."

"Who am I talking to?"

"Duh, it's Sydney. Richard was a good guy. Arcane attacked him out of anger. He—"

Her head shoots up, turning toward me she says, "Fucking liar, man! She's a psycho whore, and I'm supposed to take the blame for her actions?"

"No one's blaming you, Arcane. How do *you* feel about Caitlyn?"

Arcane's expression is that of disdain and irritability, but he replies anyway.

"As much as Garrett and I care about her, she's still a whore. Caitlyn doesn't use protection and fucks anyone."

"She can't help it, Arcane. It wasn't like she lived a normal life."

"No shit, *Nick*. I've been the one trying to protect her."

"And you were doing a good job." As soon as I say it, I realize Arcane will jump on it.

"What do you mean 'were'? If it wasn't for Garrett and me, Caitlyn would have created more destruction."

"Did Caitlyn kill Carolyn, Arcane?"

Her face changes again and she turns her back and goes to the window. She massages her temples and then presses her hand and forehead against the window.

"Don't listen to him. Arcane thinks we're always ganging up on him."

"And you would be…"

She turns toward me and shakes her head from annoyance.

"Sydney! Why do you keep asking for my name? Do you want me

to spell it for you?"

"I apologize. I don't mean to be rude."

"You're exhausting me just like I'm exhausted from all the covering up I had to do for Caitlyn."

"What do you mean?"

"She got worse with her paranoia and became more dangerous. We all tried to keep tabs on her, but she'd always find some way to escape without notice. Like when she went back to Chicago and killed Carolyn."

"Why would Caitlyn want to hurt Carolyn?"

"Because she felt like Carolyn betrayed her. Caitlyn found out that Arcane was in jail, so she thought Carolyn failed as the adoptive mother. She relied on Carolyn to take care of him. Caitlyn thought Carolyn adopted one of her sons. Carolyn tried to explain that she didn't know what Caitlyn was talking about and then threatened to call the police. Caitlyn repeatedly hit her over the head. She gets crazy when she thinks you're lying. After Caitlyn killed her, she put her in the trunk of Carolyn's car, drove it to the airport and flew back to Seattle."

I want to hear more of Sydney's story. As bad as I feel for Caitlyn, I find her personalities interesting, so I ask, "Why did she think Carolyn adopted one of her sons?"

This is the first time I have been able to 'summon' all of Caitlyn's personalities in one meeting.

Arcane whips around locking his eyes on me. He throws his head back, laughing, and slaps his leg.

"You are dense. Caitlyn went back to the adoption agency every year to find out where her sons were. She gave permission to a public file in case her sons were searching for her. Someone from the adoption agency called and gave her some information about one of her sons still being in the Chicago area. Caitlyn went to Carolyn's house instead of the people who actually adopted him. She's so stupid—Caitlyn flip-flopped the numbers on the address. Dumb bitch."

"So, one of her sons was trying to find her?"

Arcane gives a sly smile and says, "I guess so, Einstein."

All of a sudden, Caitlyn is shaking now and she starts to cry, burying her face in her hands.

"What's wrong?"

"I'm sad you think I'm crazy. I know Garrett has a mother."

"You're right, Caitlyn. Garrett does have a mother—and that mother is you. You are Garrett's mother."

Her demeanor loosens up and her face becomes complacent with this thought. I allow her time to let the idea sink in that her stories aren't entirely wrong.

After a few minutes, I reach over and place my hand over hers and say, "I believe, if you understand your personalities, and learn to control them, you will get better."

"So, it was a waste of time to give you my journal? You won't get me out of here?"

"I *am*, Caitlyn. Your journal helped me understand who *you* are along with your other personalities. It wasn't a waste of time and you should continue to write in it."

"To have you discredit it?"

"I believe the stories are real in your head. We just need to talk about them to separate what's real from what's not. I will continue

visiting and talking to you every week…if you'll have me. If you're not in the mood to talk, then I'll just hold you."
I get up and pull her close, taking her chin in my hand and turning her to face me.

"I am always here for you, Caitlyn. We will get you out of here, but I need you to believe that I wouldn't do anything to hurt you. I hope you know I believe in you."

"You do?"

"I do. I believe your writings, because it's how you feel. Now I need you to believe a little in me, so you can get out and come live with me."

"I'd like that, Nick."

I kiss the top of her head.

A nurse taps and opens the door.

"Time's up," she says politely.

Caitlyn looks at the nurse then me, quietly repeating, "Time's up."

"I'll see you next weekend?"

Caitlyn returns her most beautiful smile and the nurse escorts her down the hallway toward her room.

As I make my way out of the hospital the administrator catches up with me.

"How's the internship going? Are you learning anything?"

"Definitely, yes…thank you," I reply. "I appreciate you letting me intern here."

"Not a problem. She trusts you and that's big when it comes to

Dissociative Identity Disorder. We're lucky to have you working with her."

I turn back toward the hallway just in time to see Caitlyn give me a last wave.

The administrator smiles sadly at me.

"You're doing a good thing here, Garrett. Your mother might not know who you are, but she adores you. She'll come back to you … someday. For the time being, she's just locked in her own mind."

Denise Baer is a native of the South Side of Chicago, Illinois. She began writing poetry in her mid-thirties and has poems published in *Danse Macabre*. Check out Denise's poetry book, *Sipping a Mix of Verse*, and her women's fiction novel, *Fogged Up Fairy Tale*.

To learn more about Denise, please visit her website at http://www.authordenisebaer.com/, and follow her on Amazon and Goodreads. She enjoys hearing from her readers, and appreciates all reviews.

Baer Books Press
Chicago   Hattingen

FOGGED UP
FAIRY TALE

Denise Baer

An Introduction to
Fogged Up Fairy Tale

Prologue

Dover, NH, 2013

The last thing I remembered was a blast of light, and a deafening sound, like you hear during cicada season. I'll never forget that light and sound; so intrusive and obscene. The stinging of glass followed and then my chest and face felt as if someone had taken a baseball bat to them. Time alone seemed to stretch on, especially when the light and sound subsided. I felt something warm dripping down my face, but my arms and legs were too heavy to lift... or were they even there? A sound broke the silence—a sound that came from me—raw and infested with fear. Too afraid of the worst, I kept my eyes closed, so I wouldn't see parts of me laying elsewhere. The car began to heat up, and I was covered in smoke. I tried to scream, but coughed instead.

In the distance, I heard a siren and its volume increased as it got closer. Someone was talking while holding my hand when the ambulance arrived. I couldn't quite grasp the words they tossed around—*horrible—get her out of there—the car's about to blow*.

Like a rag doll, hands pulled at my flimsy extremities. Periodically, my eyes squinted open to only be abused by light and blurred images whizzing by, so I closed them to stop the dizziness. I was moved to the ambulance bed, an oxygen mask put in place, and darkness came over me. For some reason, a man popped into my mind, and my continuous visions of him were burned onto the backs of my eyelids.

The next thing was me waking up in a hospital room with the man, who I saw in the darkness, sitting next to me. He rose from the chair when he heard me, and took my hand in his. I didn't know him, which scared me more. Why was a stranger sitting in my hospital room? What happened? I wiggled my hand free and pulled myself into a seated position. I reached up to touch my face and found patches of cloth in areas. I looked back at the man—eyes narrowing now with more confusion and fear.

A nurse came into the room. She was short and heavy with a friendly smile. "Well hello. It's so nice to see you up and awake."

I touched my head again. "What day is it?"

"It's Thursday, Sweetie."

"How long have I been here?"

She let out a hearty laugh. "Five days. I guess you needed your sleep."

I squinted down at my legs trying to remember. "A week? What happened?"

"You were in a car accident." I turned toward the man who spoke to me.

"An accident?" I shook my head to jiggle everything back into place. It didn't work. "What accident?"

The nurse started taking my blood pressure and remained silent.

The man placed his hands on the bed rail. "You hit another car, and then your car spun around, smashing into a tree."

"Was anyone else hurt?"

"No. The other driver walked away with minor cuts and bruises."

Tears began to fall. White light and noise; maybe it erased the tragedy—masked it for a while. The nurse gave me a box of tissue as she continued to fiddle around with IV's and took vitals. Similar to walking through a muddy stream, my murky thoughts kept getting stuck. When one thought came into mind, it sunk away as I pulled at another. The nurse finished, patted my hand, and left the room after telling me the doctor would make his rounds soon.

The room got colder.

The man cleared his throat before asking, "How are you feeling?"

"Fine."

"You'll feel better once you get home."

I balled up the covers in my fists, pulling a little more at a time, focusing on my feet. What was happening? How could I make sense of what was going on? To calm my breathing, I pressed a hand against my chest to ease my breathing, hoping the air would cool down the heat inside my lungs. He put his hand on my arm, but I pulled away while at the same time leaning toward the other side of the bed.

"Fine. I won't touch you." He put his arms up in surrender and walked over to the foot of the bed, looking out at the gray day. "You know I should be the one pissed. If you weren't trying to text, you wouldn't have been in the accident." He turned and looked at me, becoming more irritated by my silence. "Say the word and I'm out of here."

I pulled the sheet up to my chin. "Who are you?"

His mouth dropped open, and then, as if in slow motion, he whispered, "Your husband."

www.ingramcontent.com/pod-product-compliance
Lightning Source LLC
Chambersburg PA
CBHW061937170626
46813CB00006B/2444